Murder by the Bookend

Also available by Laura Gail Black

The Antique Bookshop Mysteries

For Whom the Book Tolls

Murder by the Bookend

AN ANTIQUE BOOKSHOP MYSTERY

Laura Gail Black

CROOKED
LANE

NEW YORK

Copyright © 2021 by Laura Stone

All rights reserved.

Published in the United States by Crooked Lane Books, an imprint of The Quick Brown Fox & Company LLC.

Crooked Lane Books and its logo are trademarks of The Quick Brown Fox & Company LLC.

Library of Congress Catalog-in-Publication data available upon request.

ISBN (hardcover): 978-1-64385-826-5
ISBN (ebook): 978-1-64385-827-2

Cover illustration by Mary Ann Lasher

Printed in the United States.

www.crookedlanebooks.com

Crooked Lane Books
34 West 27th St., 10th Floor
New York, NY 10001

First Edition: September 2021

10 9 8 7 6 5 4 3 2 1

For my husband, George,
whose support and encouragement
have never wavered.
I love you.

Chapter One

"How do you think it's going?" I peeked out through the curtained doorway from the back room.

I'd inherited the bookstore three months ago from my uncle, Paul Baxter, who had not quite creatively named it Baxter's Book Emporium. Two months of soul-searching and intense waffling had finally forced me to admit I had fallen in love with the small, quaint town of Hokes Folly. The people had accepted me with open arms, and I was pretty sure I'd finally found a place I belonged, a place I could truly call home. As a result, I had taken it upon myself to rename the bookstore, but I had rejected the idea of putting my own last name on it, since Quinn's Book Emporium wouldn't have been much better.

Rita Wallace rolled her green eyes at me as she snagged two fresh pots of coffee, one decaf and one regular. My friend and next-door neighbor had offered to help with tonight's grand reopening event. "Jenna, it's only been twenty minutes since folks started coming in. Why don't you ask me when it's all over?"

I sighed, resisting the urge to grumble about how friends were supposed to lie to you at times like this in order to make

1

you feel better. After grabbing another box of the commemorative coffee mugs I'd splurged on as giveaways for the guests, I followed the chuckling redhead as we threaded our way toward the coffee station at the front of the store.

Rita leaned toward me as she poured the coffee into the urns. "Take a deep breath and chill out a bit, hon. It'll be fine," she whispered before easing her way through the crowd to return the empty pots to the back room.

I smiled as I pulled a mug from the box and ran my thumb over the store's new name, printed in a deep smoky-gray-blue on one side of the mug. "Twice Upon a Time." Uncle Paul would have approved. I'd come to Hokes Folly, nestled high in the mountains of North Carolina, at his invitation. He had offered to help me get back on my feet after recent trauma in my life. I had arrived, looking forward to reconnecting with an uncle I hadn't seen in almost a decade, only to find him dead.

Before I let my thoughts move in a too morbid direction, I took a steadying breath and finished unpacking. As I turned back to the crowd, I scanned the faces, recognizing some. A handsome form in a black tux held up a couple of plastic shopping bags as he walked in the front door. Keith winked a chocolate-brown eye at me, and my heart pitter-pattered like a tap-dancing poodle. I just hoped it wasn't wearing a tutu. In the aftermath of solving not only my uncle's murder but also a second murder, I'd begun dating Detective Keith Logan, and I shot him a playful grin. At least I hoped it looked playful rather than somewhat nauseous, which was how I felt. After all that had happened, I needed this to go well.

Keith set his bags behind the counter and planted a chaste kiss on my cheek. "I bought three of each, so there is no way we can run out of coffee tonight."

I had brought in enough sparkling wine for everyone to celebrate, but I hadn't thought to replenish my dwindling supply of coffee. Before I could thank Keith for stepping in and saving the day with his emergency run to the grocery store, a lithe brunette in an elegant, black evening gown stepped in front of us and held out her champagne flute to Keith for a refill.

"What a charming little party this is." The woman's bored expression made a mockery of her words, but her husband's firm grip on her elbow made her clamp her lips shut before she said more.

"Now, Selina, dear, I think Miss Quinn has done a truly delightful job of bringing together those truly interested in books." He turned to me. "I must apologize for my wife's rudeness."

I'd been mentally counting to ten, and I took a slow breath before responding to the director of the Hokes Folly Community Library. "That's okay, Mr. March." I nodded slightly at him, again hoping my true feelings didn't show through.

In contrast to his wife's obviously expensive gown, he wore a cheap, brown suit that clashed with his ruddy complexion and dirt-colored hair. Although his tone and face had remained calm, I noticed he didn't release the tight hold on his wife's arm.

To help smooth things over, I turned a tentative smile to his much-younger wife. "That's a lovely gown, Mrs. March."

Selina slid her hands down the black, sequined material. "Yes, isn't it? I've always liked wearing Vera Wang. Haven't you?" She narrowed her eyes, and her mouth took on the tiniest hint of a sneer.

My teeth ground together as I choked back the catty response I wanted to blurt out. Her dress may have cost more than a month's take-home pay from my store, but that was no reason for me to be rude. Okay, maybe I could be a little catty.

"When it's all I can find." I tilted my head and smiled sweetly, ignoring the frown that whipped across Selina's delicate features.

Keith stepped forward with the refilled flute. "Both dresses are equally stunning, though everyone knows it's the woman who makes the dress beautiful, not the other way around." He smiled and handed Selina her glass.

Selina's mouth opened in a small "O," and a gasp left her lips. However, before she could speak, her husband tightened his grip on her elbow and led her away through the crowd.

As they moved away, Selina ranted at her husband. "Did you hear what he said to me? The gall! Anyone can see that thing she has on came straight off the sale rack at K-Mart."

Douglas's jaw tightened, but his response was too softly spoken for me to hear.

I glanced down at my own far less expensive dress, which I had purchased from Kohl's, thank you very much. I'd spent too much on the black sheath dress, but the sleeveless gown hugged me in all the right places, and I hadn't been able to resist buying it. And the fact that Keith couldn't keep his eyes off me tonight made it worth every penny.

A glass of sparkling wine was pressed into my hand, and I turned to look into Keith's eyes. "I can't drink this. The last thing I need is for it to go straight to my head. It's all I can do to keep track of who's who as it is."

"Oh yes, you can. You look like you need it." He placed a hand on the small of my back, gently guiding me toward a quiet corner. Once in a slightly less crowded spot in the store, he blocked my view of the room for a moment, giving me a bit of a break from the crowd.

I tensed and relaxed my shoulders a few times and rolled my neck to loosen the tightness. "I just want everyone to have a good time."

Keith shifted a bit, unblocking my view. "Sweetheart, look around you." He gestured with his glass at laughing couples, several people contentedly browsing the shelves, and small conversation groups, which had sprung up around the room. "Everyone *is* having a good time."

I inwardly winced at Selina March's rudeness. "Some don't seem to be."

Keith chuckled. "Don't worry about Selina. Tomorrow, you'll probably be her best friend. She's just in one of her moods. From what I hear, she's pouting because Douglas put his foot down and wouldn't let her stage a late-nineteenth-century ball at the inn."

A picture of the elegant turn-of-the-twentieth-century mansion, which was now the five-star Hokes Bluff Inn, popped into my head. Built in the early 1900s and intended to outshine Biltmore in Asheville, the estate had over three hundred rooms, a bowling alley, two indoor swimming pools, and more. I could just see a ball in the grand ballroom, a stringed orchestra playing period pieces while ladies in beautiful dresses danced with dashing men, all in period dress.

My eyes wandered over my own little soirée, with my new coffee mugs and my rented but inexpensive champagne flutes. I took in my guests, dressed in everything from nice dresses and suits to true formal wear. Next to the image of a late-1800s ball, I could see why Selina would see this as a bit of a letdown.

Keith slipped his arm around my waist and gave me a little squeeze. "Your grand reopening is a smashing success."

I smiled up at him, relaxing at his warm touch, and paraphrased Rita's words. "Let's just hope you can still say that when it's all over."

Soft strains of classical music wafted from the stereo my only employee, Mason Craig, had set up behind the front counter, the soothing notes relaxing me further. I took a small sip of the sparkling wine, enjoying the way it tickled across my tongue.

Keith stroked the back of my neck softly, his warm fingertips drawing random patterns across my skin. "You look beautiful tonight. You should wear your hair up like that more often."

"Stop that." I reached a hand up to check the artful twist Rita had arranged in my shoulder-length, dark blonde hair, hoping to bluff my way past the warmth that signaled a blush creeping across my face. Yep, all still in place since the last time I'd nervously checked it.

I once again scanned the room, and as I was about to take another sip of the wine, I saw Mason Craig frantically waving at me from the front door. I'd hired him during the investigation into Uncle Paul's murder, and in spite of his personal past with my uncle, I hadn't regretted the decision.

I nodded at Mason and handed my glass to Keith. "No rest for the weary. I need to go see what's happening."

This time, I traversed the store more quickly, sidestepping guests' questions and well-meant compliments. I reached the door to find a flustered twenty-year-old Mason blocking the entrance. I placed my hand on his arm. "Is there a problem?"

"This is Linus Talbot."

Smiling warmly, I extended my hand in welcome to the tuxedoed man, recognizing the name as belonging to the town's Director of Antique Books at the library. Hokes Folly might be a small town, but due to the historical significance of the Hokes Bluff Inn, the library had a rare book section that was the envy of many larger cities. "I'm so glad you could make it, Mr. Talbot."

I turned back to Mason. "Is his name not on the list? If it's not, it was an oversight. I did send Mr. Talbot an invitation." Again, I shot a warm smile at the older gentleman.

Mason looked down at the clipboard in his hand. "Yes, ma'am, his name's here. But—"

"But," Linus interrupted, "I don't go places that don't also allow Eddy to come."

My gaze followed Linus's gesture, and I noted the medium-sized dog sitting quietly beside his master, his head barely reaching Linus's knee. The wavy, golden-red coat and white chest were well groomed, and deep-brown eyes returned my stare. A giggle burbled up when I noticed the black bow tie around the dog's neck, which exactly matched the one Linus wore.

"He's well trained, he's dressed formally for the occasion, and your invitation did say 'Linus Talbot and guest.'" Linus raised his hand. "We solemnly swear that Eddy will not chew anything, disturb other guests, or make a mess in any way."

My heart melted for the dog when I saw Eddy sitting with right paw raised, his eyes glued to Linus. Why the heck not? I preferred not to alienate someone who had been helpful to me in the past and whose assistance I was likely to need again. "All right, you can both come in. But I'll hold you to that promise." I tore two tickets off the roll on a stool beside Mason and handed them to the librarian. "One for you and one for Eddy. You'll need them for tonight's drawings."

Linus and I walked into the store, leaving Mason to cover the door.

"You've really done a lot with this place in the last couple of months," Linus said, his brows up and a speculative gleam in his eyes.

I nodded slowly. "It took us weeks, but we finally organized everything. Thank goodness I had Rita and Mason to help, or I'd probably still be working on it."

Linus chuckled. "I do remember the mess in which Paul kept things. It's amazing he could ever find anything in here, but he seemed to know where every book was hidden. Are those refreshments?"

I blinked, startled by his abrupt change of subject, but I understood when I followed his line of sight to the table I'd set up. "Yes, we have coffee and sparkling wine. If you'd like, I can scare up a bowl for Eddy to have some water." I reached down and stroked the dog's head, receiving a tail wag in response.

"There's no need. Eddy loves to drink from those little Styrofoam cups. If he gets thirsty, I'll make sure he has something. But I think I'll go help myself, if you'll excuse me."

I smiled and watched the book specialist walk away, Eddy trotting beside him, never moving more than a foot from his master. What would it be like to have a pet that devoted to me? Maybe I should consider getting a kitten or puppy now that I'd decided to give living in Hokes Folly a try.

Rita waved from across the room and pointed at her watch. I glanced down at mine and realized it was time for my welcome speech.

I stepped to the front counter and cleared my throat. "Excuse me. May I have everyone's attention, please?"

The sounds of conversation slowly died as faces turned to me expectantly.

I tamped down the butterflies in my stomach and took a deep breath. "I'd like to thank you all for coming tonight. As you know, Uncle Paul loved this store and this town." As I continued my speech, the nervousness left me. This was my town now. I belonged here. "In the past few months, I've come to love them too. You've all opened your hearts to me, and I hope to serve the community as well as my uncle did."

Determined not to bore anyone with a long speech, I wrapped up. "So please, everyone enjoy your time here tonight, and don't forget to take a commemorative mug home with you."

A brief round of applause echoed through the room before guests turned back to their conversations. A man stopped to give Eddy a quick pat before chatting with Linus. Again, I wondered if a pet might be a good idea, as the guests seemed content having the dog in the store.

"Ms. Quinn."

My daydream about pets ended, and I turned to see who had spoken.

"Bradford Prescott." A man extended his hand, his other resting at the waist of the woman beside him.

"Mr. Prescott, I'm so glad you could make it tonight." I took his hand momentarily, recognizing the candidate for state legislature from a speech I'd watched him give recently. "How is your campaign going?"

"Beautifully, thank you." He gently nudged the woman forward with his hand. "This is my wife Becky."

Bradford and Becky? Their matching shades of blond hair and their elegantly coordinated attire marked them as one of the few couples in Hokes Folly that could be considered our version of a power couple, and I remembered Bradford's wife worked at the district attorney's office, although I had her listed in my records as Rebecca. Their almost alliterative names were a bit cutesy, but I figured no one would dare say so and risk offending them. I shook the perfectly manicured hand the petite Becky held out.

"I'm so glad to see you allow animals in your store." Bradford gestured toward Eddy, who sat patiently at Linus's side as the librarian talked to another guest.

I smiled again at the odd pair, the proverbial man and his best friend. "Consider this a trial run."

"As you know, stronger animal cruelty laws are part of what I hope to accomplish should I be elected to the North Carolina House of Representatives next month."

Stifling a groan, I turned the smile toward Bradford. "Oh?" How could I get out of this? I really had no desire whatsoever to listen to his mini-stump speech, as I'd already heard much of his political opinions at the town meeting Rita had forced me to attend with her. He'd verbally danced circles around his opponent, his political savvy and intelligence impressing me even when I had disagreed with a few of his stances, although I thought he was spot-on regarding animal welfare. After the Howell bribery scandal had broken last week, completely discrediting Bradford's opponent, I figured Bradford was a shoo-in for the position. No one wanted to reelect a corrupt official.

I tuned him out as I subtly searched the crowd for Keith's dark head over the crowd. *Darn.* He was deep in conversation with Phillie Hokes, the last member of the Hokes family still living in Hokes Folly. She and her sister had owned a vintage and antique clothing store next to my bookstore. Phillie had recently closed the store, although she was still disposing of the remaining inventory and fixtures and had thrown herself more fully into her love of gardening. I thought of the gorgeous flower beds I'd seen in her backyard. She was probably filling Keith's ear with information on what plants she thought I should include in my display windows as we approached the holiday season, ignoring her knowledge of my completely brown thumb. Plants and I did not get along.

Next, I scanned for Rita's flaming hair. No luck there either. I caught a glimpse of her back as she walked into the back room, probably to make more coffee or grab more sparkling wine. Mason was a bust, too, as he still had his hands full at the front door. Resigning myself to a political chat, I returned my attention to Bradford as he droned on about his agenda.

"I do feel more funding of the animal shelter could stop this problem, don't you?"

Uh-oh. I had no clue what he was talking about, and I racked my brain for a vague way to answer that wouldn't let him know I'd been ignoring him. "I think any extra money the shelter receives would help every problem they face, Mr. Prescott."

He nodded as if I'd just said something extremely wise, and I wondered if he really thought I was that smart or, more likely, if he was too seasoned a politician to risk making a constituent feel foolish by pointing out her lack of attention based on her weak answer.

When he took a deep breath, as if to launch into another speech on his platform, I jumped in, cutting him off. "Here comes Mr. Talbot now with Eddy. I'm sure he'd love to hear about your ideas on animal rights." I gestured toward the approaching duo.

Bradford turned to see Linus approaching, and he paled a bit and took a step back when Eddy raised his hackles. A low, humming growl rumbled in the dog's chest.

Linus knelt and spoke softly, settling Eddy before rising to speak to the politician, a cold look on his face. "I see you're still using that hypocritical platform to get elected."

Fire flashed in Bradford's eyes, and his jaw clenched for a brief moment. He seemed to gather himself, relaxing his jaw and smiling before speaking in the silky tones he used to sway others to his point of view. "I would have hoped by now you would either have taught that dog manners or put him down."

My brows shot up, my moth dropped open, and a gasp burst from my throat. What the hell?

Bradford turned and placed a hand on my arm in a way I assumed he meant to be comforting rather than sending an icky chill up my spine. "This animal's a known danger to others. I hadn't realized it was this particular dog when I saw him across the room. I truly hate to see any animal put to sleep, which is why I adamantly support having no-kill animal shelters. However, dangerous animals, such as this dog, should not be allowed to threaten the safety and security of the good people of this city."

Linus's voice came out in a low rumble, sounding remarkably like Eddy's growl. "You lying sack of slime. We both know where this dog came from, and after tomorrow, so will a great many more people."

Chapter Two

B radford blanched again, a light sweat breaking out on his forehead. "Now see here! You have no right to slander me publicly!"

Oh crap! The loud voices were drawing people's attention. This was *not* how I wanted the evening to go. A spectacle had definitely not been on the agenda.

"I have every right, especially when it's not slander." Linus reached down to stroke Eddy and moved off into the crowd, leaving me to pacify the agitated politician.

At least it was over for now. I scanned the crowd, saw Keith making his way toward me through the onlookers, and shook my head. He stopped, eyebrows raised. I mouthed, *I've got this*, and he nodded once and stopped to talk to someone who seemed to want to gossip about what had just happened as she gestured wildly in our direction.

I refocused my attention on Bradford, who had returned to a more normal color and was blotting the light sheen of sweat from his forehead. Becky patted his arm, cooing words I couldn't hear, and he seemed to take strength from them.

"Mr. Prescott, since I run a bookstore, I'd like to hear more about what you might do for small business owners if you're elected to the legislature." Thank goodness I'd come up with something that might pull his attention away from the run-in with Linus.

A few other guests moved closer, and the suave politician persona came to the fore, his dulcet tones instilling confidence in the listener. I listened long enough to be polite before I moved away, rolling my eyes when I heard someone who apparently had no clue what had just happened drag him back into talking about his shelter policies by saying, "Isn't it wonderful the owner allows dogs into her store?" I hoped it didn't trigger another scene.

I eased my way through the room to the refreshment table, jonesing for a cup of java. I arrived at the same time as Rita, who was bringing two fresh pots of coffee from the back, and I held the urn open while she poured in the aromatic liquid. "Thanks. I don't know what I'd do without you tonight."

"That's what friends are for." Rita smiled, took the empty coffeepots, and grabbed a couple of empty wine bottles, careful to hold them away from the emerald-green dress that emphasized her voluptuous curves. "Go mingle. I've got this covered."

"I owe you one," I said as she walked away.

I smiled at the "Oh yeah, in a big way" she tossed over her shoulder on her way to the back room.

Holding a Twice Upon a Time mug under the spigot, I let the aromatic brew flow. I'd used beans from a local company, figuring if I wanted them to buy my books, I needed to support their business as well. The little bit extra I paid for the coffee turned out to be more than worth it. The smell and taste were out of this world. I blew across the hot liquid until it cooled enough to take a tiny sip without peeling my tongue, and the flavor slid through my mouth, awakening my senses and giving me just the pick-me-up I needed.

I sighed, wishing I could simply stand here a while and enjoy the sensations, but I was a hostess tonight, and I had guests to keep happy. I turned and scanned the room and noticed a woman standing alone, looking uncomfortable in her baby-pink dress. Her full figure was not flattered by the profusion of ruffles or the puffy sleeves on the outdated style, and her frizzy, mousy-brown hair showed streaks of gray. As I approached, she stared deeply into her own coffee cup, her eyebrows pulled together in concentration.

When I was close enough, I cleared my throat, hoping not to startle her into sloshing her coffee all over the books. "Is there a specific area of interest I could show you? Things are arranged a bit differently from when Uncle Paul was here."

"You must be Jenna Quinn." The woman's face erupted into a smile that brought beauty to her round face. "I'm Alice King. And yes, Paul did keep things in a piled heap. It's why I never came into the shop just to browse. I couldn't stand the mess. He would call me if he found something he knew I'd want, and I'd pop over to pick it up."

"I'm glad you joined us tonight, Ms. King." I racked my brain, and while I remembered the name from the card file Uncle Paul had kept on his best customers, I couldn't recall what types of books the plump woman preferred. "I hope you'll visit more often now that things are a bit more neat and orderly."

"I will, thanks. But it's just Alice. 'Ms. King' makes me remember how old I am. I prefer to think of myself as much younger." She giggled, making the rows and rows of ruffles bounce up and down like a swarm of butterflies.

Well, at least one person seemed to be having a nice time. "Is there anything I can help you find?"

"Poetry."

"Right this way." I led the woman to the correct section and pointed out shelves containing such authors as Tennyson, Shakespeare, Byron, and Shelley. "We do also have a few nice editions on an endcap."

Alice followed me to the end of one row where I'd set up a display of elegantly bound antique books. As I reached and pulled a book from its shelf, a flurry of movement caught my eye. A woman swept past, and her swinging purse strap snagged the corner of the book in my hand and sent it flying to the floor, where it landed on its edge.

I gently picked up the book, eyeing its damaged spine, and whirled to see who had been responsible. I should've known. Selina March. Before I could say anything, the woman whirled on me.

"How dare you stick that book out in my way! It could have damaged my Gucci handbag. Do you know how much this would have cost you to replace if it had?" The woman's voice carried through the store as she shook her handbag at me.

I drew on my mother's lessons in manners and counted to ten before I replied. "Mrs. March, you knocked the book out of my hand, and I would appreciate it if you would pay for the damage."

"Pay for it? You must be joking. I have absolutely no intention of paying for that piece of junk." She rounded on Alice and sneered. "Why don't you buy it? Maybe you could pawn it off on someone else and make a few bucks."

Alice's face lost all color, and she took a step back. "How dare you?" Her voice came out in a raspy whisper.

"I'm terribly sorry." Douglas stepped from behind the shelf. "I'll pay for the book. How much is it?" He pulled his wallet from his jacket pocket.

I peeked inside the cover for the cost code I'd lightly penciled in a corner. Although not a low price, at least it wasn't hugely expensive. "Mr. March, it's—"

"You will *not* buy that book!" Selina's screech silenced the whispers of the crowd that had gathered. "I did nothing wrong."

Linus pushed his way through the crowd that had gathered to see the spectacle. "I may be able to fix the book. It won't be the first one I've had to repair due to this woman. However, as always, it will drop the value."

"Those were not my fault!" Selina's voice continued to rise in pitch and volume. "I'll have you fired if you keep saying they were!"

Eddy stepped between Linus and Selina, a low growl rumbling in his chest.

Good grief, first the state legislature candidate and now Selina March? Was it a good idea to have animals in the store? I looked up to see Keith working his way through the crowd, and this time I didn't wave him away. I might need backup, although I did wonder whether I should ask Linus to take the dog home or ask Douglas to take his wife home. After all, the dog was simply protecting his master from a screaming banshee.

Selina took a step back, her voice rising yet again. "Keep that mangy mutt away from me! He's probably the one who tore up those books, and you're trying to blame it on me!"

Linus reached to stroke Eddy's head, calming the dog, and gave him a quiet command to sit. The dog immediately obeyed, and Linus focused on Selina. "If they weren't your fault, why did your husband pay out of his pocket to have them repaired?"

Ouch. I knew I should step in, as this was not the memory I wanted people to have of my store, but my inner nosiness pushed to the fore. I know it was petty, but the woman had been catty with me, and a small part of me, a part my mother would have condemned as unladylike, wanted to see Selina put in her place.

Selina's face reddened, her fists clenching and unclenching as she stared daggers at her husband. "*What?* You *paid* for them? You know damned good and well any damage was *your* fault, not mine! How *dare* you humiliate me like that?" Selina stormed out of the store, with a groveling Douglas trailing pitifully behind her.

Stunned, I stood holding the damaged book as Keith finally made it to my side. I opened my mouth to speak to him, but I honestly had no clue what to say.

Keith put his arm around my waist and gave me a squeeze, dropping a kiss on my hair in front of the gathered crowd. "It's okay, sweetheart. With a gathering of this size, there are bound to be personality clashes."

Linus gently took the book from my hands. "I'm sorry there was such a scene."

"I'm still not quite sure what just happened." I relinquished the damaged tome, glad to have Keith's support.

Linus chuckled. "No one ever is when she's around. Now, if you'll show me to your back room, I think I can repair this with a bit of book glue. I know Paul used to keep some on hand for such emergencies."

I shook my head and motioned toward the back room. "This way." I led him through the dispersing crowd and into the small storage and office area at the back of the store. "You'll find everything you need in the top desk drawer. And thank you."

"No problem. I'll let you know when I'm done." He settled himself at the desk, and Eddy curled up at his feet.

Pasting a smile I didn't feel on my face, I moved back out into the store, determined to put the remaining guests at ease and ensure the mood lightened after the disastrous display. Noticing a familiar pink-clad form, I eased my way through the crowd.

"Alice, I am so sorry about that incident. I apologize for Mrs. March's rudeness."

"What an awful woman." Tears glittered in Alice's eyes. "Some people just won't let things die."

Not knowing what else to do, I patted her shoulder. "I'm sure she didn't mean to upset you so badly."

"Yes, she did." The plump woman took a deep shuddering breath. "And she succeeded." She closed her eyes and swallowed hard. Abruptly, she changed the subject. "I'm not interested in that book."

It took me a second to make the mental leap. "If Mr. Talbot can't repair it properly, I can knock a bit off the price for you. But he seems to know what he's doing, so I'm sure it will be as nice as it was before. If you'd like, I can go ask him how it's coming."

"Linus Talbot is a pompous, self-righteous jackass who thinks everyone is beneath him. Just the fact that he's touched the book ruins it for me. He's another one who won't let things die. One day, if he keeps destroying people's dreams, someone will put him in his place for good."

I barely managed to keep from taking a step back at the vicious fervor in Alice's voice. Before I could think of how to respond, the plump woman swept down the aisle toward the poetry section in the rear of the store. I hoped she intended to pick another book to purchase, but I didn't follow her to find out. At least she hadn't run from the store in a huff like Selina March had.

As that thought passed through my head, I caught sight of the woman herself. Selina had returned to the store and was slipping into the back room.

I all but ran through the store, hoping to stop any more altercations before they happened. Enough was enough.

"Is there something I can do for you?" I asked as Selina exited the back room. Although I forced myself to smile sweetly, I hoped my firm tone left no room for doubt that I wasn't really pleased to see her back in my store.

"I left my fur." Selina's reply was equally aloof as she gestured to the mink coat draped across her arm. "Don't worry. I'm not staying in your nasty little flea-infested store any longer than it will take me to get to the door again."

"I'll see you out." I followed her to the front to ensure she was truly gone this time.

Selina flew through the store, almost dislodging several more books as she swung the arm holding her coat. I breathed a massive sigh of relief as the door closed behind her.

"I'm sorry, Jenna. I couldn't stop her from getting her coat." Mason clutched his clipboard tightly.

"It's okay." I rested a hand on Mason's shoulder and felt him relax a bit at the friendly gesture. "You did the right thing. She's gone now, and I'm glad, although I wonder where Douglas was."

Mason pointed to The Weeping Willow, the small pub across the street. "They argued on the sidewalk after they left. Then she stormed off, and he went in there. I can't say I blame him.

That woman would drive any man to drink." As we watched, the library director stepped through the pub's door, shoulders slumped, trailing after his wife as she plowed down the sidewalk on the other side of the cobbled street.

"Poor guy," I muttered under my breath, looking toward the parking lot at one end of the historic district. "I'd hate to be in that car on the drive home."

"Ain't that the truth?" Mason shook his head.

I inhaled deeply and let the breath out slowly, to clear my head, as I took in the picturesque historic street. The Hokes Bluff Inn drew guests to the town, and the historic district completed that step-back-in-time feel the Town Council wanted. The district had been rezoned years before, ensuring only businesses that could have been present at the turn of the twentieth century could inhabit the spaces along the cobblestone street. The ends of Center Street were blocked, allowing only foot traffic down the sidewalks. Long warehouses, once used as part of the cannery that had supported the town decades ago, had been converted into stores with apartments above. Tourists loved the quaint feel, and locals appreciated the number of customers the historic district drew to the area.

I squared my own shoulders, giving Mason's a final squeeze before letting go. "You're doing a great job. Keep it up."

"Yes, ma'am. I'll do my best."

I steeled myself for another round of damage control as I eyed the whispering groups, obviously gossiping about Selina's flamboyant return and departure. *Please don't let anything else happen tonight.*

I moved deeper into the store, mingled with guests, answered questions as tactfully as I could, and made small talk, hoping to soothe any jangled nerves, especially my own. Things settled down, and laughter and merriment flowed as everyone seemed to let go of the night's previous drama in favor of enjoying the free alcohol and opportunity to socialize.

As the evening wore on, so did the blisters forming on the backs of my heels. I hadn't worn shoes like these in months, and my feet were not happy about being forced to remain in the black pumps with three-inch heels for the last few hours.

At nine PM, I moved to the front of the store and again requested everyone's attention. "It's time for the drawing, folks!" I shouted over the crowd. My mother's voice rang in my head, berating me that a lady did not bellow. Well, this lady's feet hurt too badly to care at the moment.

Mason stepped behind the counter and began moving the items into view. He placed a vintage set of blown-glass book-ends and an antique reading lamp on the counter and brought a three-foot-tall, solid wood bookshelf around to sit on the floor in front of them. Lastly, he pulled a one-hundred-dollar store gift certificate from the cash drawer and laid it on the counter near the other items.

All but the gift certificate had been donated by Phillie as she cleared out her vintage store. Since she didn't want the items back and hadn't taken a ticket, she had offered to help with the drawing.

Rita moved through the crowd with coffeepots, pouring refills, and Keith did the same with a bottle of sparkling wine.

"The first item tonight is this lovely antique reading lamp." I gently held up the delicate brass lamp, its shade the shape of a large bluebell flower, the petals made of translucent mother of pearl edged in brass.

Phillie reached into the bowl and read out the number on the ticket. An excited patron came forward to claim the gift, and Mason packed it gently into a box he'd brought from the back room.

"Next is a beautiful set of bookends made of hand-blown glass." I picked one up, its tall glass spire twisted gracefully over a glass block base. As I turned it in the light, its interior prisms sent rainbows of color across the room.

Again, Phillie read the number, and this time Linus Talbot stepped forward as winner, Eddy close at heel. I hadn't seen them exit the back room, and I smiled at the loyal dog while his owner happily accepted the open box bottom Mason had found to hold the bookends.

Two more patrons happily won the ornately carved bookcase and gift certificate, and congratulations were extended to each winner as everyone headed out to the parking lots at either end of the historic district, commemorative mugs in hand.

A touch on my arm caught my attention, and I turned.

"I've repaired the book as best I could with what you have in the back room. The fact that it's now been damaged and repaired will devalue it somewhat." Linus shook his head. "It's a shame too. It was a lovely copy."

I followed the librarian back through the store to the back room and stood gazing at the repaired book. To my untrained eye, I couldn't see any remaining damage. However, I knew I couldn't sell something to a customer without disclosing the damage and repair.

My fingers trailed across the brass binding surrounding a white cover with black and gold scroll work, an ornate cutout in the center. Green grosgrain material backed the cutout, on which "MILTON" was stamped in gold lettering, matching the gold gilt edging on the pages. Who had read this book over almost two centuries since its publication in 1853?

"It's still in wonderful condition, in spite of the repair."

Linus's words pulled me from my walk into the past, and I turned as he headed into the front room.

"How long until I can safely put it back out on the shelf?" Even knocking down the price a bit, I could still get a nice sum for the book.

Linus furrowed his brow. "I'd say around two days. That should be sufficient time for it to set."

I thanked him profusely for his time, since he had been here as a guest, not to work on my books, and waved to him as he left, the faithful Eddy at his side.

"Well, that was sure a party." Rita leaned on the front counter and slipped her heels off. "At least I wasn't wearing a hoop skirt and crinoline, not to mention a corset." She rubbed her hands down her ribs.

I joined her, both at the counter and in her barefoot state. "We did have folks dressed from informal to formal. You would have fit right in with one of your work outfits."

Rita worked at the inn as head of the makeup and hair artistry department. People who visited the inn were swept back in time with period events, formal dinners, and more. Each guest was dressed and coiffed in period style, and the staff, including Rita, dressed the part as well.

I sagged against the counter, taking weight off one of my tired feet. "All drama aside, I think it went reasonably well."

Warm arms snaked around me from behind. "It went beautifully." Keith planted a kiss on the back of my head. "You'll be the talk of the town."

Mason exited the back room with one of the rental glassware racks in his hands. "Especially if everyone hears about all the brouhaha that went on." He set the rack on the counter and moved about the room, picking up half-empty champagne flutes.

Rita threw a balled-up napkin at Mason. "It all smoothed out in the end." She leaned over, put an arm around me, elbowing Keith aside, and squeezed my shoulders. "For now, we can relax. Mason can do a little bit of the cleanup tonight, but we can leave most of it for tomorrow. I have the morning off and can help out."

Too exhausted to care, I nodded and walked to the front door. As I checked the lock, a red and white streak ran past the front windows. Eddy?

Without thought for my stockings, I unlocked the door and yanked it open. "Eddy!"

Keith followed me out the door. "You saw Linus's dog?"

"Yes, he ran past as if the boogeyman was after him." I pointed down the street in the direction I'd seen the animal run.

Keith took off at a jog, calling softly, while I ran through the store to the fridge in the back, hoping I could find treats to coax the frightened dog. What had scared him so badly? And where was Linus?

Pushing that thought out of my mind, I raced out the door again, lunchmeat in my hands, to see Keith walking toward the store, a large bundle in his arms wrapped in his jacket. I held the door open, and he brought the terrified dog inside.

Carefully Keith set the dog on the floor, and I knelt to soothe Eddy, offering him a treat. A dark stain covered his feet.

"Keith, is that . . ."

Keith knelt beside me and picked up a paw. "Blood."

"Linus . . ." My stomach tightened.

Keith stood and strode out the door. I jumped up, jammed my feet back into my high heels, my aching feet forgotten, and raced after Keith in the direction we'd seen Linus go when he left the store.

As we neared the parking lot, I could see a lone car in the lot, its passenger door open and the dome light on, the soft dinging of the door chime echoing through the air.

Keith's stride took him to the car considerably faster than I could run in high heels if I didn't want to risk breaking an ankle. I skittered around the open door to see Keith kneeling beside a still body. A shattered blown-glass bookend lay on the asphalt, shards immersed in the dark puddle that oozed out from under Linus's head.

Keith turned. "Go call the police. Tell them I'm here securing the scene."

"Is he . . .?" I couldn't finish the sentence as a lump rose in my throat.

Keith's jaw clenched. "Tell them we'll need the coroner."

Chapter Three

Detective Frank Sutter yanked open the front door and plowed into the store. I groaned inwardly. The tactless detective, with his piercing stare and accusatory manner, had the people skills of a rock. Keith swore Sutter got amazing results, but how the belligerent man had managed to move up that far in the police force, I would never know.

"You again." Sutter huffed to a halt in front of me and reached for the little notebook I knew he kept in the breast pocket of his coat. "I should have known."

"Well, hello to you too, Detective Sutter. It's nice to see you again. How have you been?" What was I saying? Snarkiness wouldn't endear me to the bull-headed detective, as his narrowed eyes and humph confirmed, but I just hadn't been able to help myself.

Keith slipped his arm around me. "Don't start, Frank. You know this isn't her fault in any way."

Grunt. "So you say." He grasped a pencil in his meaty fingers and pinned me with his gaze. "Why don't you tell me about tonight's shindig?" *Grunt.*

I cringed at the grunting, an irritating sound that reminded me all too much of my first terrifying encounter with the abrasive detective—an encounter I'd prefer to forget. Resisting the urge to run, I took a deep breath and steadied my nerves. "We held the grand reopening event tonight for the book elite of Hokes Folly."

I proceeded to tell Sutter about the night, the kerfuffles that had occurred, the drawing, and finding the body. When I finished, he remained silent for a few moments while he completed the notes he'd been furiously taking while I spoke.

"Do you have a copy of that guest list?"

I nodded and motioned to Mason, where he and Rita still sat calming the dog. He rose and strode across the room, his brow furrowed and his lips pursed.

"Mason, can you get your copy of the guest list, take a photo of each page with your phone for our records, and then give the original to the detective, please?" Mason's copy would have the attending guests' names checked off, so Sutter wouldn't have to bother those who hadn't shown up.

Mason nodded and wordlessly disappeared into the back room, Sutter trailing behind him.

A hand touched my arm, taking my attention away from Sutter's retreating back. I turned to find Keith holding out a cup of coffee.

"You look like you could use this."

"You have no idea." Gratefully I took the Twice Upon a Time mug and lifted it to my lips, letting the warm liquid fortify me.

Keith raked a hand through his wavy, dark hair. "Believe me, I know. And I feel so useless."

"Useless?" My hands gripped the warm mug, trying to leech warmth back into my icy fingers. "Why? Shouldn't you be helping Sutter question everyone?"

Keith shook his head. "It's policy. I was present at the event and found the victim with you. I'm a witness and therefore can't take part in the investigation."

"Oh no. There's no one to rein him in." A wave of pity washed through me for those Sutter would question in the coming days, tinged with a bit of dread for my own continued encounters with the bullying man.

"Not this time." Keith sighed. "He has no idea how to deal with people. He's like a bull in a china shop with everything he does. He keeps saying he'll retire, but he won't set a definite date. But as rough as he is, I'd rather have Frank Sutter on the case than anyone from County."

Almost as if he sensed our conversation topic, Sutter left the back room and moved his bulky form across the store to where I stood with Keith. "Your employee, Mason Craig, said tonight was an invitation-only event. How did you select the guest list?" He waved the stack of papers in my direction.

"Rita and I went through Uncle Paul's client listings. He kept careful notes on which special clients bought what types of books and how often. That way he could contact a suitable buyer if a really nice book fell in his lap." I took a sip of the coffee Keith had brought, letting its warmth soothe my nerves as it slid down my throat.

Grunt. "This was the cream of the crop of your uncle's customers?"

I nodded. "Tonight was only for a select few. More of a PR event than anything else. Tomorrow morning we'll begin a weeklong grand reopening sale, which is open to everyone."

Sutter nodded and made a note in the little book he always kept handy.

I flinched inwardly, realizing the rumors that would swirl around my sale. How many customers would choose not to come out of fear or a sense of propriety? This was hardly how I envisioned my full leap into the world of selling books.

However, my possibly lost sales were nothing compared to the grief a family would feel tonight when receiving the news of a lost husband, father, or friend. My brow wrinkled. I'd talked to the librarian a few times on the phone and had finally met him in person for the first time in the store that evening, but I knew relatively little about him other than his vocation and the few vague tidbits I'd gathered based on his interactions with other customers and his dog.

Sutter's gravelly voice dragged me back into the conversation. "In the meantime, we'll also need a full accounting of who left early."

I nodded. "If Mason hasn't marked it clearly on the list, he should be able to walk you through that. I wasn't at the door, so I'm not the best person to ask." I craned my neck to search the room for my employee.

"Not so fast." *Grunt.*

Sutter's hand on my arm made goosebumps prickle up to my shoulder. I turned to face him.

"How well did you know the victim?"

"I spoke to him on the phone briefly after Uncle Paul died, regarding a book he had appraised prior to my uncle's death." I saw no reason to add *which* book that had been and reopen a case best left closed. "I've spoken to him a couple of other times since then about books I've run across that might hold value. However, we met in person for the first time tonight."

"Oh?" *Grunt.* He narrowed his eyes as if looking for a reason to suspect me. "No old flame there? No college friend's dad or friend of a friend? No other connection?"

I gritted my teeth at being the brunt of yet more of Sutter's smarmy insinuations. I'd had enough of those a couple of months ago. "Mr. Talbot was invited because he was one of Uncle Paul's loyal customers, and he enjoyed expensive antique books. There's nothing more to it than that." I was doubly grateful I held the coffee mug. It gave my fingers something to squeeze, keeping me from succumbing to the urge to throttle the man.

"And where were you at the time of the murder?"

Keith jumped in before I could answer, which was probably just as well, since I was very close to going off on the irritating detective.

"Jenna and I were both cleaning up after the guests left, as were Mason and Jenna's neighbor, Rita Wallace. They can both confirm Jenna never left the store."

"Really? I'll have to check into that." *Grunt.* Sutter's sneer said he doubted the story, but he flipped his notepad to a new page and moved off to find his next target.

I heaved a sigh of relief, glad I'd managed not to blow my top at him. "How do you work with him without strangling him?" I asked Keith.

Keith chuckled. "I've developed a thick skin and a warped sense of humor." He shrugged.

I humphed and pinched the bridge of my nose, trying to stave off the headache that had begun to pulse behind my eyes. "I suppose I'll have to come up with a way to spin this."

"Look on the bright side." Keith tossed me an irreverent grin. "Once word gets around there was a murder in the parking lot after your event, people will line up to get in to see the store. Just be ready to sell them all some books."

In spite of the macabre situation, I couldn't help but chuckle. Thank goodness I had Keith. Last time I'd been in Sutter's sights, Keith and I hadn't known one another. Even then, however, he'd stood up to Sutter on my behalf, and one thing led to another . . . and here we were. I looked down at my now-cold coffee I still clutched in one hand. *Why not?* I took a sip and knew why not when I almost gagged at the taste. It seemed temperature really did matter. I looked up at Keith again. "He doesn't really think I had anything to do with all of this, does he?"

Keith looked across the room at Sutter, who spoke quietly with another officer. "He's still frustrated that his pet theory about your uncle's and Norman Childers's murders didn't pan out."

"So he wants to nail me with this one? Is he crazy? Does he really think I'd kill someone—even if I wanted to kill someone in the first place—in the parking lot near my store, right after an event that places me here?" Mentally I counted to ten. Surely the man couldn't be that vindictively narrow-minded.

"As nutty as he is, Sutter does get results, though I'm not quite sure how," Keith assured me. "Besides, he can't pin it on you. There are too many people who will vouch for the fact that you were inside with us when Mr. Talbot was killed."

I stopped myself before absently taking another swig of the cold coffee, instead handing it to Keith. "I suppose you're right." I glanced toward the front of the store and noticed Mason slumped on a stool behind the counter while Sutter knelt on the floor beside Rita and Eddy, checking the dog's paws.

Mason raised his gaze to meet mine as I approached. "Hey, boss lady. Not a great way to end a party."

"No, not exactly the pleasantly memorable evening I had hoped for." I leaned on the counter next to him.

"At least it will be memorable." He shrugged his shoulders.

"Keith says morbid curiosity will bring in the customers." I wondered how fast the gossip mills would churn this out and at what point they would it turn into a free-for-all shooting spree—inside the store, no less—with multiple victims.

"Sure it will," agreed Mason. "We should use it in our advertising. 'We have books to die for.'"

My eyebrows shot up. "That's awful!" I clamped my lips together to control the inappropriate giggle that wanted to burst out.

"How about 'Twice Upon a Time: Home of the Killer Deals'?" His hands swept in front of him as if he envisioned a marquee.

I managed to stifle my mirth again, guilt quickly replacing it. "Linus Talbot was a nice man, and we shouldn't make fun of his death."

Mason wilted on his stool. "You're right. I use humor when I'm under stress."

I patted him on the arm. "It's okay. We all handle things differently. Just don't let the police hear you say something like that."

"Not everyone thought he was nice, though." Mason fidgeted with his tie, loosening it before pulling it over his head to toss into a heap on the counter.

I sighed deeply. "No, I suppose they didn't."

Motion out of the corner of my eye caught my attention, and I turned to see Rita frantically waving me over to where she still sat with Eddy. Sutter had cornered Keith, and the two seemed deep in a heavy conversation. I scooted over to where Rita sat.

"What's up?" I squatted and stroked Eddy's head, relieved to see the dog looked far calmer than he had when Keith had brought him inside.

"Frank Sutter is what's up!" Rita's cheeks were flushed, and her gaze sparkled with fury.

I turned my head to look at Sutter and Keith. "What happened?"

"He called animal control," Rita sputtered.

My head whipped back around to stare at Rita. "What?"

"I can't believe it. If I could take him home with me, I would, but my lease won't allow it. After all this poor baby has been through, now he's going to a cold cell at the pound?" A single tear slid down her face, either from anger or compassion or maybe a bit of both.

My own anger flared at the injustice. Flashes of Eddy flooded my mind, looking adoringly at Linus, staying at Linus's side, stepping up when he felt a threat to Linus, and finally running in terror and helplessness when he'd seen his owner, his best friend, murdered in front of him.

I stood. "Oh hell no, he's not." I gritted my teeth, whirled, and marched toward the two detectives.

"Sutter!" I called as I stormed across the room.

Sutter turned and glared at me while Keith's brows rose and concern leapt into his gaze, probably because he could sense his new girlfriend was about to go all psycho on him. I didn't care. Let them see my anger. When I had spent time in jail for something I hadn't done, at least I'd understood what was going on. Poor Eddy would never understand.

Keith stepped forward as if to stop my rampage as I plowed to a stop in front of Sutter.

I spit the words out in staccato fashion. "You. Will. Not. Send. That. Baby. To. The. Pound. Got it?" Had Keith not angled himself slightly between Sutter and me, I likely would've poked Sutter in the chest with each word. Even my mother's voice, usually admonishing me to be ladylike, was silent in my head, as I knew she would have been just as outraged on Eddy's behalf.

Sutter didn't seem fazed. *Grunt.* He tilted his head. "What do you propose we do with him? Turn him out on the street to starve or get hit by a car? Or do you plan on taking him home with you?"

That brought my internal steam roller up short. What *did* I propose to do with the dog? I honestly hadn't thought about that. All that had filled my mind was keeping Eddy out of doggy jail. I blinked and took a step back. Before I could stop myself, words pushed from my throat, almost as if of their own accord. "Yes. I'll take him home with me, so you can call off your animal control buddies. Do you have a problem with that?"

Sutter smiled, and I barely kept my jaw from dropping open in surprise. While it didn't make him handsome by any far stretch of the imagination, it made him seem a lot less unpleasant. Until he spoke.

"Well, then, I guess you'll be staying put, seeing as how you'll be taking responsibility for our prime and only witness to the crime." His smile now seemed less friendly and more I've-got-you-right-where-I-want-you. "I know you're not a permanent citizen of Hokes Folly yet. A few weeks ago"—Sutter gestured at

Keith—"Logan, here, mentioned you hadn't made the full decision to stay yet. I hope I don't need to remind you not to leave town until this is settled."

I laughed openly at him. He couldn't really be that dense. It had to be an act. His confused expression sobered me. A little. "Detective, if you look around, you'll notice this was a grand reopening party. That one thing should have told you I've chosen to stay. Permanently. I have no intention of leaving for any reason."

Sutter grunted again and nodded. "Then I think we have all we need for now."

I pasted on what I hoped was a helpful expression, when what I really felt was the need to bodily toss him out of my store. "If there is anything else we can do, please let me know."

As Sutter walked away, I leaned into Keith, who had slipped his arm around my shoulders, probably in preparation for holding me back should I get another wild idea to chase Sutter down again. "Gads, what a night."

He dropped his arm to my waist, turned me, and pulled me snuggly against his solid chest. "It's over for now. Do you want me to go upstairs with you?"

I stepped out of his arms, smiling, and placed my hand on his cheek. How had I gotten so lucky? "No. I'm okay. I just want to be alone for a while, if that's all right."

Keith placed his hand over mine and turned his face to kiss my palm, closing my hand over the kiss when he was done and almost melting me where I stood. "There's a kiss for later if you need one. If you need more than one, I'm only a phone call away." He winked saucily at me, but I knew his intent was to get my mind off the night's macabre event and off the swirling red lights I knew would stay in the parking lot at the end of the district until well into the wee hours.

Rita chose that moment to approach. "If you two love birds are done making goo-goo eyes at each other, I'll say my goodnights." She leaned in to give Keith and me each a quick hug. "I'll be down here first thing tomorrow morning to help clean up, but I have to leave by ten to go primp twenty ladies for a one o'clock tea event at the Inn. I'm headed home to crash into bed. I'm glad you kept the dog. Call me if you need me." She said this last to me.

I nodded and waved as Rita left the store, knowing she would need all the rest she could get. Her job as a makeup, hair, and fashion artist, primping, powdering, and preparing each lady as a turn-of-the-twentieth-century work of art for the formal dinners and events at the Hokes Bluff Inn, could be an exhausting one. Mason, who had to open the store the next morning, followed Rita out.

Keith slowly stepped over to where Eddy lay curled in a tight ball under the coffee station table. "Hey, buddy. Take care of our girl tonight, okay?" He gently stroked the dog's head, earning a tiny tail thump in return. Keith stood and held something out to me. "Here, it's my cummerbund."

I took it reflexively but wasn't sure why he'd handed it to me. "You might need a leash to get him up the stairs."

My heart melted even further, if that was possible. This man was almost too good to be true. My skin tingled and my breath caught as he gently kissed me goodnight before exiting and leaving me alone with a frightened dog.

I turned to look at Eddy, and my stomach sank at the sight of the still-bloody dog cowering in as tiny a ball as he could form, huddled under a table. *Poor sweet puppy.*

I approached him slowly, held out my hand, and was greeted by a few tentative licks on my fingertips. I stroked the dog's head, my heart breaking as he whined. "Well, boy, we can't leave you here, can we?"

He thumped his tail once on the floor in answer to my question.

I slid my fingers under his bow tie collar and tugged gently. When he resisted, I crouched down to the dog's level and rubbed his ears, glad Keith had thought to give me something to use as a leash. Eddy tucked his head into my lap and sighed. I crooned softly, hoping to soothe him. I could only imagine his grief. He'd watched his master get murdered.

After a few minutes, I stood and again grasped his collar. Eddy hesitated a moment, then stood and took a few tentative steps forward. I continued crooning as I slowly led him toward the stairs. Unsure if Eddy would stay at my side as he had Linus's, I slipped Keith's cummerbund through the bow tie around Eddy's neck.

"Come on. That's a good dog. Let's go."

The dog paused, his pleading eyes glancing back and forth between the front door and the stairs, obviously torn between memories of his owner's death and the thought of following me.

"It's okay." I reached to stroke his head again. "You can come home with me. I'll make you a nice bed with some blankets on the floor, and we'll see if we can find you a better home tomorrow." No way was I letting Sutter ship him off to some pound where he'd stand as much a chance of being put to sleep as finding a new home.

At my gentle tugs on the makeshift leash, Eddy slowly followed me up the stairs, pausing with me as I unlocked the apartment door. I coaxed with soft words and a few head strokes, finally untying the cummerbund after we were locked safely inside. He took a few steps, sat, and looked at me as if to say, "Now what?"

I went to the kitchen, looking for something to feed the dog, letting him follow when he was ready. When he heard the can opener, he trotted into the kitchen and sat expectantly.

After putting the bowl of canned chicken on the floor, I leaned down and stroked the dog again. "Sorry, boy, but this is all I have for now. Just don't get used to it. Your new owners might not feed you so well."

He wagged his tail without looking up.

I left him eating the last of the chicken, glad to see his appetite hadn't disappeared, and walked to the bathroom and turned on the water to warm up. Eddy couldn't go to bed with his owner's blood still all over his feet, even if it had dried by now.

Eddy's face peeked around the corner, and at the sight of the water running into the tub, he jumped over the side and sat. Well, that was easy. I'd expected to have to fight him into the bath, worried I might further traumatize him. But it seemed he liked baths. Who knew?

After soaping, rinsing, and toweling Eddy thoroughly, I pronounce him as clean and dry as I could possibly make him and turned him loose into the house to explore. While he poked around, sniffing his new, albeit temporary, home, I pulled blankets from the closet, folded them into a pallet, and positioned it in a corner of my bedroom.

I couldn't hold back the tears that welled up to sting the backs of my eyes when I turned to see him already snoring, curled in a tight ball on the foot of my bed.

Chapter Four

"We're sorry, there's simply no room." The woman's compassionate tones seeped through the phone lines. "Have you thought of keeping the dog?"

I sighed deeply. "I've been asked that a dozen times already. I hadn't planned on getting a dog at this point." I knew I'd thought about it when I saw Linus with Eddy at the party, but I hadn't meant *now*. I didn't have anything a dog would need. I hadn't prepared. I'd just reopened Uncle Paul's store, and I had new time commitments. I wasn't ready.

My eyes closed. *"You do realize you're making excuses again."* Mom's voice echoed through my head.

"I really hope you change your mind," the woman said. "If you've tried all the other rescue groups and the local no-kill shelters, the only place left is the pound. Since he's an adult, he won't have but twenty-four to forty-eight hours there before they put him down."

After thanking the woman, I hung up and looked across the room at Eddy sprawled comfortably on the couch and snoring lightly. He raised his head when I spoke.

"It looks like I just inherited a dog." I walked to the couch and crouched down to pet him, eliciting a wagging tail in response. No way was I letting this dog be put to sleep just because he had the bad luck to have his best friend murdered. "Since I'm officially a dog owner now, I guess we'd better find you a real collar and leash and something better to eat than canned chicken."

I glanced at the resting dog and quickly tripped down the stairs to check on Mason and Rita. I'd gone down earlier, but they'd all but shoved me back up the stairs to work on finding Eddy a home.

"How'd it go?" Rita was slipping her coat on. "Find him a home?"

"Yep." I swept an arm up the staircase toward my apartment. "The new owner has never had a dog, has nothing for a dog, knows nothing about caring for a dog, and has little time for a dog."

Rita all but squealed and hugged me tightly. "How wonderful! He's just what you need."

"We're keeping him?" Mason grinned as he stacked the last crate of rented glassware on the counter. "Will he come to the store during the day? I can help walk him."

I disentangled myself from Rita's hug, laughing at their enthusiasm. "I don't know. I hadn't thought that far. I hadn't considered any of this. I just didn't want him to go to the shelter. Not after everything else." My heart squeezed again.

"However it turns out, as always, you're not alone." Rita grabbed her purse and headed for the door. "Except for now. I have to get going or I'll be late for today's primping session. Have to get myself gussied up first."

As the door chimes tinkled at her exit, I turned to Mason. "The store looks great." I looked around at the sparkling counters, vacuumed floors, neatly packed glassware ready for the rental company to pick up, and full trash bags by the doorway to the back room. "Thanks for handling this."

Mason grinned. "What else could a store manager do?" He leaned casually on the counter.

My eyebrows rose. "Manager?"

He scuffed a shoe across the carpet. "I guess I thought . . . since you're the owner . . . I thought maybe . . ."

"Mason, stop." I put a hand on his arm. When he whipped his head around, gaze startled, I held my hands up. "Easy there. You don't have to panic every time we have conversations like this." I smiled, hoping I was putting him at ease.

Mason swallowed hard. "I don't want you to think I'm trying to take advantage of you or anything. You've already done so much for me, and it's just a title. And if you don't like the idea, that's fine with me. Really. It's okay. We can forget I mentioned it." He reached for the vacuum cleaner he'd left behind the counter.

"Mason, please stop." I repeated the command, softer this time.

He froze and turned, standing stiffly with pursed lips to cover his embarrassment.

"I think it sounds like a wonderful idea. You often open and close. You have made bank deposits for me. You've tracked inventory and have been invaluable with your customer skills. Without you, the store would not have done half as well over the last few months." As I spoke, I realized just how important Mason was to the store. "I agree a raise in title is in order. However, I insist it also come with a raise in pay."

When I tossed out a new number, Mason whooped and pumped a fist before sobering. "Sorry, didn't mean to be too unprofessional." He straightened his spine. "You won't regret this. I promise." He turned, marched through the store, grabbed the two trash bags, and headed out the back door toward the dumpster in the alleyway.

I chuckled as I headed up the stairs to grab Eddy. "I already don't," I murmured under my breath.

I entered the apartment and looked around for Eddy. No dog. I looked in each bedroom, the bathroom, even the laundry room. Nope. My stomach tightened. Had someone come in and taken him? I checked the front door. Locked. He had to be here. He couldn't have gotten out on his own. I stopped, calmed myself, and considered. If I were a scared dog suddenly left alone right after my owner was murdered, I'd hide someplace I felt safer.

I checked the bathtub, the closets, and the pantry. Finally, I knelt and looked under my bed, catching the glow of his eyes.

"Hi, baby," I cooed softly, extending a hand under the bed. "Did you think you'd lost someone else?" I wedged myself as far under the bed as I could, my fingertips brushing against his soft fur.

"I'm sorry I left you." I rubbed a velvet ear. "I promise I won't again. Where I go, you go from now on, okay?"

The dog's tail thumped the ground, as if he understood.

"Why don't we find a better spot to snuggle than this, huh?" I eased out from under the bed but stayed on the floor where Eddy could see me.

After a moment, the dog edged out from under the bed, and I sat up. He climbed into my lap and pressed himself against me.

I managed to keep my tears at bay as I kissed him on the head and told him what a good boy he was. I should've considered how he would feel if I left him alone in a strange place too soon. I guessed he really would go with me to the store every day.

When the dog calmed a bit, I grabbed the cummerbund-cum-leash, slipped it through the bow tie collar, and went out the front door. Relief flooded me when I realized I hadn't parked my car in the same lot where Linus had been murdered. I turned Eddy's nose the opposite direction and headed across the walkway in front of my neighbors' doors. After loading the dog into the car, I called Keith as I started the ignition.

"Logan."

"Hi. I hope you like dogs."

Keith chuckled. "And good morning to you too."

"I'm serious," I said. "I've spent the morning calling every shelter and every rescue group within thirty miles. No one has room. The soonest anyone can take him is in six months."

"I wish I could take him, but I just can't," Keith said. "My landlady would have a fit. She only rented to me because I didn't have a pet. Have you thought about keeping him?"

I glanced in the rearview mirror at the dog sitting quietly in the back seat. "Oh, I wasn't asking if you wanted to take him. I wanted to make sure you wouldn't hate it if I had a dog from now on."

"That's fantastic. And I love dogs."

"I'm actually calling to get Linus Talbot's address so I can go pick up his food, a real collar and leash, and maybe his bed and some of his toys." I put the car in gear. "If that's not possible, I'll have to run to the pet store and pick up a few things. I was not prepared to become a dog mom today."

"I don't think it would be a problem to get his things. But I'll warn you, Sutter is likely to be over there already. Want me to come along as a buffer?"

"Absolutely."

* * *

I stood with my mouth slightly agape, staring up at the monstrosity looming up out of the ground. Not in the oh-my-gosh-this-is-so-amazing sort of way. More like the what-in-the-world-is-this sort of way. Learning that Linus had lived in the same neighborhood of historic homes as Phillie Hokes, I'd pictured a large, elegant home. What I saw looked like it had fallen, all dark and dreary, straight out of a gothic suspense novel. The menacing look was compounded by turrets, peeling paint, a crooked shutter on one of the windows, and a gargoyle weathervane on the highest peak. The only things missing were sinister music and maybe a few bats flying around the roofline.

Rather than continue to be critical of Linus's run-down home, I opened my car door to let Eddy out, shut the door, and strode up the walk, noting the tarnished brass lion's-head door knocker and the slightly rusty door lock. Flower boxes hung from the windowsills flanking the front door, and large glass "stones" filled the top over the dirt. At least here, Linus had planted something happy to offset the overall tone of the home.

A young police officer met me at the door and informed me Keith was waiting for me inside. I thought of the old adage about not judging a book by its cover and bravely followed the officer through the huge, creaking front door, hoping the inside of the home was more cheerful than the outside.

Sadly, this was not the case. The hardwood floors groaned when stepped on, and a lamp in the parlor to the left showed carpets that were far past well-worn. Although the room seemed neat and tidy, the cushions on the heavy, Victorian furniture were definitely threadbare, and the velvet drapes, which made an attempt to block out the sun, were faded and riddled with holes I suspected had been caused by moths.

Keith strode from the room, arms outstretched as if to give me a quick hug. However, Eddy had other ideas. He tugged me into the room and dove under the couch, backing out with a worn plush toy of indeterminate age, which still squeaked as the dog happily chewed.

"Looks like I know which guy wins out." A silly grin slid across Keith's face.

"He definitely has more fun with a squeaky toy than you would." I sashayed up to Keith and planted a kiss on his cheek. "But I don't think you really have anything to worry about."

Keith's eyes darkened for the briefest moment before he cleared his throat. "Okay, then. Let's get Eddy's things."

As most of the officers seemed to be working downstairs, we started upstairs. I followed Keith and our police officer escort from room to room, silently taking in the home as the two men spoke quietly to one another, I assumed about the case. In each room, the sad display of yesteryear's worn-out finery continued. But with each opened door, Eddy poked his head in eagerly, as if expecting to find his missing owner. My heart broke a little more each time his excitedly wagging tail slowed at the sight of an empty room.

We finally stumbled into what appeared to be the master bedroom. A huge four-poster bed dominated the large room, and an equally imposing dresser and chest of drawers stood against other walls. I cringed when I saw the gaudy mural painted on the ceiling. Although faded, I could make out several cherubs surrounding a man and woman in bed while they slept. There was no way I would have been able to sleep under that.

Eddy tugged me to a corner on the other side of the bed where a large dog bed lay. Several toys littered its surface, and Eddy sniffed each one before putting his feet on the side of the bed to peer over the top, again seeming to look for Linus.

I noticed a patch of dog hair on the bed's cover, and I smiled, remembering the feel of the dog snuggling against my feet at the foot of my bed. I'd never had a dog before, and I could definitely get used to that.

I knelt and stroked Eddy's head. "It's okay, sweetheart. I know Linus would be here if he could. He loved you so much. You're such a good boy."

Eddy licked my cheek once and settled onto his dog bed, head on paws and a forlorn look on his face.

"Is he okay?" Keith knelt beside me.

I shook my head. "He keeps looking for Linus."

"Poor guy." Keith scratched the dog's head. "I wish there was some way to make him understand."

I looked into the dog's eyes. "I think he does. He just wants to be wrong."

Another officer had been sent to the kitchen to find a garbage bag, and he returned, offering it to Keith.

"Okay, boy, let's get your bed and toys packed up." He stood and motioned to Eddy, who slowly stood and stepped off the bed, watching with a drooped tail as his belongings slid into the black plastic bag.

I wrapped my arms around him and gave him a kiss and a hug. "It'll all be okay, sweet boy. I promise." With a lump in my throat, I stood and grasped the makeshift cummerbund leash again.

The second officer took the items to the front parlor to wait while we looked for more of Eddy's belongings. In the kitchen, we discovered his real leash and collar of sturdy leather. I shook my head at the deceased librarian's sense of humor. The bronzed tag inset on the leather collar said "Edition." So that was Eddy's full name.

After replacing the dog's bow tie and Keith's cummerbund leash with Eddy's own matched-leather set, I located a large bin filled with dog food, a scoop lying on top of the bin, and laid the makeshift leash set on top of its closed lid.

As we moved through the first floor of the house, I looked for a reason to snoop, hoping to find something, anything, which would say I wasn't to blame for Linus's death, that his time in my store hadn't been the trigger, that his death so near my store and so closely following the event was merely a cosmic coincidence, that I wasn't responsible for the broken heart of the sweet, sad boy at my heel.

I moved through the downstairs, looking into what would be called a family room today, a formal dining room, a solarium, and of course the parlor where Eddy had found his squeaky toy. I peeked into one last room, one that seemed to be a library-study combo. Here, at least, there was order. The furniture seemed to uphold the antique theme, as with the rest of the home.

My gaze slid around the room over the ornately carved wooden shelves full of what seemed to be old, likely antique, books. A huge desk with a brass desk lamp dominated one corner, and a big, comfy-looking, corduroy chair and a long couch with several cross-stitched pillows on it stretched along the right wall.

A lateral file cabinet stood behind the desk, and papers lay stacked on both the desk and the coffee table in front of the couch. The room seemed clean and orderly, and it gave the impression of a welcoming warmth.

"It's almost cozy in here." I ran my gaze over a colorful granny-square afghan draped across the back of the corduroy chair.

"It does look like he spent all his time in here when he was home." Keith stepped up beside me.

I pointed at the couch, pillows piled high, and another crocheted afghan draped over one arm. "Maybe he slept here, too, sometimes." I remembered the ugly cherubs above the master bed and knew I'd prefer this room to that one.

Grunt. "Apparently Talbot spent time in here researching old books he'd purchased on his buying trips for the library and staying up to date on the latest trends in book repair and binding techniques." Sutter's grating voice sounded behind my shoulder.

I turned to view the rumpled, older detective. "Nice to see you, Detective." I knew my smile didn't reach my eyes.

Over Sutter's shoulder, I spotted a yellow tennis ball under the ornate wooden desk. *Bingo!* This time when Eddy tugged, I released my grip on his leash, hoping it looked like an accident. The dog raced to get his toy, and I followed him into the room, stooping to gather his leash. As I stood, I glanced quickly over the desk and noticed an open appointment book.

"Miss Quinn, please control the dog. This is an active investigation." Sutter's rough voice made me jump.

Oh crap. Busted. How had he crossed the room so silently? "I'm sorry. Eddy saw a toy and pulled out of my grasp. I came in to get him. But while we're in here, could we look for his vet records and license records?"

"Fine." *Grunt.* Sutter gestured to my tagalong police officer to look through the file cabinet in search of pet records. His eyes narrowed when he glanced at the desk's surface, and he flipped the appointment book closed. "But I think you can wait in the parlor for us to bring them to you."

He herded me into the parlor where I sat with Eddy, me on the surprisingly comfortable Victorian sofa and the dog on the floor, while Keith carried the dog's items to the car. I gnawed my bottom lip, processing what I'd seen in the appointment book, judging its worth.

"Keep your nose out of this, Miss Quinn." Sutter plopped a folder onto the table. "Let us do our jobs."

"Of course, Detective. I wouldn't dream of interfering." A man had died after an event I'd invited him to—a man I liked and respected—and he'd been killed with a prize he'd won at said event. Yes, I would let the police handle it . . . if Keith were involved. But he wasn't. Couldn't be. And I knew for a fact how Sutter could get things twisted up and miss the boat when it came to finding a killer. However, I pasted what I hoped was a demure smile on my face, scooped up the folder, and headed for the door.

As I got into my car, Keith leaned in my window. "Do you want to come to my place, or should I meet you at yours so you can tell me what was in the appointment book?"

Chapter Five

"**B**ut I have to go talk to her." I resisted the childish urge to stomp my foot. I was not giving in on this. I plopped down on one of the bar stools beside my kitchen island and crossed my arms.

"And what are you going to do if that makes you a target? For all we know, Talbot was killed for what he was about to tell her." Keith stared me down, hands on hips and fire in his gaze.

"Look, I can't help it that I happened to notice the name of the reporter he had an appointment with today." I knew I was being churlish, but I couldn't help it.

"No, but you can be sensible and not go off half-cocked to talk to her." Keith flung his hands up in the air and let them flop down in a what-am-I-going-to-do-with-you gesture.

"I am not half-cocked!" I rounded on him. "I am not breaking any laws by speaking to a reporter, and I don't need your permission to do so." I jabbed my finger in his direction to punctuate my statement.

Keith plopped onto the stool next to mine. "No, I suppose you don't." He raked a hand through his hair. "But I don't want to see you get hurt. Or worse, see you come crosswise with Frank Sutter. You know how he can get."

That took the wind out of my sails, and I sighed and sagged back against the island. "I know. But I can't just sit here. The man died leaving an event in my store. I invited him there. It's likely I also invited his killer. I even provided the murder weapon. In a roundabout way, it's my fault." A lump formed in my throat, and tears threatened to fall. How could I make him understand I needed to see this through?

Keith turned my stool to face his and encircled me in his arms, letting me bury my face against his shoulder. "It's not your fault, Jenna. You didn't kill him."

I leaned back, looking up at him. "But—"

He put a finger against my lips. "No buts. Whoever killed him would have done it, whether after your event or at another time. You didn't cause that."

"No, I guess not." I wiped at a stray tear that trickled down my cheek. "But I still feel like I need to do something."

Keith lifted my chin so I would make eye contact with him. "Until we know who killed him, I want you to promise me you'll be careful."

I nodded and leaned my head into his shoulder again, letting his warmth chase away the chill of murder.

* * *

Two hours later, after repeatedly promising to call Keith the moment I was through, I waited in The Weeping Willow, a glass of sweet tea in front of me. I thought about the first time I'd been inside the pub, the day I'd seen the news blurb about Mason's arrest for my uncle's murder. I shuddered and turned my back on the wide-screen television that hung behind the bar, choosing instead to think of the pleasant meals I'd had since that day.

A tall, willowy woman entered and crossed the pub in my direction. "Jenna Quinn?" She extended her hand.

"Yes, and you must be Deandra Lynoir." I smiled as I shook the woman's well-manicured hand. I'd have to remember to ask her secret. Comparing her nails to mine, I realized how awful my hands looked, probably from handling dry books all day long.

"Call me Dee." She turned to the just-arrived server and ordered a beer, then returned her attention to me. "I'm glad you called. I wanted to ask you a few questions about the events after your party."

I watched her pull a tape recorder out of her purse and switch it on. "Ms. Lynoir . . . Dee. Wait."

She pressed the "Stop" button and looked at me expectantly, her thumb still on the "Play" button.

I pointed at her recorder. "I didn't call you to spill my guts about last night. I called to ask you why Linus Talbot had an appointment to talk to you today."

Dee leaned back in her seat and studied me through narrowed eyes. "I see. And what do you plan to do with this information? Are you selling it to another reporter? Is it Gary Long over at WHTC?"

My eyebrows rose. "No, I'm not selling anything, and I've never heard of Gary Long. I only want to find out why a man died after my event."

Leaning forward, Dee placed her elbows on the table. "In that case, we'll exchange information. I'll tell you something, and you tell me something."

I hesitated, searching for a way around the woman's offer. I really didn't want to sensationalize anything that had happened in the store, and I knew anything I told her would end up in the next edition of the paper. But then, that could be a good thing, as I'd control what she knew. Maybe I could avoid the gossip mill's eventual bloody-massacre version. After a moment, I nodded.

"Why was Linus Talbot at your store last night?" Dee asked.

"I inherited the store from my uncle, who passed away a little over two months ago. Last night we had our grand reopening event. Mr. Talbot was one of my uncle's valued customers, so he was on the guest list, along with quite a few other people."

"This is the same store that was owned by Paul Baxter, the man who was murdered inside that store recently?" Dee scribbled notes on a pad she'd pulled from a briefcase she'd brought with her.

"Yes. It's the same store." I wondered how long it would take before the first thought into people's minds when they heard of my store wasn't about my murdered uncle.

"I see." Dee made another note. "And what was the relationship between you and Linus Talbot?"

I swiveled my chair to face her and crossed my legs, my hand fidgeting with my tea glass on the table. "I believe I've answered two of your questions so far. I think you can answer one of mine."

Dee flashed a smile. "Sure. Shoot." She put her pen on the table and picked up her just-delivered beer to take a sip.

"Why was Linus Talbot coming to speak with you today?"

"Let's just say he was coming to see me about a dog." Dee winked.

I folded a napkin and placed it under my tea, soaking up the condensation where it had puddled on the table. She wasn't going to get away with giving me vague hints when I'd been open with her. "I'm assuming you mean his dog, Eddy. Why would Eddy interest you?"

Dee leaned forward and placed her elbows on the table. "Because the dog used to belong to Bradford Prescott."

My eyes widened, and my jaw dropped. I snapped it shut again and tried to fit that piece into what I'd witnessed between Linus, Eddy, and the state congress candidate. I realized Dee had spoken again. "I'm sorry, can you repeat that?"

"For the third time, what was your relationship with Linus Talbot?" Dee held her pen poised.

I shook myself and answered. "There was no relationship. Uncle Paul and I both used him as a resource to authenticate rare books, should one pop up. Last night was the first time I'd met him in person. Now it's my turn again. How did Linus end up with the Prescotts' dog?"

"I asked him that." Dee flipped through her pad of notes. "All he would say is that he'd adopted the dog from a local shelter after Prescott dragged it back in when the press coverage died down."

Dee apparently recognized the confusion in my gaze. "You have no idea what I'm talking about, do you?"

I shook my head and sipped my tea, letting the cold, sugary drink clear my thoughts.

Dee leaned back and crossed her legs. "I forgot you're relatively new to town. The election is next month, so you've missed all the campaign tactics and theatrics. In a nutshell, Prescott has pushed hard. He's pulled out all the stops to show himself as the everyday man, the working man, the professional man, the man of leisure, the animal lover, the education advocate, and the town's best friend. He's made every effort to point out where his competition is doing a poor job—at least in Prescott's mind—and presenting how he would have handled it and will handle it when, not if, he is elected."

"Isn't that a rather broad platform?" I swirled my tea in my glass, fidgeting as my mind tried to piece together how Eddy fit into all of this.

"It is." Dee nodded. "But Prescott has backers with deep pockets who are assisting with expenses. They've laid the ground-work, making every effort to ensure their candidate walks into that state house in the spring."

"And the dog?"

"The dog was a PR stunt. One of Prescott's platform points is better animal cruelty laws and better funding for local no-kill shelters in the state." Dee leaned forward and ticked items off on her fingers. "First, he gets a dog from the local shelter. Second, he makes sure the media knows. Third, he ensures he takes the dog to events where dogs are allowed, and he makes sure the press is there to see it and notice, giving him a chance to give a spiel on how wonderful he would be in office. Fourth, he includes the dog in every home photo, every home-based inter-view. Fifth, he openly plays with and walks the dog in full view of the community."

"So, what went wrong?" I had a feeling I wasn't going to like what I heard.

"The public got bored." Dee chuckled and sipped her beer. "The news media makes money when the public is interested enough to buy newspapers, watch the news channels, and buy the news magazines. When sales start to dip because the headlines aren't fresh enough, the press moves on to other issues. After a month, the dog was simply no longer news. He slipped quietly out of the picture, unnoticed and unremembered. Prescott pulled that stunt too far before the election."

"And Bradford took the dog back to the shelter?" My heart broke for the dog, who seemed only to want to be loved, and I gulped down a swig of tea to push away the lump forming in my throat.

Dee nodded. "Apparently not in the best of shape. It was a couple of months later. I went by the shelter, and according to the staff, the dog was half starved, his coat was a mess, and he cowered in the corner any time there was a loud noise or someone moved too fast. It was nowhere near the sweet dog they'd adopted out to Prescott. He'd originally belonged to an elderly lady who had passed away. He'd had no emotional issues, other than missing his first owner, when Prescott adopted him."

"But he says he wants to adopt another dog!" I plopped my tea glass back onto the table with a hard thump, which echoed through the room.

My loud words caught the attention of other patrons, and heads turned our way.

I took a deep breath and unclenched my hand from the death grip it had on my tea glass. "He told me just last night that he plans to adopt another dog, since we all need to support our shelters more."

Dee laughed loudly, drawing more attention from our fellow diners. She leaned in and spoke quietly. "He can't. No matter how badly he wants the press again now that the election is closer. The shelter has put Prescott on the no-go list for future adoptions and has put out the word to quite a few rescue groups."

The knot in my stomach loosened a bit, glad no other dog would go through what Eddy had. No wonder he was grieving for Linus so deeply. Linus had been kind and loving to Eddy, a far cry from the home Bradford and Becky Prescott had provided. The fact that they'd used a sweet, helpless animal as a publicity stunt and had abused him and neglected him afterward made it a sure bet I would never vote for Bradford, no matter who his opponent was.

It also raised Linus a notch in my estimation. "I take it Linus Talbot wanted everyone else to know what a snake Bradford is?"

"Yep, seems that way. But without him as a confirming witness to what had happened, I have no story. It would be hearsay. And no one at the shelter wants to get involved. They'll only talk to me off the record." Dee waved a server over to our table. "Now that I've answered all your questions, you can answer a few more of mine. But let's order and eat while we chat."

The next hour was a mix of salad, sweet tea, a bit of extraneous information about the grand reopening, and friendly chitchat. However, my mind could not let go of the fact that Bradford Prescott had something to hide.

Chapter Six

Mason whistled low and leaned back. "That's just not right, I don't care who you are."

During a late-afternoon lull in the store, I'd explained what I'd learned from Dee, and Mason and I had spent the next hour scouring the internet for articles and videos about Bradford and the dog. We'd also looked at his campaign website, which was still littered with references to Eddy.

I looked over at Eddy, stretched out in a patch of sunshine streaming through the front windows, and anger surged again. How could someone treat such a sweet animal so badly? Considering all he'd been through, he was doing remarkably well. Okay, so his appetite was a bit off; he was somewhat lethargic, at least in my opinion; and he was a little on the clingy side, not letting me get too far from him at any given time. However, he wagged his tail when I talked to him, loved tummy rubs, and had stopped hiding behind the sales counter when customers came in. That was definite progress for less than twenty-four hours.

"At least he can't hurt another animal." I'd told Mason about how the shelter had blacklisted Prescott and had spread the word to the rescue groups.

"But still. To be that mean to such a cool dog." Mason rose and strode to the dog's side, kneeling to stroke his soft fur.

In response, Eddy, showing he had not lost all trust in humans, rolled onto his back, seeming to encourage Mason to pet his belly. Mason obliged, eliciting a slow tail wag from the dog. Too bad Mason couldn't take him. They'd be great together.

At the jingling bells over the door, Eddy jumped to his feet in one swift movement, but instead of running to my side, as he had with every other customer, he began to wiggle and wag excitedly.

"Benson!" The young woman squealed in delight and threw herself on the floor beside the dog, a curtain of long, silky blonde hair cascading over Eddy's fur while she planted a multitude of kisses on the wriggling and writhing dog. "Oh my gosh, you're really here!"

My heart squeezed. Had someone just come in to claim my dog? *Hmm . . . my dog.* I guess somewhere in the back of my head, I'd begun to like the fact that he was mine. But I wanted what was best for him, and this girl seemed to be his favorite person in the world right now.

"Benson?" Mason, my protective young employee, still knelt on the floor.

The blonde yanked her head up, eyes wide, as if suddenly realizing she was not alone. "Oh. Oh, I'm sorry." She scrambled to her feet, a still-wiggling Eddy snuggled up against her leg, giving her goo-goo eyes.

I smiled and extended a hand, pleased b
without hesitation and shook it firmly. "I'm J
seems to really like you. But you called him
She smiled shyly in return, and her soft
and tentative. "Eddy? Is that his name now?
happened to him." Her hand dropped to hi i
stroking him.

I really had fallen for this dog, but it see
did have a history with him. "Would you li
Then we can sit and chat." I motioned to the
At her agreement, I poured two mugs of
stocked up on and led her to a set of cushy a
ner of the store, where I hoped patrons woul
to sit and explore books they'd chosen whil i
ones to purchase. Eddy trotted along with us
feet when we sat.

In the face of her shy silence, I opened the
only had Eddy one day, and I want him to h
Would you like to have him?" *Please say no,*
say no. I almost sagged with relief at her respo
"I can't. Daddy would be angry if I broug
Back? "Back?" I echoed my thoughts
before?"

She nodded, and I stifled a chuckle w
openly staring at her, seemly swept away by t
silky strands of her hair when she moved.

"Yes. I'm Bethany Prescott. I'm Bradford
ter. Benson—Eddy—was our dog for a wh
down and absently stroked him again, careful
mug held away from him.

"At least he can't hurt another animal." I'd told Mason about how the shelter had blacklisted Prescott and had spread the word to the rescue groups.

"But still. To be that mean to such a cool dog." Mason rose and strode to the dog's side, kneeling to stroke his soft fur.

In response, Eddy, showing he had not lost all trust in humans, rolled onto his back, seeming to encourage Mason to pet his belly. Mason obliged, eliciting a slow tail wag from the dog. Too bad Mason couldn't take him. They'd be great together.

At the jingling bells over the door, Eddy jumped to his feet in one swift movement, but instead of running to my side, as he had with every other customer, he began to wiggle and wag excitedly.

"Benson!" The young woman squealed in delight and threw herself on the floor beside the dog, a curtain of long, silky blonde hair cascading over Eddy's fur while she planted a multitude of kisses on the wriggling and writhing dog. "Oh my gosh, you're really here!"

My heart squeezed. Had someone just come in to claim my dog? *Hmm . . . my dog.* I guess somewhere in the back of my head, I'd begun to like the fact that he was mine. But I wanted what was best for him, and this girl seemed to be his favorite person in the world right now.

"Benson?" Mason, my protective young employee, still knelt on the floor.

The blonde yanked her head up, eyes wide, as if suddenly realizing she was not alone. "Oh. Oh, I'm sorry." She scrambled to her feet, a still-wiggling Eddy snuggled up against her leg, giving her goo-goo eyes.

I smiled and extended a hand, pleased when she took it without hesitation and shook it firmly. "I'm Jenna Quinn. Eddy seems to really like you. But you called him Benson?"

She smiled shyly in return, and her soft voice was delicate and tentative. "Eddy? Is that his name now? I never knew what happened to him." Her hand dropped to his head, her fingers stroking him.

I really had fallen for this dog, but it seemed this girl really did have a history with him. "Would you like a cup of coffee? Then we can sit and chat." I motioned to the coffeepot.

At her agreement, I poured two mugs of the local brew I'd stocked up on and led her to a set of cushy armchairs in one corner of the store, where I hoped patrons would feel comfortable to sit and explore books they'd chosen while selecting which ones to purchase. Eddy trotted along with us, curling up at her feet when we sat.

In the face of her shy silence, I opened the conversation. "I've only had Eddy one day, and I want him to have a good home. Would you like to have him?" *Please say no, please say no, please say no.* I almost sagged with relief at her response.

"I can't. Daddy would be angry if I brought him back."

Back? "Back?" I echoed my thoughts. "You had him before?"

She nodded, and I stifled a chuckle when I saw Mason openly staring at her, seemly swept away by the swaying of the silky strands of her hair when she moved.

"Yes. I'm Bethany Prescott. I'm Bradford Prescott's daughter. Benson—Eddy—was our dog for a while." She reached down and absently stroked him again, careful to keep her coffee mug held away from him.

Oh, holy cow on a cracker! I managed to clamp my lips together an instant before my jaw could drop open or I could blurt out my thoughts. Mom would have been proud of my fast recovery into gracious hostess mode.

"I take it you still live at home?" I wondered if I'd misjudged her age, assuming it was close to my own twenty-six years.

"Yes, at least until I finish high school in the spring." She sat up a bit straighter. "But I have plans to go away to college after that."

I sipped my coffee while I considered what she'd said and what she hadn't. Her subtle eagerness to leave Bradford's home might mean he wasn't always nice to her any more than he'd been to Eddy. I hoped I was wrong. "That's great. What will you study?"

She smiled widely and scratched Eddy again. "I've already been accepted at North Carolina State University. I'll get a degree in animal science with a concentration in vet bioscience. After that, I hope to get into their veterinary school and become a vet."

Thank goodness Mason hadn't seen that smile. He'd have been a goner for sure. But a customer had entered, and my ever-professional employee had snapped into salesman mode and was leading the woman to the aisle that held both romance and diet and health books. I wondered idly which one she'd asked for.

My attention back on Bethany, I racked my brain on how to bring up Bradford's treatment of Eddy. "I'm sure your parents are very proud of you."

Her smile fled as quickly as it had come, replaced by a furrowed brow and a shake of her head. "No. They're not." She gripped her mug tightly.

My eyebrows rose. "Why not?"

She sighed and seemed to wilt into the chair, her former excitement completely gone. "Daddy says he refuses to have a daughter who plays on the floor with animals all day. He says he won't pay for it if I don't go to law school like he and Mama did."

I gritted my teeth, took a sip of coffee to give my mouth something else to do other than blurt out that Bradford was a royal jackass, and leaned forward. But before I could speak, Bethany's soft words cut me off.

"But I showed him." A slow conspiratorial grin crossed her face, and her backbone straightened. "I got scholarships. My guidance counselor at the school helped me find two academic scholarships that will cover all the costs of books, tuition, and housing. And I got a job three weeks ago, working part time at a local vet clinic, helping clean up. They've already said they'd help me find a vet clinic job in Raleigh when I get to college."

My estimation of this girl went up by a huge leap. "Why doesn't your father want you going to vet school?" Vets made decent money, and it was a respectable profession, full of compassion, heartache, joy, and love.

"Daddy doesn't like animals." She shrugged.

Bingo! "I thought part of his election platform was that he wanted better support for local no-kill shelters and stronger animal cruelty laws."

Bethany shrugged again, a guarded look skittering into her gaze. "That's true." She stared at me a long moment before looking around the room as if to ensure no one was close by. She leaned in and whispered. "It's all just to get elected. He knows a lot of people love animals, and he thinks no one else is doing much about it on the state level, so he grabbed it as part of his 'I care about the people and I'm a great guy' platform." She wiggled her fingers in air quotation marks to punctuate her statement. "He even adopted Benson—Eddy—as part of the show."

I matched her whisper, hoping to keep her talking. "Adopted? From a shelter?"

"Yeah." She sighed. "Daddy made a big production of it. He called news channels, papers, magazines. He had a bunch of press people there, and Mama and I had to dress up and go with him to pick the dog."

"Wow, that's a lot of effort just to adopt a pet." Again, I tamped down my anger at a man who would use a sweet and trusting animal in such a way.

Bethany leaned back as the door tinkled, letting us know the customer had left. I looked up to see Mason once again staring, likely internally drooling over the beautiful girl. He caught me looking, grinned, shrugged, and shuffled toward the back room. I stifled the eye roll I wanted to aim at Mason's retreating back.

"Daddy let me pick Eddy. That was part of his 'family is always the most important aspect of my life' angle." More air quotes. She reached down and scratched the dog's head again, looking at him with a gaze full of love. "I knew he was the right dog the moment I saw him." She sobered and straightened. "But if I'd known how Daddy would treat him, I would never have chosen him. Not that any dog deserved that."

"Your dad wasn't nice to him?" I leaned back and crossed my legs, hoping I didn't look too eager for her answers.

She shook her head. "Not after all the news people lost interest. After that, Daddy left him in the backyard on a chain. It was summer and hot, and I'd go out and replace his water all the time. Daddy didn't even give him a doghouse for shade. If he ever went in the backyard for something and Eddy tried to jump on him, he would kick Eddy or shove him or yell at him. He would only let me feed him once a day, but I would sneak him treats." Her eyes glistened with tears.

I reached out and squeezed her hand. "But he's safe now."

Bethany gave me a watery smile. "Yes." A deep, shuddering breath whooshed from her lips. "But that was blind luck. One day when Daddy kicked him, Eddy tried to bite him. Daddy was so mad, he dragged Eddy to his car and took him to the shelter to have him put to sleep for being vicious."

"Really?" *This dog? This sweet, protective, loyal dog?*

Bethany's brow furrowed and she leaned forward. "He's not! I swear he's not! It wasn't his fault! He's a good and sweet and loving boy. It was Daddy who was the mean one." She seemed to realize she was speaking too loudly, and she shrank back into the chair. "When Daddy got home, he wouldn't tell me what had happened, and I cried for three days until Mama finally told me there was a man there who stopped Daddy. He'd come to adopt a dog and saw Daddy dragging Eddy in and heard him say he wanted Eddy put down. The guy demanded to take Eddy, even signed papers waiving liability because Eddy had tried to bite Daddy. But I never knew if it was really true until this morning."

"What happened this morning?" I motioned to Mason to bring the tissue box, pantomiming blowing my nose and pointing at the counter where the tissues were.

Mason's brows rose, and he rushed to grab the tissues and offer them to the distressed girl.

Bethany smiled another watery smile, this time at Mason. The poor guy. He was definitely a goner now.

"The police came to talk to Daddy about what happened last night at your store." She delicately dabbed at her eyes. "They said they'd been told there was a man here with a dog who had growled at Daddy, and they'd had an argument. Daddy said it was the dog we'd adopted but who had turned vicious. He said the man wanted to tell the newspapers he'd abused the dog. Daddy was furious and asked if he could take out a restraining order on the man."

Sounded like either Bradford hadn't known Linus was dead, or he was a wonderful actor. After seeing his ads with Eddy in them that he'd posted on his website, the way he pretended he loved the dog in order to pander to his constituents, I knew it could go either way.

"But then they told Daddy the man had been murdered, and Daddy got really quiet." Bethany sniffled and blew her nose. "Daddy took the police into his office then and shut the door, so I couldn't hear any more. When the police left, I followed them and asked what had happened to Eddy. They told me you'd kept him overnight. I came here hoping you'd know where he was now. I wanted to make sure he was okay . . . that someone hadn't hurt him again."

"He's fine." Mason knelt beside her and the dog and stroked Eddy's head. "No one is going to hurt him ever again. I promise."

I had to hand it to Mason. He didn't pepper her with questions—likely because he knew I'd spill the beans once she was gone. Instead, he played the gentle knight in shining armor, coming to her emotional rescue with the one reassurance he knew would make her smile again, this time at him.

And smile she did. I wondered if Mason would become a puddle of goo at her feet that I'd have to scrape out of the carpet.

Bethany took a deep breath and stood. "Enough of my weepy self. Since I'm in a bookstore, do you guys have any veterinary science books or biology books?"

Mason leapt to his feet and led her to the science section, where the two disappeared down an aisle, Eddy at their heels. I sat back in my chair, my mind spinning, sipping the now-tepid coffee as I rehashed the conversation.

Bradford had known Linus wanted to ruin his chances of winning the election. Had it been out of spite or out of concern for animals? Did it matter? What did matter was that Bradford was furious about it. But was he furious enough to kill over it?

Chapter Seven

Saturday morning dawned bright and sunny, and I had high hopes for the foot traffic for my store. I still liked that phrase: my store. It hadn't been too long ago that I'd hit rock bottom, on trial for embezzlement and a murder I hadn't committed, crimes that had yet to be solved. However, I hadn't been the culprit.

Now I was a store owner with roughly a million dollars in the bank, thanks to my uncle's generosity in his will. My heart twinged, the familiar feeling of sorrow and regret surging up at the missed opportunities to reconnect with him fully before his death a couple of months ago. But I would do my best to make him proud of my efforts with the store, just in case he was looking down on me from the great hereafter.

I showered, grabbed a quick bite and a cup of coffee, fed Eddy, and took the dog out for a walk before the store opened. After cleaning up and disposing of his morning efforts, the two of us headed to the store, approaching it from the street side and entering through the front door, making Mason look up, seemingly eager to help the first customer of the day.

Mason's smile fell. "Oh, it's just you."

"Wow, and good morning to you too." I chuckled and took off Eddy's leash, turning him loose to find a comfortable corner for a nap.

"Oh, sorry." Mason turned and busied himself dusting the back shelf behind the counter where we kept reference books and books on hold for customers.

I leaned on the counter. "Were you expecting someone else?" At his not-so-casual shrug, I prodded further, remembering our visitor from the previous day. "Maybe a cute blonde with an affection for the new four-legged member of our staff?"

Mason turned and shrugged. "Maybe." He ducked his head and fiddled with the duster in his hand. "Not that it matters. A girl like that wouldn't be interested in a guy like me. Besides, she's leaving town in a few months."

"A guy like you?" Trying not to sound like I was pitying him, I added a joking tone to my voice. "You mean a guy who likes dogs and books and is a true gentleman?"

Mason shook his head. "No." He plopped down on one of the stools behind the counter. "I mean a guy with no prospects."

I stifled the surprised laughter that tried to burble up and instead pasted what I hoped was a serious look on my face. "Mason, you're not even twenty-one until next month. Your whole life is one big prospect. You can do anything you want."

He shook his head again. "No, I can't. Not like girls like her can. I don't have a rich dad who can put me through college. Even with my new raise—which I appreciate so much, by the way—I don't even make enough here to put myself through junior college."

Ah, there was the true issue. "Where would you go and what would you study if you could?" A kernel of an idea formed in my mind.

"Promise you won't think it's dumb?" He twirled the duster in his hands, sending little puffs of already picked-up dust back out into the air.

I swept my fingers across the left side of my chest in a big X. "Cross my heart."

Mason's gaze met mine. "I looked online at what was offered at the local branch of the John. J. Hokes Community College."

I nodded my encouragement when he paused. I'd heard of the college, which had started as a community center that held general classes in cooking, home economics, and auto mechanics for local residents but had grown into a widespread and fully accredited junior college over the span of twenty years.

"Well . . ." Mason pursed his lips a moment before pushing out the staccato words. "They offer an associate degree in accounting. I know you were an accountant too, and I know you don't want to be one anymore, but I figured it was something I could do online, and maybe you could help me if I needed it, and it's something that I could do here in Hokes Folly, because I don't really want to move to another city. Not that it matters, though, because at the rate I'll be able to pay for classes, I'll be thirty before I graduate."

How did this kid not quite six years younger than me manage to bring out my previously unknown motherly instincts? He was right, though. I'd turned my back on the accounting world when I'd moved to Hokes Folly. Frankly, the accounting world had turned its back on me when the marketing firm for which I had worked had fired me after accusing me of embezzlement.

I shook my head and refocused on Mason's current dilemma. "You've really given this a lot of thought."

"Yes and no." Mason shrugged and stood. "It's been in the back of my mind for a year or so, but after yesterday, it's kind of in the front of my mind now."

I knew Mason had come from a disadvantaged background. His father had skipped out with his secretary while his mother was pregnant with him. Mason didn't even know who or where his father was. His grandparents had passed away when he was young. His mother, a loving and strong woman, had passed away a little over a year and a half ago, leaving Mason pretty much on his own with no safety net. After getting in with a rough crowd during his grief and a short stint of drug usage, Mason had gotten his head on straight again and was moving forward with his life.

Well, everyone could use a fairy godmother, if one was available. I mentally waved my magic wand. *Bibbidi-bobbidi-boo.* "Mason, I think Uncle Paul would have wanted you to go to college. What if I help pay for your school expenses?"

I expected him to be excited, happy, joyful—something positive. However, he turned and stalked down an aisle, duster in hand. Loud sniffing ensued, and I crept to the end of the aisle and peeked around in time to see him brush a tear off his cheek and suck in another loud sniff.

"Dust getting to you?" I walked into the aisle and leaned against the shelves near his efforts, knowing dust wasn't the issue.

Mason cleared his throat and sniffed once more. "Yeah. This shelf was pretty bad. I must have missed it last time." He turned to face me, duster forgotten. "I appreciate your offer, but I can't accept it. You've already done too much, helping me get my own apartment and all. Now there's the raise, which will help me get a new car. I can't keep mooching off you every time I need something. A man has to stand on his own two feet."

I nodded and crossed my arms, understanding his quandary. "Fair enough. I'm sorry if I upset you with the offer. So how about this one instead? How about a student loan? I'll loan you the money to go, and once you start making money as an accountant, we can come up with a fair payment plan to pay me back."

He cleared his throat again, straightened his shoulders, and nodded once. "I think that's an option we might consider."

Mason turned back to his dusting, and I figured it was time to leave him to regain his composure. I strode behind the counter, sat, and woke the laptop up. We'd finally completed setting up our point-of-sale system on the new computer. I'd also hired a girl to build us a database to input customer requests or their interests, so we could ensure we contacted the right people when certain types of books came through the store.

Now I needed to write personal letters to each of the people who had been on the guest list for Thursday's event, whether they had attended or not, asking them to stop by or call. While Uncle Paul had been able to keep all of their information straight in his head, I needed the computer to remember everything. How he'd managed it, I would never know.

The bell over the front door tinkled, announcing a customer, and I turned to see the plump woman I'd met at the event. What was her name? It started with an A . . . Alice! That was it. Alice King.

"How are you today, Alice?" I stepped from behind the counter, my hand extended.

She grasped my hand in both of hers and shook it, her hands soft and slightly clammy. "I'd be better if we weren't all grieving as a community for poor Linus." She let go of my hand and pulled an obviously used tissue from her purse and dabbed at her eyes.

I resisted the urge to wipe my hand on my jeans and reach for the hand sanitizer as I nodded. "Let's get some coffee and sit for a bit."

She remained silent as I poured coffee into two of my store-logo mugs, led her to the seats in the corner, and handed her a mug.

"Linus was such a good man." She half sobbed into her tissue the moment we sat. "I can't believe he's really gone."

My eyebrows shot up. This was opposite of the sentiment she'd expressed during the event, foretelling doom.

Apparently, she caught my odd look, and she hurried to explain, pushing her words out at a gushing pace. "Oh, I know I said someone would put him in his place for good, and there were times when I wanted to myself, but I never would have actually killed him, and now he's gone, and even though he was such a nasty man to me, it's so unkind to say mean things about the dead, so I'm trying to be nice, since he can't be here to defend himself." She sniffed again, as if to punctuate her pseudo-grief.

I stared at her, my brows still up, unsure of how to respond as she came to the close of her rant. "Alice, I'm sure no one thinks you had anything to do with Mr. Talbot's death."

"That rude policeman does. He all but tried to force me to confess." Her tearful remorse at Linus's death was momentarily replaced by a righteous indignation. "As if I'd be that stupid, even if I had done it."

I couldn't believe I was about to come to Sutter's defense after all he'd put me through. "Detective Sutter is just doing his job. He has to solve a murder, and he knows the killer could be someone who attended the event. I'm sure he was trying to eliminate you as a suspect." Although I'd intended them to help, it seemed my words had the opposite effect.

Alice paled and began to shake hard enough her double chin wobbled. "You think the killer was there?" Her voice rose an octave and came out in a semi-squeak. "In this store? Possibly right next to me at some point?" Her hand clutched at my arm, her fingers digging painfully into the skin.

I gently but firmly pried her vise-like grip from my arm and wished I'd been more careful with my words. "There is that possibility, but the police will find out who did it."

Alice's eyes held a frantic glaze now. "I wasn't the only one who didn't like Linus. Selina March couldn't stand him. And she's mean enough to kill someone. You saw how she acted. And she came back to get that god-awful fur coat of hers. She flashes that thing around, because she thinks it makes her look classier, so she couldn't just leave it here. Poor Douglas buys whatever she wants, and she bleeds him dry. He's a saint to put up with her, I tell you. And it was right after she left with her coat that everyone else left."

"We did have the drawing after Selina got her coat, which means Linus was killed at least half an hour after they left." I patted her gently on the shoulder, trying to calm her a bit.

Alice shook her head. "No, you don't understand. It had to be her. She really hated Linus after the whole car incident." She nodded emphatically, as if confirming her opinion, and took a large swig of coffee.

"Car incident?" I racked my brain, searching for any information about Selina and coming up with nothing.

Alice settled into her chair, the tears in her eyes replaced by a predatory gleam, the tissue wadded in her hand. "Oh, I forget, you're not from here, so you don't know. Well, let me tell you then." She giggled. "About twelve years ago, when Selina was a senior in high school, she and a couple of her friends got drunk at a party on Linus's street one night, and they stole his car for a joyride. They wrecked it. The other two girls got away, and Selina would never reveal who they were. However, she passed out drunk in the front seat. Linus pressed charges, which put a felony on Selina's record. Since she hadn't been in trouble like that before, she got three years of probation instead of jail time. But she also lost her scholarship to the University of Virginia, where she hoped to join a sorority and find a rich husband."

College again. I sipped my coffee as I let it roll through my mind. "She was mad at Linus because she didn't get to go to college after she was the one who broke the law?"

Alice shook her head. "She went to college. Her daddy could have paid for her to go anywhere she wanted. But after that incident, he insisted she stay home and go to the local junior college so he could keep an eye on her. All of her hopes for a rich husband and moving away from here were crushed."

"How did she meet and marry Douglas? They seem an unlikely couple." I pictured the drab older man with the wilted look in his eyes.

"Oh, that?" Alice leaned in, glee at gossiping sparkling in her gaze. "She met him while she was studying at the library. He's fifteen years older than she is, and his father had money. She thought he was her ticket out. Three years after they married,

Douglas's father died and left his fortune to the library in a trust, to be used only to maintain the building and create additions as deemed needed by the library board of directors. Poor Douglas didn't get a dime because his father saw through Selina's fake-sweet act. He pegged her as a gold digger from day one, and he refused to support that. Frankly, we were all surprised when she didn't divorce Douglas on the spot. But she'd entrenched herself as queen bee socialite in town, and she didn't want to start over with a divorce on her record."

Alice revived her tissue and dabbed at her eyes again. "Selina forces that sweet man to live like a pauper in order to support her spending habits." She stood, shoved her tissue into her pocket, and thrust her mug at me. "I really should go talk to that detective again."

I caught the mug, sloshing a bit over the edge onto my hand, glad it wasn't still terribly hot, and scrambled to my feet. "Before you go, might I talk to you about what types of books you would like me to hold for you if I find them?" I walked toward the computer.

A smile, genuine this time, crossed her face. "I'd be happy to talk books for a few minutes."

After I entered her information into our new searchable database of customers—okay, customer, since she was the only entry so far—I spied the book I'd almost sold her at the event. I pulled it off the shelf behind the counter where I'd stashed it and forgotten it and held it out to her. "We do still have this one available. Linus did an amazing job repairing it. You can't even tell it was damaged."

Alice recoiled, as if I'd tried to hand her a snake. "I have no interest in taking that book or any other book Linus Talbot touched. Not after . . . well, I don't want it. That's all."

Eddy, who had been asleep behind the counter, chose this moment to stand, stretch, and walk out into the store.

Alice stumbled backward. "Is that Linus's dog?"

I smiled and nodded. "Yes, I've decided to give him a home." And I really had. After my reaction the day before when Bethany Prescott had visited and I'd briefly thought I'd be losing him, I couldn't deny how quickly I'd formed a strong attachment to the dog.

"Just keep that mutt away from me." Alice curled her lip and clutched her pocketbook to her wide stomach, as if using it as a shield.

Eddy eased in front of me, his hackles raised at her aggressive tone.

Alice stepped backward to the door. "Maybe if Linus had paid more attention to the world around him instead of to that stupid dog, he'd still be alive."

My eyebrows shot up, and by the time I could stutter out a rushed "please come again," the only sound I received in return was the jangling bells over the door.

Chapter Eight

I smoothed my deep-crimson pencil skirt as I sat on the chair Keith had pulled out for me in a gentlemanly manner. He rounded the small table and sat opposite me.

A server placed hardcover menus in front of each of us and stepped back. "Would you like to order drinks?" She smiled.

Keith and I had been to this sushi restaurant twice in the last three months, and he already knew what we'd both want.

"Yes, we'd like a bottle of nigori sake, chilled, and a pot of hot jasmine tea, please." As she left the table, he opened his menu.

I'd already opened mine, scanning the list of mouth-watering temptations on which we would gorge ourselves until we could barely walk back to the car. We discussed what we would share for dinner and ordered when the server returned, the smile still on her face.

As she left, Keith leaned back and sipped from his tiny cup of sake. "So, Alice went a little bonkers on you, huh?"

I chuckled, jumping back into the conversation we'd started on the way over. I'd explained about the plump woman's wildly swinging moods and had told him what she'd said about Selina March. "That's one way of putting it. She was so weepy and mournful over Linus to begin with, then went all psycho about it later. I have a feeling what she expressed at the end is closer to her true feelings than the tears and sentiments she tried to push out."

Keith sobered. "Sounds like she's awfully intent on pointing a finger at someone else." He leaned in and reached for my hand. "Be careful about trusting either Alice or Selina for now. Or the Prescotts, for that matter."

My eyebrows rose. I hadn't discussed my chat with Bethany Prescott with him yet. "Why do you say that?"

"Sutter is zeroing in on Prescott as the most likely suspect. He's convinced it had to do with his election campaign and a fight he'd had with Talbot over a dog." Keith squeezed my fingers. "Your new dog."

I flipped my hand and wove my fingers into his, reveling in their warmth. "I know."

"You know? How?" Keith pulled me closer. "Jenna, you can't go around interrogating people. You know Frank Sutter will have your hide for it."

I slid my fingers out of his grasp, leaned back, and crossed my arms. "Why is your first assumption that I'm meddling in your department's investigation? Where's the trust?"

Keith narrowed his eyes and studied me a moment before nodding once. "Fair enough. I'm sorry. How do you know? And what exactly do you know?"

I relaxed the tension that had gripped my shoulders, internally letting go the irritation I'd felt at the oh-so-minor accusation. "Bethany Prescott dropped by the store, hoping we'd know what happened to Eddy." I smiled briefly, remembering their reunion. "She told me about what happened with the dog and why Bradford hated Linus."

Keith shook his head, chuckling. "I swear, for someone so new to town, folks sure love to chat you up and give you all sorts of information. I really am sorry I jumped to conclusions." He reached over and uncrossed my arms, sliding his fingers into mine again. "Forgive me?"

The rest of my irritation fled at the genuine contrition in Keith's gaze. "I do." Catching sight of our server weaving her way toward us with our food, I added, "I'll tell you about it while we eat."

Thirty minutes later, stuffed with as much sushi as I could possibly eat, I sat back as a sigh of contented pleasure escaped my lips. "I can't move. You'll have to help me waddle to the car."

"We'll both have to help each other." Keith chuckled. "Seriously, though, how narcissistic do you have to be to make sure your wife, kid, and even dog have names that start with the same first letter as yours? I mean, come on. Bradford, Becky, Bethany, and Benson?"

A giggle burbled up. "At least if they're into monograms, they could all share the same stuff."

At his guffaw, I shushed him and glanced around the restaurant to see if we'd disturbed anyone. No one seemed to care. As my gaze swung back toward my date, I caught sight of a familiar fur coat sweeping through the restaurant behind a startled hostess. Angry words followed.

"I can't believe this place still doesn't have a coat check. After all the times I've requested they set one up." Selina March's arrogant shrill echoed through the dining room, drawing the attention Keith's loud laughter had failed to summon.

Of all the rotten luck. The server seated the Marches at the table next to ours.

Selina's head swung around the room, her gaze settling on me. "Is there something you want?" Her demanding question ended abruptly. "Don't I know you?"

I nodded but before I could speak, a sneer spread across her face, and she wrinkled her nose in seeming distaste.

"Oh yes, the little bookshop girl who accused me of damaging her stupid books."

My mouth dropped open, and I sucked in a breath, ready to let her have it. How dare she? Keith's shoe kicked my foot under the table, stopping me before I could cause a scene. He must be in league with my mother's voice inside my head, which was demanding decorum and politeness, even in the face of blatant rudeness.

Keith's soft voice was just loud enough for the Marches to hear. "Yes, Jenna owns Twice Upon a Time. You were there for her event, where you created a tacky scene, weren't you?"

Okay, so not so much in league with Mom after all. I'd have to thank him profusely later.

Selina's screech cut through the room again. "Who do you think you are?"

"Now, Selina, dear, calm down." Douglas's hand gripped Selina's arm, and I noted he wasn't quite as simpering tonight as he had been previously. "Let's enjoy our dinner." His gaze slid to me, seeming to silently plead with us to simply let it go.

Keith picked up the check our server had brought to the table, and we walked toward the front of the restaurant to pay, passing behind Selina as we left.

A snarky comment, offered to her husband in a loud whisper I was sure was meant to be overheard, hissed out of Selina's lips.

"I can't believe that woman expects me to be sorry about her stupid book. The only thing that keeps everything in that store from being yesterday's trash is that some of them seem to actually be valuable. God only knows why."

Keith slid his arm around my waist, keeping me from turning around and continuing what could soon become a very unladylike brouhaha. Firmly he guided me toward the front of the restaurant, stopped to pay, and walked me to the car.

I slid into the car as he held the door open, crossing my arms in a pout when he closed the door and walked around to get in on the driver's side.

"Honey, the last thing you want to do is provoke that woman if she really is the killer." He leaned on the armrest between us.

I snorted. "I doubt she'd want to mess up her precious fur coat." I turned to look out my side window, purposely ignoring his steady gaze.

Keith's fingertips touched my shoulder. "Jenna."

When I didn't turn, he slid his fingers down, gently grasping my wrist to again uncross my arms and tuck his fingers into mine. "Jenna."

Man, this guy was irresistible, and I figured he knew it. I huffed once more and turned. "She makes me so incredibly mad. I have never met anyone that openly and intentionally rude and hateful in my life!"

At my raised voice, Keith chuckled. "Seriously? Have you met Frank Sutter yet?"

I caught the playful look in his eyes, and my anger melted as laughter popped out. "Wow, could you imagine them as a couple?"

Keith belly laughed and kissed my fingertips before letting them go so he could start the car. "I'm not sure who would lose out more in that deal. Have you looked at Douglas? He looks like a ragman next to her."

I sobered, picturing Douglas's worn, off-the-rack suit, scuffed shoes, and ragged hairstyle, as if he hadn't had a decent cut in several months. Mentally I compared it to Selina's sleek and polished look. Her manicure alone would have cost a fortune, and I'd have to spend at least two months' salary from the bookstore on the dress that had hugged her slim form. I could only assume her bag and shoes were equally expensive, even though I'd not seen them. "She does seem to spend only on herself."

"I don't think I could do it." Keith cleared his throat. "Thank goodness I've found such a cheap girlfriend."

"Uh-huh." I mock-glared at him, knowing he was joking, still attempting to ease the earlier tension. "But seriously. I keep thinking about the other night and Linus saying she had damaged other books. I thought she didn't like books."

"I asked about that." Keith turned onto my street. "From what I've been able to find out, she pitched a fit at Douglas one day at the library, pissed off that he wouldn't let her spend six thousand dollars on a pair of Bengal cat kittens. She thought they'd look pretty walking them while she wore her fur coat. Seems her temper tantrum included yanking books off the shelves and throwing them at Douglas while screaming at him like a fishwife."

"And Linus repaired the books?"

Keith nodded as he turned into the driveway. He put the car in park. "Yep. The ones that weren't damaged beyond repair." He got out and walked around to my door and opened it.

"I can see why that stuck in Linus's craw. But she said those damaged books weren't her fault." I led the way to my front door, unlocked it, and walked through, looking forward to a time when I would be greeted by a wiggling dog who rolled to his back demanding tummy rubs. For tonight, however, Eddy had been left next door in Rita's excellent care.

Keith followed me in, walking to my kitchen and stepping behind the bar to the small wine fridge built in under the counter. "She says it was Douglas's fault." He pulled out a bottle of Chardonnay and opened it.

"What? How?" I accepted the wineglass of wheat-colored liquid.

He led the way to the couch and sank into one corner. "Seems she feels if he'd just let her have the kittens, she wouldn't have been angry. Therefore, it was his fault the books got damaged, not hers."

I kicked off my heels, tucked myself into the opposite corner of the couch, and propped my feet in Keith's lap. "Wow. Talk about deflection."

"She blames him for everything. If your customer, Alice, is to be believed, she likely even blames him for not inheriting from his father." Keith ran his thumbs up the sole of one foot, gently massaging.

A soft mmmmmmmm purred from my throat at his ministrations. "It's almost like she's punishing him for being average rather than stinking rich. She's sucking him dry. How does he do it?"

Keith shook his head. "I know I sure couldn't." His hands moved to my other foot. "So, tell me more about your idea for Mason's college tuition."

I melted back into the couch, savoring the massage. "I guess I'm still trying to figure him out. I know Uncle Paul would want me to help him, but Mason doesn't seem to want my help."

Keith chuckled as he kneaded the arch of my foot. "He wants it. But he doesn't want 'help.'"

I raised my head. "Got it. He wants help, but he doesn't want help. That makes a lot of sense. Thanks." There was no possible way for him to miss my sarcastic tone.

"Think about it." He reached for my other arch. "He's trying very hard to be a man who stands on his own two feet. Yet at every turn, you're there like a mothering safety net."

"I am not." Yes, I was. And I knew it. "I only want him to be happy. He just brings out that instinct in me."

"Yeah, well, you need to ignore some of that instinct before you either turn him into a leech, although I doubt that will happen, or he stops letting you know if he needs something." Keith picked up his wine glass and sipped. "Wouldn't you rather help him figure out how to do things on his own instead of handing him your own easy answers each time?"

I considered this as I slid my feet from Keith's lap and tucked them underneath me. "I see what you're saying. Help him find a way to help himself. Don't hand him money or find him a place to live."

"Exactly." Keith scooted over next to me on the couch and draped an arm across my shoulders. "Even if he has to work harder for it, that's how it has to be. Without his own hard work, he won't have the satisfaction of accomplishment. That sense of 'I did this.'"

It went against the grain, but I knew Keith was right. Mason had to struggle in order to build resilience.

"Should I rescind my offer of a loan?" I swirled my wine glass, watching the golden liquid circle the bowl.

"No." Keith planted a kiss on my head. "I think the loan, which he has to pay back, is okay. But stop offering to bail him out without him having to work for it in the future."

I nodded. "Got it."

Apparently sensing a closed subject, Keith asked, "Are you going to pick up Eddy tonight?"

I shook my head. "No. Rita said she was turning in early, so I'll go get him in the morning."

"Isn't it a bit too early?" He twisted his wrist to look at his watch. "It's only nine o'clock."

I chuckled and tucked my feet up onto the couch. "Actually, I think she said that in order to give us more time together without distraction. She's probably wearing fleece pants and binge-watching old movies, snuggled in bed with my dog."

"How's he doing with the new situation?" Keith finished his wine and set the glass on the coffee table.

"Overall, better than expected." I thought of his actions in the store. "He's still a bit skittish with people coming in and out downstairs, but I think he'll get past it."

"With all of this attention, he'll adjust in no time." Keith squeezed my shoulders once more and stood. "I'm sure I'll get over the idea of another guy living with my girl." He winked.

I giggled and rose. Gads, what was wrong with me? I didn't giggle. Yet I just had. "I think you'll live." I grabbed a blanket from the back of the couch, draped it around my shoulders to ward off the evening chill, and followed him to the door.

Keith slid his arms into his coat. "I'm actually glad he's here. It's not a bad idea for you to have a watch dog."

Before I could answer, he tipped my chin up and placed a soft kiss on my lips. "Be careful, Jenna. I . . ." His voice faded.

I looked into his liquid gaze, losing myself in what I saw there, afraid to hope it was real.

He shook his head. "I don't know what I'd do if something happened to you." He pulled me into his arms for a deeper kiss before striding though the door and down the walkway toward the parking lot.

Chapter Nine

Sunlight filtered through the buttercream-yellow organza curtains I'd hung in the primary bedroom. After a month in the windowless spare—which reminded me all too much of the three months I'd spent in jail for a crime I did not commit—I'd finally moved my things into what had been Uncle Paul's bedroom. It had taken two more weeks to get past the twinges of guilt, the feelings that I was intruding on a space that should never have been mine, before I'd finally shaken myself and told myself I was being ridiculous. Uncle Paul had wanted me to be here. I belonged.

Letting my eyes crack open to take in the bright room, I inhaled deeply, appreciating the smell of coffee wafting in from the kitchen, where I'd set the coffeepot to automatically brew at seven AM. What a lovely way to wake up. I smiled and sat up, stretching my arms overhead and yawning widely.

I rose, showered, dressed, and padded into the kitchen for that first delicious cup of coffee, all the while reveling in Keith's kiss from the night before, suspecting he had almost said those three special little words. We'd only known each other for a couple of months, but I knew I loved him. However, I suspected he needed a bit more time to come to that same conclusion.

I enjoyed a simple breakfast of Raisin Bran before slipping on a pair of lined clogs and all but skipping toward my front door to go get Eddy. I opened the door and saw Rita already headed over from her apartment, Eddy at her heels.

She stamped her feet as she walked, as if trying to warm them. "It's freezing out here." She pulled her sweater tighter around her waist.

I opened the door wider, and she followed Eddy inside.

"Eddy's already been walked." Rita handed me his leash and made a beeline toward the coffeepot. "And I can't feel my toes anymore."

I leaned down, unclipped the leash, and hung it on one of the coat hooks beside the front door. "I could've walked him after you brought him back." I chuckled.

Rita picked up her now-full mug of coffee and wrapped her fingers around it. "Mmm," she hummed contentedly as she sagged onto a barstool beside the island. "Warm."

Eddy danced around my legs, happy to see me, and I knelt to scratch the dog before getting my own cup of coffee.

"How did he do last night?" I sipped the hot liquid carefully and sat on the stool next to hers.

Her eyes popped open, and she glanced at the dog. "We told ghost stories, braided each other's hair, talked about boys . . . oh, wait, that was with you."

I almost spit out the coffee in my mouth but managed to contain the laughter.

Rita grinned. "He was great. He snuggled with me on the couch while I watched *The Philadelphia Story*. Man, Cary Grant and Jimmy Stewart in the same movie? What could be better? They don't make them like that anymore."

I'd have to be sure to tell Keith I'd been right about Rita's evening activities. "Sounds fun. Did he sleep okay? He can be restless."

"He did get up once and need to go out." Rita swiveled her stool toward the dog and continued in a baby voice. "But we had fun, didn't we? Yes, we did."

Wow, okay. That just happened. My friend was losing her mind. My thoughts must have been mirrored in my expression.

Rita rolled her eyes. "Oh, stop it with the who-is-this-crazy-woman look. Have you not ever talked like that to a pet before?"

I shook my head, watching as Eddy jumped to the couch, turned one circle, and curled up with his head on his paws. "I've never had a pet before. Mom was allergic to cats and dogs, and Dad didn't like putting animals in cages, so hamsters, turtles, and lizards were out. I never had the desire to have a fish."

Rita's brows rose. "Okay, then. You really are a newbie at this." She shook her head in seeming amazement. "Well, if you haven't ever done it, give it time. You will."

"If you say so." I shrugged and set my mug on the counter. "Can I ask you something?"

"Sure." Rita swiveled back around to face me. "Shoot."

"It's about Keith." I stood and walked around to the coffeepot.

"And?" Rita held her mug out for a refill.

I shrugged again. "I don't know. I guess I want to know how to really tell if someone is into you." I looked up at her to see her jaw drop.

"Okay then. I guess pet ownership isn't all you're new at." She sipped her coffee. "What brought this on?"

I sighed and dropped onto the stool again. "It's been a couple of months, and I don't know . . . it seems to be going really slowly. Maybe I'm misreading things or wishfully thinking."

A slow smile spread across Rita's face. "You like him." She leaned in and looked at me more closely. "You *love* him."

"Maybe." I raised my mug and gulped too-hot coffee, trying to cover my embarrassment.

Apparently sensing my discomfort, Rita reached out a hand and squeezed my shoulder. "Hon, it's okay. I didn't mean to tease. But I'm a bit confused. I thought you'd been in serious relationships before. Weren't you engaged before you came here?"

I let my mug plop onto the counter with a thud. "I try not to think about that. But since you mention it, yes. I've been in relationships before, in high school. In college, I was too busy, too driven, to get into anything serious. Once I started working, my long hours eliminated most of the possible dating pool. Blake Emerson was the first adult relationship I'd had. He wined and dined me, and it was all rather whirlwind. A month after we started dating, we were living together and he had proposed."

"No chance to stop and think it through, huh?"

I chuckled. "Not even one second."

Rita sat quietly for a moment, draining her mug of coffee. "You're worried that because Keith is taking things more slowly, he's not that interested?" At my nod, she continued. "Honey, let me tell you this much. I've watched how that man stares at you when you're not looking, and I can tell you he's way beyond interested."

"If you say so." Then what was the deal?

"Has it occurred to you he's being patient to give you a chance to be ready? I'm sure you told him about Blake."

My head snapped up, and my jaw dropped. "I hadn't even considered that. What do I do?"

Rita waved a hand in the air. "Girl, be patient. Give it time. When it's right, there honestly is no need to rush." She thunked her twice-emptied mug on the counter. "Except when it comes to those books. I only have one day."

"Oh my gosh, I almost forgot." I snagged her mug and put both mine and hers in the sink before grabbing Eddy's leash, waking the dog, and heading downstairs.

"The boxes are in the back." I led the way toward the back room, where a shipment of thirty-eight boxes of books had arrived. I'd purchased the lot of them at an estate sale two weeks ago, my first since inheriting the store. I couldn't wait to see what was inside, and I was tickled Rita had offered to help out when I'd dropped Eddy off the night before.

"Do you have any clue what's in any of them?" Rita reached for a box cutter, careful not to damage the books inside the closest box as she slid the cutter along the tape that sealed the box shut.

I looked over her shoulder into the box. "Not a clue."

She looked up at me, and I grinned.

"It'll be like Christmas." She flipped the flaps open and pulled out a stack of 1970s copies of Agatha Christie paperbacks.

I flipped through the stack, recognizing titles and mentally preparing space on a shelf for them. They would sell well.

"How are things at the inn this week?" I opened another box and peered inside at old cookbooks. Oh well, every box wouldn't be a winner.

"Oh, didn't you hear?" Rita plopped down a stack of Louis L'Amour Westerns. "Selina is throwing a turn-of-the-century ball next week."

My head popped up, ignoring my newly opened box. "What? I thought Douglas told her she couldn't do it. I think Keith's words were that he finally put his foot down."

Rita snorted. "Douglas March wouldn't know how to put his foot down when it comes to that woman if his life depended on it. Although he did try. But she threatened to divorce him if he didn't let her have her way."

"Wow." I shook my head and looked down into my open box to see current romance novels. I picked one up and turned the picture of a man and woman in a steamy embrace to face Rita. "I guess they don't have this kind of relationship."

"Not for a long time, honey." Rita opened another box. "Although from what I understand, he does love her deeply. I've never figured out why."

"Isn't a week's notice a bit short?" I dropped the romance back into the box, refusing to get dreamy thinking of Keith's kisses.

"Yep, which is why we're all pushing hard to get it all ready. We're lucky we're not also working on a Sunday." She dusted off her hands and reached for another box, gingerly sliding her box cutter through the shipping tape and opening the flaps. "Jackpot!"

I stepped over and peeked inside. "Aren't you glad you're here instead?"

Gently, I pulled four matching volumes from the box. Gold lettering stood out from brownish-burgundy covers, and I picked up one of the books. *Shakespeare's Works: Falstaff Edition, Volume I.* Golden scrollwork elegantly encased the title, and gold gilt edges shone in the overhead lights. Black embossed scrollwork decorated the front cover. I eased it open and turned the first few pages. A black and white artist's rendering of Shakespeare, a thin rice paper half page to protect the rendering, a title page noting the publisher. I turned a few more pages and found what I sought. The preface was dated 1859.

A grin split my face. "Jackpot is right. This will bring a pretty penny."

We found several more books of similar quality in the box, setting them on the desk to inspect later before turning back to the remaining boxes. Three more boxes revealed additional 19th-century volumes in amazing condition.

Although we hoped to find more boxes such as these, the remaining boxes contained more cookbooks, Westerns, romances, and the odd box of older mystery paperbacks, including books by Elmore Leonard, Dorothy L. Sayers, Mickey Spillane, and more by Agatha Christie.

"All in all, not a bad haul." I surveyed the open boxes, smiling again as my gaze settled on the stacks of antique books we'd discovered. "Tomorrow, I'll get Mason to price and shelve most of these, but we'll have to do some digging on the antiques. I'm still pretty new at this, so it takes a while to research, and I still have to call Linus . . ." My voice faded as I realized what I'd said. My book friend would no longer be on the other end of the line.

Rita stood and hugged me. "It wasn't your fault." Her stomach rumbled loudly. "Let's go grab a bite to eat and clear our heads." She looped her arm through mine and tugged me away from the back room.

Eddy lay sleeping in the sunlight pouring through the front windows.

"I can't leave Eddy alone yet." I smiled when the dog raised his head at the sound of his name. Here was a male who wouldn't break my heart.

"I knew a lady who put her dog on the doggy version of Prozac when her other dog died. Maybe something like that would help Eddy through all of this." Rita leaned down to scratch the dog's head. "Might be worth a call to a vet."

I thought of the vet records still lying on the dining table where I'd dropped them when I got home from Linus's house the other day. "I can look to see who Eddy's vet is and give him a call later. For now, let's call in an order and eat it upstairs."

After ordering and retrieving our food, we walked upstairs, and Eddy settled on the couch while Rita and I set the food on the kitchen bar.

We ate quietly for a few minutes before Rita spoke.

"I never would have thought Linus would have so many enemies." She stabbed another bite of her salad with her fork. "He seemed so nice the day we talked to him about Paul's book."

Rita had been present the first time I'd spoken to Linus. Shortly after I'd moved to Hokes Folly, I called Linus about a book he had authenticated for Uncle Paul . . . a book that had ultimately been at the root of my uncle's murder.

"I've spoken with him on the phone quite a few more times, and he was always happy to help me with a book's general value." I laid my sub sandwich on my plate and brushed off my fingers. "We never talked about anything personal, so I can't say I really knew him. Only that he loved books as much as Uncle Paul had."

"I don't know." Rita gestured with her fork. "If I ended up at a party with several people who hated my guts, I think I'd have been more careful going back to my car alone in the dark."

I swiveled and looked at Eddy. "He wasn't alone," I said softly.

Rita's gaze followed mine. "I guess not."

"Well." I abruptly stood. "I think I'll get back at those book boxes. You ready?" I rewrapped the remaining half of my sandwich and walked to the refrigerator. It would make a nice lunch on Monday.

"Sure." Rita hopped off her stool and took her now empty Styrofoam box to the trashcan in the pantry. "Let's get back at it while I'm still around to help."

I grabbed Eddy's leash, and we took him for a quick walk before heading back to the store. As we approached, I saw Phillie Hokes unlock the door to the shop next door and step inside.

"Come on." I motioned to Rita and headed toward the now half-empty vintage store, where I rapped on the glass door, waving at Phillie when she looked up.

With a smile on her lips, she rushed to the door, turned the lock, and pulled the door open. "Come in out of that cold wind."

"Is it okay if we bring Eddy in with us? He's a little skittish about being alone." I gestured toward my furry companion.

"Absolutely." Phillie motioned us in, leaning down to scratch the dog's head as he passed her.

"Nice jeans." I grinned at the older woman. I'd never seen her in anything so casual.

Phillie twirled around. "I've never had a pair before, and I can honestly say I like them."

"Never?" Rita stepped back a couple of paces. "They look great on you."

"Livie wanted us to live like we were elderly spinster sisters from the nineteen fifties, because it fit her vision of who she was. It's part of why she loved all the historical books and why she loved this vintage clothing store so much." Phillie locked the door behind us and walked toward a seating arrangement still set up in one corner. "The way we dressed, the way we spoke, the way we did everything. It's like she wanted to live in Mayberry, and it was easier to let her have her way."

"And now that she's gone?" I prompted.

"Now that I'm on my own for the first time in my life, I'm figuring out who Phillie Hokes really is. I'm no longer just Livie Hokes's sister." Phillie gestured at her jeans-clad legs. "And for now, that includes blue jeans." She took a few empty boxes off delicate-looking vintage chairs, gesturing for us to sit. "What brings you ladies here today?"

"I wanted to thank you again for donating the items for my event and helping out with the drawing." I gingerly sat on one of the dainty chairs, hoping it wouldn't wobble, and was pleased to find it sturdier than it appeared.

Phillie waved her hand around the store. "I'm glad to find homes for these things. What with Livie gone . . ." She pursed her lips after mentioning her sister. "Let's just say I won't miss this business. It was her love, not mine. All I can say is thank God for eBay."

I tried to picture the tiny, older woman selling vintage clothing on the auction site and couldn't manage it. "What will you do now instead?"

A sly smile cross Phillie's lips. "You should already have guessed that, dear. After all, you're the one who put the idea in my head."

"A garden shop!" Rita clapped her hands and squealed. "It's perfect for you."

"Pshaw." Phillie waved her hand. "Nothing is ever perfect. You girls need to learn that. But it will definitely be a lot more fun than this store ever was."

I grinned at Phillie's reference to twenty-six-year-old and forty-four-year-old women as girls. Maybe I was closer to it than Rita, but neither of us were children. And after all I'd been through in the last year, I felt a lot older than my chronological age.

"Oh, stop that." Rita waved her hand back and forth. "You aren't that much older than I am. You're what, forty-nine?" She shot Phillie an impish grin.

Phillie snorted. "I am not embarrassed that I'll be sixty-five next spring. I went through a lot to get to this age, and being this old means I survived every bit of it." She punctuated her sentence with a curt nod of her head, and an impish smile curling her lips.

I chuckled. "And we're glad you did. So, where will your nursery be?" I hoped it was close enough to still see the woman regularly.

"I found the best spot, with room for large greenhouses and room to expand. It's just outside town." She patted us both on the knees. "I expect you both to visit. I still need to teach you"— she pointed at me—"how to keep Paul's plants alive. You haven't killed them yet, have you?"

I shook my head. "No, ma'am." I hoped she hadn't seen the drooping leaves on the ficus tree in the front window of my apartment. To take her attention off my lack of a green thumb,

I changed the subject. "Would it be all right if I asked you a few questions about Linus Talbot?"

Phillie's demeanor changed, sadness replacing the earlier sparkle in her gaze. "Linus Talbot was a good man." She shook her head. "I still can't believe it."

"Had you known him long?" Rita leaned in and rubbed the older woman on the shoulder.

Phillie drew a deep breath and released it. "I've known Linus since grade school." A wistful smile touched her lips. "I had a terrible crush on him in fourth grade. But he had eyes only for Janet Chrisforth. I got over my crush, and he eventually married her. I know this will sound terrible, but I'm glad she passed away years ago. I don't know how she would have handled him being murdered."

I plunged forward. "Can you think of anyone who would want to harm him?" Gads, now I sounded like a cheesy cop show.

She tilted her head to the side, her brows drawn together. "Oh, quite a few folks didn't like him. He was set in his ways, and everything was black or white for him. There was no gray area on any matter. But to kill him? I don't know."

I told her what I'd found out about the politician's pet plat-form and what Alice had told me about Selina. "Do you think either of them could have done it?"

Phillie thought for a moment before shaking her head. "Honestly, I don't know. I do know Selina couldn't stand him. And from what you said, Bradford Prescott had a solid reason to dislike him as well. But you need to add Alice into that pile. She likes to tattle on others, but she had her own reasons to hate Linus."

"She has seemed a little hot and cold on the subject of Linus Talbot, from what I understand." Rita shifted in her chair as if trying to find a comfortable position.

I ignored my own numbing backside from the pretty but hard chair. "Do you know why she hated him?"

"She loved him." Phillie shrugged.

"Wait, she loved him, which is why she hated him?" Rita shifted again.

"About six years ago, right after Janet passed, Alice started working at the library. As she had an associate's degree in library science, she was a shoo-in for the job. They put her working with Linus in the rare book section, helping him catalog new items donated or purchased and learning to care for and repair antique books. As the months progressed, she began brokering minor antique books. She found some through your uncle, which she sold to various buyers, although I don't think he was her only source."

"I remember Paul had a wish list from her in case he found books at estate sales," Rita stated.

Phillie nodded. "At least she didn't develop a crush on him too."

"Too?" Gads, I hoped her garden center would have more comfortable furniture. Anything but the miserable chairs from this store. I shifted my weight to my least-numb hip, trying not to be jealous of Eddy snoozing at my feet. It seemed even the floor was more comfortable than my chair.

Phillie smiled sadly and shook her head. "Yes, Alice had a habit of falling in love with men who were simply being nice. She didn't come from the best family, and when someone showed her affection, she latched on like there was no tomorrow.

Apparently Alice mistook Linus's kindness to her while he taught her about antique books as attraction. She'd been working there around two years when she tried to kiss him, and she told him how she felt. He put her in her place, assuring her he was still in love with his deceased wife and always would be. She was crushed. She yelled at him that the only other thing he loved were musty old books, and he'd die a lonely, bitter old man. Pitched herself quite a fit." Phillie waved her hands in the air above her head. "Ran around waving her arms and crying and screaming at Linus like a banshee. Got herself fired over it."

"Is that why she refuses to touch a book that Linus has repaired?" I'd already told the older woman about Alice's attitude at my store.

"No." Phillie shook her head. "Seems right after she was fired, one of her clients brought in a book to have Linus authenticate it. The man had heard rumblings that Alice was passing off fakes as the real deal. Buying replicas and using repair techniques to age the books and make them appear genuine, or something like that."

Rita sat up straighter, eyebrows raised. "Linus caught her at it?"

"He did. The book the man brought was nowhere near the age Alice had claimed. She'd sold him a book for several thousand dollars, but it was worth maybe thirty at most. She'd done a good job of it. But Linus was good at his job too. He told the buyer the truth, and the man spread it through antique book circles that she was intentionally selling fakes." Phillie frowned and pursed her lips. "The sad part is that she was really good at finding just the right books for her clients. After it all came out, then we knew why. Now she works at a gas station on the outskirts of town. She blamed Linus for that as well."

"Wow." I let out a low whistle. "No wonder she can't stand him. He got in the way of her sweet deal. At least in her mind."

"The worst part was she was still convinced he loved her up until that point. So not only did she lose her scam income, her dreams of setting up housekeeping with Linus were dashed to bits as well." A soft chime from a grandmother clock behind the counter drew Phillie's gaze. "Lordy, it's already three thirty. I'm going to be late to meet the realtor to finalize the papers for the nursery property. I need to get a move on, ladies."

Rita and I both stood when Phillie did and followed her out of the store, waiting with her as she locked up.

I touched her on the shoulder. "Miss Phillie, would you like us to walk you to your car? I mean, after what happened . . ."

Phillie chuckled. "No. That's not necessary. I refuse to live in fear. Linus's death wasn't random. It was too personal." She snapped open the pocketbook she'd put over her arm. "Besides, I still have several of Papa's old security items."

I managed to keep my jaw from dropping when I spotted the large revolver in her purse, lying across a few tissues, a couple of ballpoint pens, and a change purse.

"Believe me, I can and will take care of myself." Phillie winked at us and snapped her pocketbook closed. "You be sure if you keep poking around in this murder that you two do the same."

As we watched her march toward the parking lot, her pocketbook swinging from her forearm, I pictured her in a Dirty Harry stance, pointing the revolver at someone and asking them if they felt lucky. Though the thought was amusing, her words held a ring of truth. We—I—needed to be more careful. What if I asked the wrong person the right questions?

Chapter Ten

Monday morning, I stood with coffee in hand, looking out the floor-to-ceiling windows of my living room area onto the cobbled street below. Many of the businesses were closed on Mondays, so the foot traffic was minimal. Instead, our animal neighbors came out to play. Eddy was especially focused on the squirrel family playing in the trees sunk into holes in the sidewalks. We'd already had our morning walk, but I knew he would love the opportunity to sniff the trees and leave his own mark, just so those squirrels knew who really owned the street . . . at least in Eddy's doggy mind.

I knelt and scratched behind his ears, draping an arm around him for a hug. He slumped to the floor, squirrels momentarily forgotten in the face of possible petting, and rolled to his back in a plea for tummy rubs. I obliged for a few minutes before standing and walking to the front door to grab the twice-weekly local newspaper I'd subscribed to.

My coffee went down the wrong pipe at my gasp, and I coughed uncontrollably for a minute before I could reread the headline at the top of the front page. *"Third Murder Linked to Local Bookstore."*

Seems I'd been sucked into another reporter's not-so-friendly mind game. I walked to the couch, letting my mug hit the coffee table a little too hard, and sank into the sofa to read the article.

Local used and antique bookstore Twice Upon a Time, formerly Baxter's Book Emporium, has been linked to the recent murder of Linus Talbot, Director of Antique Books at the Hokes Folly Community Library.

In early August, new store owner Jenna Quinn found her uncle, Paul Baxter, dead in his bookstore. Baxter's pursuit of an antique diary of town founder John Hokes led to not only his death but also the murder of Norman Childers. Talbot's death makes the third death to be linked to the store in four months.

Thursday night, Talbot attended a grand reopening event at Twice Upon a Time, where he won a set of antique, blown-glass bookends, one of which was used to bludgeon him to death in a parking lot outside the historic district in downtown Hokes Folly minutes after the event ended.

"Uncle Paul and I both used him as a resource to authenticate rare books," said Quinn. However, she claims she had never met Talbot in person prior to her event.

Before his death, Talbot had set an appointment with a Hokes Folly Tribune *reporter regarding the background of his beloved dog, Edition, who previously belonged to North Carolina House of Representatives candidate Bradford Prescott, and who is now in Quinn's custody.*

Hokes Folly Police Detective Frank Sutter confirmed the Police Department is looking at the death as a homicide. However, he would not confirm whether Prescott is currently a person of interest in the murder.

Should anyone have information regarding the murder, please notify the Hokes Folly Police Department.

I flopped back into the couch cushions as I let the paper drop into my lap, emotions warring in my head.

My stomach clenched. I was furious. At Dee Lynoir for suckering me into talking to her about the event. At myself for being so stupid as to trust a reporter after being relentlessly hounded by reporters in Charlotte, where everything I'd said, or sometimes hadn't said, had been twisted into sensationalism, until I'd finally hidden out in a run-down motel. And then I'd received Uncle Paul's invitation.

Before I let the past swamp me, I stood and tossed the paper onto the coffee table and strode to my bedroom to stare at the clothes in my closet. Eddy followed me and hopped onto the bed, flopping down to stare at me while I tried to decide what to wear for the day. The clothes I'd worn in my previous life in Charlotte hung in garment bags in the guest room closet. I had no need for power suits or high heels here. Eventually I'd have to get rid of these items, although I'd likely keep one or two dressier outfits. Maybe I could get Phillie to show me her tricks for offloading clothes on eBay. I smiled, glad to think of my friend acting more like the sixty-five-year-old woman she was rather than someone three decades older.

Dragging myself back to my current wardrobe, I slid my hand past the jeans I preferred to wear most days and pulled a pair of slacks out of the closet. I laid them across the bed and pulled open a drawer to remove a mauve sweater. "What about this, Eddy?" I gestured to the outfit.

Eddy, ever helpful, thumped his tail once and closed his eyes.

I showered and dressed, walked Eddy once more, and took him downstairs to the store.

A low whistle met me. "Wow, you look great." Mason stood on a ladder, placing books on the overstock shelf. "What's the occasion?"

"I'm surprising Rita at the Inn for lunch." I reached down and ruffled Eddy's fur. "Can you watch Eddy while I'm gone? I've already walked him, and he shouldn't need anything before I get back, but he gets stressed when he's left alone."

Mason deftly jumped to the floor. "Sure thing, boss." He strode across the room, knelt in front of the dog, and scratched him under the chin. "It'll be just us guys, boy. You up for that?"

Eddy swept his tail back and forth and gave Mason's face a quick lick.

Mason stood, wiping his cheek. "Yeah, I think we've got this covered. Have fun."

As I walked down the sidewalk outside the store, I glanced back in, catching Mason playing a rousing game of chase with Eddy. I stopped and watched, smiling at the boyish antics, which ended with Mason on the floor cuddling the dog, whose tongue hung out of a goofy grin.

With a light heart, I drove toward the historic estate. After parking in the lot near the inn, I accepted a footman's help into one of the horse-drawn carriages. To give guests an experience as immersive as possible, the inn required all cars to park in a gated and guarded lot a couple of miles from the inn. Guests were then driven to the estate in horse-drawn carriages that were replicas from the first few years of the 1900s.

Enjoying the carriage ride down the tree-lined drive, I let time and stress slip away. Sun dappled through the leaves overhead, and the crisp, clean air invigorated me. As I slipped from the carriage at the inn's steps, I tipped my driver and pulled two carrots from my pocket, which I had grabbed before I left my apartment, giving one each to the horses who had brought me up the lane. Their whuffing sniffs and velvety lips tickled my palms as they took my offered tip, and I left them happily munching as I strode up the steps and entered the building.

Built in the last few years of the 1800s, the inn was a veritable museum to life at the turn of the twentieth century. Designed to compete with George Vanderbilt's estate, Biltmore, in Asheville, the mansion that had, almost two centuries later, become Hokes Bluff Inn had been designed to be a fully self-sustaining estate. The soaring architecture and the intricate woodwork took my breath away every time I entered the vast entry-hall-cum-lobby.

I strode to the front desk and asked for Rita to be paged. While I waited, I explored the expensive paintings, originals, hung in ornate frames at intervals down the long entry hall. Steps approaching and the rustle of skirts caught my attention, and I turned.

"Hi! What brings you here today?" Rita approached, arms outstretched for a hug.

"Hi, yourself." I took in her gorgeous green day dress patterned after those in the early twentieth century. The long skirt, piped in darker green in several horizontal rows near the bottom, belled out below the knee, and her button-up boots peeked out from underneath the hem. A white ruffled shirt with a high collar, buttoned to the top of her throat, and a green long-sleeved jacket with velvet lapels completed the ensemble. As she was indoors, she wore no hat, but her red hair was piled on her head in delicate waves.

Careful not to muss her, I leaned in for the hug. "I'm here to take you to lunch in the dining room. I know you're swamped with the upcoming event, but you do have to eat."

Rita linked her arm through mine. "Invitation accepted."

As we entered the dining hall, a long room that had once housed a massive table but was now scattered with smaller tables, a shrill voice hit my ears, and I turned.

"I don't care if you have someone else scheduled for the dining hall that night." Selina March leaned in toward Elliot Burke, the inn's manager. "Cancel them. I'm paying you good money to host this ball."

Elliot's soft voice, too low to make out, wafted across the room, but apparently his comments didn't soothe the savage beast.

"I. Don't. Care." Selina's voice rose in volume with each word. "Find a way and fix it." She turned on her heel and stalked across the room.

Before she'd taken more than a few steps, Elliot caught her elbow, this time close enough for his words to carry to us. "Mrs. March, I'm sure we can find a way to accommodate both events. We do have a secondary dining hall, which sits very near the great hall where the ball will be held. We prefer to reserve it for exclusive events, but we would be willing to open it up for your event. Shall we go view the room?"

I had to hand it to him, he knew how to smooth ruffled feathers.

Selina almost purred at the term "exclusive," and she looped her hand through his offered elbow. "Darling, why didn't you tell me about this secret room earlier? It sounds like exactly what I need."

They crossed the room toward the door, which would take them past our table. I tried to duck behind the menu, not wanting another conversation with the irritating woman. However, Selina had already caught sight of us.

"You." Selina's tone now sounded a bit accusatory, and her face formed into a sneer. "Trying to see how a real event should be handled?"

"Oh, hello, Selina. I didn't realize you were here." I carefully closed my menu and laid it on the table.

Selina's raised brows implied she didn't believe me. "If you really want to snoop about it, I can try to get you a position on the serving staff. If you learn how they should be done, maybe your little events won't be so boring in the future." A nasty grin slid across her face. "You shouldn't have to resort to providing a murder weapon for a guest's death to spice things up."

My mouth opened, and my shin felt a sharp pain. I looked across at Rita, whose pursed lips and narrowed gaze told me she'd kick me under the table again if I angered Selina enough that Elliot lost the business.

Chagrined, I took a deep breath and plastered a fake smile on my face, not really caring if she could tell it wasn't real. "I appreciate the offer, but I'll be busy that night."

Elliot tugged gently on her arm, turning her away from our table. "Mrs. March, we'd better hurry before someone else manages to book the private room."

Flashing a blazingly white-toothed grin at her escort, Selina let herself be led away. "Do tell me more about this room."

When she was out of earshot, I leaned in toward Rita. "At least I won't have to threaten to divorce someone to force him to pay for my ego trip of an event."

Rita picked up her menu and flipped it open. "I can't believe she fell for the 'secret and private exclusive room' schtick."

I laughed and looked up from my own menu. "You guys don't really have one?"

The server approached, and we quickly ordered before Rita answered.

"Oh, there is a room." Rita handed her menu to the server, who turned and left. "But there's nothing secret or exclusive about it. We use it to hold the overflow of the main dining hall. If an event is big enough, it's generally used to feed and entertain the kids while the adults are in the main dining hall."

A burst of laughter erupted from my throat, which drew a couple of stares from across the room. "She's basically being put at the kids' table?"

Rita smiled and primly rearranged her skirts. "Don't you think that's where she belongs?"

This time I kept my laughter at a lower volume, but tears leaked from my eyes before I could contain my mirth again. "Do you guys think you'll be able to get everything ready in time for her ball? I heard it was supposed to be on Friday. That's only four days away."

Our food arrived, and Rita unwrapped her flatware and placed her napkin in her lap. "We'll make it. With how everyone has pitched in, plus a bit of sheer luck in finding an available florist over in Asheville, who will deliver arrangements to us on short notice, we'll be ready with time to spare."

I swallowed a bite of crisp salad greens. "Will you work the night of the event?"

"Nope. Everyone will show up already dressed. Nothing for me to do." She sipped her iced tea. "I'll leave a few of my people available to help the staff with their clothing, but I've done about all I can with my department to help prep for the event."

"Well, you're missing a lot of fun at the bookstore. We're sure to have a lot more customers after today's article in the paper." I shoved a cherry tomato around on my plate.

A crease slid across Rita's brow. "Article?"

I sighed and leaned back, dropping my fork on my plate. "Remember that day when I went to talk to the reporter that Linus was supposed to meet?"

Rita nodded and chewed.

"Seems she wrote an article that implies Twice Upon a Time is murder central."

"No!" gasped Rita. "She didn't!"

"She did." I shook my head. "I should've known better. I, of all people, know how they can twist innocent comments into sensationalism in order to sell papers."

Rita reached across the table and patted my hand. "Honey, the folks in this town know you're a good one. They loved and trusted Paul, and they love you too. This will blow over, and things will be fine."

Later, on the carriage ride back to the parking lot and the drive back to the historic district, my mind spun with worry over the bad publicity sparked by the newspaper article. And after Selina March's insulting comments and her hateful selfishness, I could easily see her jumping on this latest way to make my store look bad.

When I entered the store, Mason shoved something under the counter and greeted me with a huge smile that looked a little forced. "Hi! Welcome back. I have everything ready for the remaining two days of the grand reopening sale."

"Was that today's paper?" I didn't feel like dancing around the issue, and I was pretty sure I knew what he was hiding under the counter.

Mason's smile slipped a little. "Today's paper?" His voice squeaked a bit.

Man, this kid was a really bad liar. I chuckled as I plopped my purse on the counter. My hand groped underneath and came up with a wad of thin paper, which I dragged into the light.

"Yes, this paper." I placed the offending paper, offending article facing up, on the counter. "It's okay, I've already seen it."

"Oh, thank goodness." Mason visibly relaxed. "I've been getting calls all day from reporters asking for quotes, so I went to buy the paper to see what the big deal was."

"I hope you had the good sense to say, 'No comment.'" I smoothed the wrinkles from the paper, this time noticing what a nice photo they'd used of the store. Of course, it was marred by the adjoining picture, a shot of the crime scene with tape surrounding it and investigators kneeling next to the body's former location, dried blood still in place.

"Duh." Mason shrugged. "Everyone knows reporters will twist your words."

I winced. Everyone but me, it seemed. "It won't matter. They'll spin what's here and turn us into the little shop of murder before it's all said and done."

Mason gestured at the photo spread below the article's title. "With shots like that, it's pretty much a definite. But at least folks will come in."

I propped my elbows on the counter and leaned my forehead in my hands, glaring at the article, wishing I could go back in time and undo that conversation. "Yes, they'll come in, but traffic of that type doesn't equate to book sales."

Mason shoved my shoulder. "Hey, we'll survive this. We did fine after Paul's and Norman Childers's deaths."

Straightening my spine, I took a deep breath. "Mason, you're absolutely right. We'll figure it out." I smiled, forcing myself to relax. Just how we'd figure it out, I wasn't quite sure.

Chapter Eleven

Tuesday morning, I overslept, having tossed and turned throughout the night, churning through guilt over Linus's death and Eddy's grief. Selina's spiteful words haunted me. *"You shouldn't have to resort to providing a murder weapon for a guest's death to spice things up."* She had been right. I had not only invited him, but I'd given the killer the weapon.

In the light of morning, as I showered to wake myself up, I wondered how Selina had known what the weapon was. I tried to mentally replay the news blurb about the murder, but I'd been so wrapped up in how to do damage control after the way the reporter had made my store seem like murder paradise that I couldn't remember if the bookends had been mentioned or not.

As I gobbled down my breakfast of cereal and coffee—I needed to expand my repertoire—I scanned the article. Yep, it had indeed mentioned the bookends. Stumped again. It would've been a great telltale sign that Selina might have killed him if the article hadn't been so forthcoming.

I stopped mid-chew. What a horrible thought. My mother would be ashamed. I could almost hear her now. *"You should not wish for the downfall of another or be disappointed that someone may not be guilty."* But was I wishing for Selina to be guilty? Hmm . . . maybe. However, I tried to convince myself it was simply a desire to find the guilty party, so Linus's memory could be laid to rest in peace.

Forcing Selina's greed and spiteful words out of my mind, I walked into the dining area to get Eddy's vet folder. Here, at least, was something positive I could do for the dog. Maybe putting him on a medication temporarily would help in the long run. Wouldn't hurt to ask. As I picked up the folder, papers slid from under it onto the floor.

I bent to pick up several sets of stapled pages. It seemed I'd accidentally been given two folders when I'd gone to Linus's house. The second folder, labeled "Inventory," must have been in the cabinet right behind the Hokes Folly Veterinary Clinic folder they'd intended to give me. I restacked the printouts and slid them into the folder. No time to go through them, though. I didn't want Mason to have to manage the store alone after that article. There was no telling what the day would bring.

Instead, I finished feeding Eddy, walked him, and we headed to the store, both folders tucked under my arm. When we entered, the store had only been open ten minutes, but the phone was ringing, and I counted five customers already there. Mason had been cornered by three women, the oldest of whom seemed to be in her fifties, and he signaled me for help, a desperate look in his eyes. I shoved the folders under the counter and went to his rescue.

As I approached, I heard him all but shout, "Look, here she is now. I'm sure she'll be able to help you better than I can." He race-walked back to the counter, where a legitimate customer seemed ready to buy.

I turned to the ladies. "How may I help you?"

"I'm Helen Grigby." The oldest woman raised her chin a bit. "And this is Lavinia Scoddin and Elizabeth North." She gestured to the other two women, each somewhere in their forties. "We're from the Hokes Folly chapter of the Women's League on Public Safety. We'd like to know what you're doing about the repeated murders in your store. We're prepared to stage a boycott if you don't provide adequate safety for patrons."

I gritted my teeth, my mother's voice ringing in my ear, demanding I be civil rather than bellow out the banshee scream that was rising from my depths. "I'm sorry you've been misinformed, ladies. There have not been multiple murders in my store."

Helen pursed her lips and clasped her purse tighter. "I read the article. I know a man was murdered here a few days ago."

I smiled sweetly. "Actually, he was murdered in the parking lot outside the historic district. I believe that would make it the Town Council's responsibility to provide adequate security and lighting, not mine. Now, if you ladies would like to discuss used or antique books, I can suggest a few you might like to purchase. If not, I need to assist other customers." I ignored my inner Mom-voice chiding me for being a bit rude. There was a time for being nice, but sometimes you had to be firm.

Helen harrumphed. "Well, I never. Come on, ladies." She turned on her heel and marched toward the door, the other two ladies flowing in her wake.

The phone was ringing again, and as Mason was helping a customer, I grabbed it off the cradle. I caught sight of Mason shaking his head and mouthing, *No, don't,* as I raised the receiver to my ear and cheerfully said, "Twice Upon a Time. How can I help you?"

"This is Jackie Lathan from WBGR in Charlotte. We've heard there's been another murder linked to this store. Are you the owner?"

Flabbergasted, I stammered, "What? I . . . yes—no comment!" I hung the phone up without giving the reporter a chance to respond. Instantly it rang again.

Mason's hand on my shoulder made me jump.

"It's been like that since I got here." He picked up the phone base and unplugged it, silencing the ringing. "I think we should leave it unplugged for a few days."

Numbly I nodded, trying not to flash back to the hounding and beating I had taken from the press in Charlotte before I'd come to Hokes Folly. It had been a veritable nightmare.

"My mom always said, 'This, too, shall pass.' I think she would have said that now too." Mason turned at the sound of the front door chimes and went to greet an entering customer.

I gathered my wits and strode behind the counter, tidying up an already neat area, giving my hands busywork until I could think straight. I'd been through so much in the last few months. Being accused of embezzlement and murder, being in jail three months, losing my job, losing my fiancé, losing my home . . . almost losing my sanity. Then I'd come here.

Looking around the store, I took a deep breath. This was mine. I belonged here. No one was going to ruin it for me. I hadn't come this far to only come this far. I chuckled, releasing the tension, when I realized a quote from an inspirational poster I'd seen had begun to flit through my brain. It seemed to fit, though, and I decided it would be my new mantra. At least for this week.

The rest of the morning ran more smoothly, without any more accusatory visits and with a silenced phone. We had a smattering of lookie-loos who wanted to gain fodder for gossip. Mason and I managed to herd them toward the door, maintaining the pleasantly bookish environment for legitimate shoppers.

When my stomach growled midday, I ran upstairs to grab the rest of a large pizza I'd ordered a couple of days ago, and we ate on the fly, gobbling bites between customers. As things slowed in the early afternoon, a soft, high-pitched whine by the door drew my attention to Eddy's need for a walk. I grabbed his leash and we headed down the walk toward a grassy area and a nice tree.

As we returned, I groaned inwardly, catching sight of Selina and Douglas March headed in our direction. I glanced around for a quick exit from their path, but it was too late.

Douglas waved at me, and I had no choice but to continue toward them.

"Hi, Mr. and Mrs. March. How are you today?" I drew to a stop next to them. "You look lovely today, Mrs. March," I added for good measure. I needed to gain inner-Mom-voice brownie points. I'd stepped over the line too many times lately.

"Of course I do." Selina struck a pose, which I figured was meant to impress me.

I caught myself before I rolled my eyes. "How are things at the library?" This was aimed at Douglas.

He shook his head and sighed. "We're managing, I suppose, but it's not the same without Linus. The funeral today was difficult, to say the least."

Oh snap, I'd forgotten! "I'm so sorry. I should have known that's where you had been today."

"Did you think we dress like this every day?" Selina pursed her lips in distaste and brushed at imaginary lint on her fur of the day, this time a black calf-length cape. "Why else would I wear all black during the day? It's just not done."

Frankly, Douglas looked as he had every other time I'd seen him, wearing a worn suit, albeit in charcoal gray today rather than muddy brown as before. Selina's all-black look was sleek, if a bit toned down for her. Her black stilettoes were only three inches, not the usual four, and her mid-thigh-length dress was almost modest and subdued. Almost.

Selina continued. "I suppose I could wear my funeral attire to one of your boring little parties and fit right in. Although I'd worry about my new fur, considering your habit of shelving books in such a way as to damage customers' belongings." A snarky smile slid across her face, and she swept her fur cape across the front of her dress, in an old-movie, Dracula-style gesture.

Douglas grasped Selina by the arm. "Enough. Miss Quinn has been gracious to us, and we will be gracious in return."

A low growl sounded at my side, and Eddy took a half step forward.

Selina gasped and stumbled backward on her stilettoes. "Douglas! That dog! Did you see her try to sic him on me? Get him away from me!"

Douglas shot me a regretful look before steering his wife to cross the cobblestone street. "I'm sure he won't follow us over here, dear. He probably responded to the fur coat, thinking it was another animal."

As they walked away, I could still hear her shrieking about how I'd tried to get my dog to attack her. I glanced down at Eddy. He still stood, watching them retreat, his legs locked and his hackles raised.

I leaned down and smoothed his hackles. "I don't know what's up with you, sweetheart, but you can't keep growling at folks. Even Selina March. Although I do understand the urge."

Eddy glanced up at me and gave me a single wag before looking back at the Marches.

I followed his gaze, watching them enter The Weeping Willow. My head turned when I caught movement out of the corner of my eye. A plump woman clad in black, a black pillbox hat with a net veil covering her face, stood in the doorway of the Hokes Folly Apothecary two doors down from the pub. When she saw me looking, she ducked inside.

At least someone had witnessed that I hadn't sicced my dog on Selina March. I'd ask the apothecary who she was, if Selina tried to push the issue. I stood, tugging on Eddy's leash, and managed to coax him into moving toward the store. We entered, finding Mason on a stool behind the counter in an exhausted slump.

"We got a bit of a lull." He leaned forward, resting his head on his crossed arms on the counter. "I'm beat."

I looked out the window behind him. "Don't look now. It looks like a tour bus must have arrived. There are quite a few folks headed this way."

Mason stood and squared his shoulders. "Round two."

The door chimes sounded, and Mason kicked into store manager persona for the next hour, handling questions, directing customers to sections of the store, and ringing up purchases.

As he worked, I pulled out my laptop and worked on the notice I'd planned for the next newspaper edition, announcing I was extending the grand reopening sale from a few days to all month long. With the traffic we'd had, I hated to end it too early.

Eddy slept at my feet, raising his head to check the door each time the chimes sounded. During the next lull, Mason walked behind the counter, and Eddy roused enough to wag his tail and solicit a good belly rub before dozing off again.

"Lazy dog." Mason plopped onto a chair, a smile on his face as he gazed at the animal. "I wish I could curl up under the counter for a nap right now."

"You're young and energetic. You'll live," I stated before turning my attention back to the newspaper notice I'd almost completed to my satisfaction.

"Uh-oh, don't look now." Mason pointed toward the sidewalk.

I swiveled on my stool and caught sight of Bradford Prescott, suit immaculate, hair perfectly coifed. He stopped and shook hands with a passerby, offering the man a pamphlet. Oh, joy. A politician soliciting. Maybe I needed to make a "No Soliciting" sign for the door.

Catching us watching, Bradford waved and strode toward our door. He entered, followed by an elderly couple. Mason perked up and swept from behind the counter, guiding the couple around the store in a mini-tour I'd seen him give several times today. I had to hand it to him; making him the store manager had done wonders for the guy.

I realized Bradford was talking. Chagrined, I turned and tried to catch up to what he was saying. Too late. He'd finished, and he was looking at me as if he expected a response.

"So, you're saying . . ." I let my words fade away, acting as if I needed clarification, and hoping he hadn't said something so simple that I was making myself look like more of an idiot.

He held out a stack of his political pamphlets. "I asked if I could leave a stack of these on the counter."

Oops, hopes dashed. Oh well. I shook my head. "I'm sorry, but if I let one organization do it, I'd have to let them all."

"You wouldn't have to push them on anyone or put them in any bags. Just let folks pick one up if they want one." He again held out the stack, a slick smile on his face.

Again, I didn't take them. "I'm sorry, I really can't." I noticed Mason waving at me from across the room. Bless that boy, this paid me back for rescuing him from the Women's League Against . . . whatever. "I'm needed to assist a customer, Mr. Prescott. I'm delighted to see you again, and I wish you all the best with your campaign efforts."

He didn't match my smile as I slipped from behind the counter. It was moments later when I heard the chimes sound, and I wrapped up with my customer, quickly returning to the front windows to make sure Bradford was moving away from my store. As I watched, he turned down the street, shaking hands as he went.

I ducked down a bit, however, when I noticed Selina and Douglas exiting The Weeping Willow, deep in conversation. They passed the store, and I breathed a sigh of relief. Again, movement at the edge of my view tugged at my attention. The black-clad woman had slipped out of the apothecary and into the pub, watching the Marches closely as she did so.

Another customer needed my attention, and I ended up deep in a conversation about vintage cookbooks. When the woman selected a few, I headed toward the counter to ring her up, noticing someone standing quietly inside the door.

Douglas March met my gaze, a smile on his face.

I nodded to him to let him know I'd be with him momentarily, completed the cookbook sale, then turned to him. "How can I help you, Mr. March?"

"Miss Quinn, I wanted to apologize again for my wife's rude comments. She really doesn't mean to be difficult." Douglas shoved his hands in his pants pockets.

Bull. That woman meant to be mean at every turn. She'd never gotten past the mean-girls stage from high school. "Of course, Mr. March. I understand. I'm sure she's just stressed about the upcoming ball. I hear it's going to be quite the bash."

"Oh, that." Douglas wilted some. "Selina does love her parties."

And furs, and expensive jewelry and clothes, and, and, and.

Douglas pulled a hand out of a pocket and pointed at the counter. "I see you're backing Bradford Prescott in the upcoming election."

Hellfire on a popsicle. The smarmy jerk had left a stack of his stupid pamphlets despite what I'd said. "I try not to discuss politics at work or let my own opinions color the atmosphere of the store. I think he left these here by accident." I snagged them and stuffed them under the counter. I'd trash them later when it wouldn't make me look rude.

"I'm sure the best candidate will win." Douglas put his hand on the door handle. "Again, I'm sorry about Selina. I'm sure you'll end up as friends one day." With a weak smile that said he didn't believe that any more than I did, he pushed open the door and left to the tinkling of the chimes.

I woke the computer and again tried to put the finishing touches on my newspaper ad, knowing I'd rather turn in finished artwork than let them create some for me after the hatchet job they'd done on my store in their article. But I needed the cheap advertisement, and I couldn't afford radio or TV ads.

The door chimes sounded again as I finished up and closed the laptop. I looked up to see the black-clad woman who had been following the Marches.

"Alice?" I asked, surprised at this completely different look on the woman. She looked almost polished compared to the little-girl pink ruffles she'd worn to the store's grand reopening event. No wonder I hadn't recognized her from across the street.

"Yes, it's me." She sniffed loudly, opening her black clutch to remove a tissue and dab at her eyes under the veil. Half sobbing, she asked, "Do you still have that book that Linus repaired last week?"

"I do." I offered her a stool to sit on.

She hitched herself onto it and propped both feet on the bottom rung. "I would like to buy it after all." She dabbed her eyes again and sniffed loudly. "It was the last thing my Linus worked on before he died."

My brows shot up, but I kept my jaw from dropping. *Her* Linus? Since when? "Yes, I can get it for you if you'll wait a moment."

She nodded and dabbed.

I left her on the stool while I rushed to the poetry section to snag the book, returning with it to the front counter. "I've discounted it a bit due to the damage, but Linus did an excellent repair job. You have to really look closely to notice anything wrong."

With trembling hands, she took the book, running shaking fingers across the cover as if caressing a lover.

Creepy! But hey, a sale was a sale. What she did with the book later was none of my business. She could sleep with it like a Teddy bear for all I cared.

I rang up the sale, hoping sentimentality didn't stretch her budget too far, and placed the book in a store logo bag along with the receipt. "I'm sorry for your loss."

She took the bag and looked inside, sniffing again. "Yes, it is a great loss. There will never be another Linus Talbot. Not, at least, for me." With that dramatic statement, she swept from the store, clutching the bag to her breast like it was the most precious item she'd ever owned.

I shook my head in amazement. Wow. Just wow. At least Eddy hadn't raised his hackles again. I looked down at my sleeping furry friend.

Another customer followed Alice out, and Mason joined me behind the counter.

"It seems Alice has done another about-face." I showed him the receipt.

"Again? Boy, she can't make up her mind, can she?" He chuckled and sat on a stool. "I think that was the last of the tour bus customers."

I printed a quick tally of the day's sales and went to the back room to put the printout in the filing cabinet beside the desk. Files. Oh snap, I'd forgotten.

"Hey, Mason, look at this." I gestured to him when I returned to the front counter. "This must've been in the file cabinet behind Eddy's vet folder, and they gave it to me by accident."

Mason took the folder I held out and opened it. "What is it?"

I laid Eddy's vet folder on the counter. "Inventory printouts. I thought we'd look at how they tagged their inventory items, so we can improve ours. I'll run it over to Keith later, and he can get it back to Linus's house."

He dragged another stool next to mine and plopped down, and I spread the stapled sets of pages across the counter.

Mason picked up a printout and flipped through it.

I grabbed another stack and scanned the categories the sheet tracked. One category was date published. I noticed all of the books on page one were antique. I turned the page. Same. I slid my finger down each page, finding Linus was only tracking the antique books. I guessed that made sense because that was his department.

"Does yours have any highlighted items?" I turned to the two pages where I'd found items that looked like he'd used a yellow highlighter on them.

Mason quickly flipped through his pages again. "Nope." He grabbed another set and flipped the pages. "But this one has three."

Quickly we checked all of the stacks, finding only the oldest and the newest didn't have highlighted items.

"Did you see the dates?" I asked, lining them up in order.

Mason leaned in and looked at the handwritten dates at the top of each set. "Hey, the first two are a year apart. Then the third one is three months after the second one. The rest are all two weeks apart."

"And did you see that the second one had about fifteen items highlighted?" I turned the pages of that set.

Mason's brow furrowed. "But what are they?"

I grabbed the set with the most highlighted items and the next dated set and turned the pages simultaneously. I snagged the next set and did the same thing. "There's a pattern." I pointed to the items. "Notice that the highlighted items are items that don't show up on the next run."

We went through all of the pages, comparing each run to the next dated run. The results were the same. With each new run, more books were missing—two to three books every two weeks.

"Were that many books being damaged?" Mason slid his fingers across the line items again.

I shook my head. "I honestly don't know. I wouldn't think so. They seem pretty careful with their collection. Although they did say Selina damaged a bunch of them one day."

"Yeah, but not every two weeks." Mason stood as the bells jingled again, signaling another customer. "Too bad he didn't print out an explanation."

Too bad indeed. I restacked the pages and slid them back into the folder. "I think I should call Keith and tell him about this. Let the police decide what it all means." I dialed Keith's number. When he didn't answer, I left a voice mail requesting he call as soon as he got the message.

I grabbed Eddy's leash. He hadn't asked to go out in a while, and I figured he'd need a walk before Keith called back, in case I had to leave him with Mason again to take the folder to the police station. I started for the door, calling the dog as I moved. Eddy didn't follow. Eddy didn't move.

Panic clenched my gut. "Eddy?" I rushed back to the counter and dropped to my knees beside the dog. "Eddy?" I shook him gently.

He raised his head, eyes not focusing, wheezing a bit as he breathed.

"Come on, boy." I patted him on the hip. "That must have been a good nap. But it's time to wake up and go for a walk."

At the shake of the leash, Eddy struggled to rise but staggered and sank to the floor again, flopping onto his side and breathing heavily.

"Mason!" I yelled across the room. Fear sliced through me, my heart racing. *No, no, no, no, no!*

Mason skidded to a stop beside me, the customer close behind.

"I need you to close the store immediately and call the vet in that folder." I looked past Mason at the teenaged boy looking over Mason's shoulder, probably there to look for a cheaper way to get ahold of the newest reading assignment for his English class. "I'm sorry, but you'll have to come back another day."

At my pointed stare, the boy nodded and left, and Mason locked the door behind him, flipping the door's sign to "Closed" as he spoke softly into his phone.

"The vet's waiting for us." Mason scooped Eddy up in his arms. "I'll drive, and you can sit in the back with Eddy."

I followed Mason out the front door, locked it behind us, and jogged to keep up with his hurried stride, grateful I wouldn't have to drive. Tears blurred my vision at the thought I might lose this sweet baby I'd come to love.

The ride to the vet was straight out of a *Fast and Furious* movie. Mason wove in and out of slower traffic, skimming through yellow lights, his emergency flashers on. We were there in minutes, and the vet met us at the door.

After the vet took Eddy back to draw blood and check vitals, I collapsed into a plastic chair in the exam room, swallowing to keep the tears from flowing. Mason paced in the tiny room, his jaw clenched. I knew he loved the dog too. Time dragged by. Although I knew it was only about half an hour, it seemed like two days before the vet reappeared.

I leapt to my feet, desperate to hear good news. *Please, let the news be good. Please.*

"I'm Doctor John Bledsoe." He extended his hand to shake mine. "I think you got him to us in time, but we need to keep him at least overnight, if not longer. I want to watch him for a bit."

My throat closed as tears of relief fell. Eddy was going to be okay.

Mason cleared his own throat. "What happened?"

"Eddy helped us with that one." The vet leaned a hip against the exam table. "He threw up all over the exam table back there, giving us a good look at what he'd ingested. The telltale smell gave it away, but we were able to find a few chunks to float in salt water to confirm. Someone fed your dog naphthalene mothballs crumbled up and mixed in with a hamburger."

My knees wobbled, and I sank to a chair. Someone had tried to kill my dog.

Chapter Twelve

M ason and I stayed at the vet's until closing time, when we had no choice but to leave Eddy in their capable hands with assurances they would check on him in their emergency wing throughout the night. By the time we left, he was in stable condition, and I was exhausted from the stress but too wired to even close my eyes.

Instead, I vacillated between agitated pacing around my apartment and collapsing in a ball on the couch.

A loud knock sounded through my front door, and I rushed to open it. Keith stood on the stoop, and I threw myself into his arms before he could cross the threshold.

His arms wrapped around me, one hand stroking my back, his lips against my hair as I shook uncontrollably in his embrace. "Honey, it'll be okay. The vet said you got Eddy to them on time."

"But what if I hadn't?" The tears I'd held back poured out, and a sob tore from my chest.

Keith scooped me up in his arms, closed the front door with the kick of a heel, and strode to the couch. He sat, snuggling me on his lap, and resumed stroking my back, adding rocking to his repertoire. "Just let it out."

His soft words were my final undoing, and I let the hurt, anger, guilt, and fear all come up in one good old-fashioned girl cry. Keith rocked me, holding me tightly, whispering words I couldn't understand over my blubbering, but the soothing warmth in his voice washed over me like a balm.

Eventually I cried myself into exhaustion and must have dozed off, because I woke up, still curled up in Keith's lap on the couch. Keith's head hung at an odd angle, and he was snoring softly. The soft light of predawn filled the room. How long had we slept in such an awkward position?

I slowly sat up, trying not to disturb him, and realized my hair was sticking up in a funky way; I had drooled on Keith's shirt, and my eyes, swollen from crying so much, had dried matter in the corners. Tossing in the fact that my mouth tasted horrible, which meant I had horrible morning breath, was icing on the cake that was my new first-morning-wakeup-with-my-boyfriend look. There was no way I could let him see me like this.

I slowly inched myself around so I could swing my legs to the floor, but I couldn't figure out how to stand without jostling him. The option to simply stay there forever, so he wouldn't wake up and see me like this flitted across my mind. Of course, he would wake up at some point. On top of that, I really had to use the bathroom. There was nothing to do but go for it.

I awkwardly shifted my weight up and off him, but about the time I was free, an arm snaked around from behind and pulled me back onto his lap.

"I had to suffer a serious crick in my neck, a wet shirt, and numb legs to finally get to spend the night with you. The least you could do is snuggle with me afterward."

He pulled me back, and I melted into his warmth again. Until reality hit. Let him crack open those eyes and get a gander at his girlfriend with her tangled hair, puffy eyes with gunk in the corners, and breath that could stop a charging bull elephant—yeah, that screamed "cuddle." *Not.*

Again I tried to extricate myself from his embrace, only to have him tighten his arms.

"I have to pee," I mumbled, trying not to open my mouth too much and let my stinky morning breath out.

"Hmm." He shifted a bit. "I'll let you go for a good morning kiss."

Oh, hot pickles on a pastry, there was no way. But my bladder insisted I at least try. In a flash, I turned my head, holding my breath, and planted a quick kiss on his lips, then slipped out of his arms, all but running toward the bathroom. His laughter echoed across the room as I shut the door.

After taking care of my morning needs, I looked at myself in the mirror and cringed. It was worse than I'd thought. I grabbed a brush and worked it through the tangles until my hair sort of behaved, giving up on the section that insisted on lying wrong. Next, I grabbed a washcloth and held it to my eyes, soothing the swelling and wiping away the corner gunk. Finally I grabbed my toothbrush and spent a good two or three minutes brushing my teeth, following it with a hefty rinse of mouthwash for good measure.

It was the best I was going to do, short of showering and changing clothes. Oh well, I at least looked a bit better than when I'd entered the bathroom. My hand turned the handle as I took a deep breath. The door swung open, and I stepped out into the main room, where the smell of perking coffee hit me.

"Feel better?" Keith poured a mug and held it out to me over the bar.

I sat on one of the stools, taking the mug and sipping it gratefully. "Yes, much. Thanks."

"You looked cuter with messy hair." He winked at me over his mug.

Heat filled my cheeks, and I nodded. "Good to know." How was I supposed to respond to that? The man looked as sexy when he woke up after an uncomfortable night on the couch as he always did. I, on the other hand, didn't even look like the same person who had met him at the door last night.

Keith leaned across the bar toward me. "Seriously. You're beautiful. Always. No matter what." He reached out and ran the backs of his fingers down my cheek.

I was pretty sure I blushed again, and I hid behind my mug as I took another swig of the blackish liquid.

"I called Doctor Bledsoe while you were in the bathroom. Eddy's doing fine." He held up the coffeepot in a silent question.

A breath of relief whooshed out of my chest. "Thank goodness." I held out my mug. "What else did he say? How did Eddy do overnight?"

"He said Eddy's vitals continued to improve throughout the night, but he still wants to keep him for a couple of days, just to make sure." Keith returned the pot to the counter and walked around to sit next to me, sliding his fingers through mine. "Eddy's going to be fine, honey."

"I know." I squeezed his fingers. "Thanks for being here last night. I'm sorry I fell apart on you."

Keith swiveled his stool to face mine, turning mine toward him as well. He lifted my chin with a finger, forcing me to meet his gaze. "Stop. Don't ever apologize for needing to cry."

I smiled. "I'm not normally like that. I promise."

"Then I'm doubly honored you felt you could trust me enough to let go." He leaned in and placed a soft kiss on my lips. "And my dry-cleaning bill shouldn't be too high."

At the sparkle in his gaze and the slight upturn in the corner of his mouth, my tension finally let go, and laughter bubbled up. "Yes, well, I did soak your shirt, didn't I?"

"Let's just say a hurricane had nothing on you last night." He leaned back, chuckling as he reached for his coffee mug, downing the last of the liquid before standing. "I need to head to work. I'll check on you later, okay?"

I stood and followed him out the door. "I'll let you know how Eddy's doing."

"Please do." He slipped his jacket on against the chill of the morning. Turning, he pulled me into his arms again, kissing me softly before letting go. "Jenna, please be careful. Someone intentionally fed poison to your dog. I don't want them to try something with you too."

I watched him stride along the walkway toward the stairs at the end of the building. As he disappeared from view, I turned to go back into my apartment and almost ran into Rita.

A grin split her face and she all but bounced on her toes. "Did I just see you-know-who leaving at the crack of dawn?"

"Yes, but—"

"And do I smell fresh coffee?" She nodded her head sideways toward my open door.

I rolled my eyes. "Would you like to come in for a cup?"

"Why, I think I would." She all but raced to the bar in the kitchen and plopped herself on a stool.

I walked behind the bar and grabbed a clean mug, filling it with coffee and sliding it across to her before topping off my own mug.

"Spill it, sister." She wrapped her hands around her mug and grinned at me again.

Moving around the bar to sit next to her, I realized she didn't know about Eddy. "It's not what you think."

"Uh-huh." She chuckled. "Sure." Apparently she caught sight of my puffy, red eyes. Her spine stiffened, and she plopped her mug onto the bar. "You've been crying! What did that man do to you? Do I need to kill him?"

"No, Rita, really. I'm fine." I reached out and put a hand on her forearm. "Keith is fine. It's Eddy. Someone poisoned him last night. But he's fine too. He's at the vet."

"What?" The color drained from her face. "Oh no. No, no, no. What happened? Are you okay?"

I nodded. "I am. Someone fed him crushed up mothballs wrapped in hamburger."

"And you're sure he's going to be okay?" Her hand clutched at mine, squeezing it tightly in support.

"According to Doctor Bledsoe, he is. He says he wants to keep Eddy a few days to watch him, though." I sighed deeply. "Keith was here because I cried myself to sleep on his lap, sitting on the couch. He didn't want to move and wake me, so he slept there too."

"Oh, wow." Rita put a palm to her chest. "That is so sweet. Guess I don't need to kill him after all."

"Please don't." I laughed but quickly sobered. "Now, whoever tried to kill Eddy? Go for it."

"Any idea why someone would want to hurt him?" Rita took a sip of her coffee and frowned before getting up to put her mug in the microwave to heat it up.

I shrugged. "The only thing I can think of is that Eddy was there when Linus was killed. Maybe the killer thinks Eddy can identify them."

"Why would they think that?" Rita cocked her head to one side, a hip leaned on the counter while her coffee heated.

"I honestly don't know." I took another sip of my coffee, amazed anew at Rita's need for her coffee to be scalding hot. Mine was a perfect temperature. I froze with the mug halfway to my lips for a second swig. "What if . . ." I plunked my mug on the counter. "Yesterday when I was at the store, Eddy growled at someone."

Rita perked up. "Who? And did they have time alone with Eddy?"

"It was actually three someones." I held up my fingers and ticked them off. "Bradford Prescott, who wanted to leave political pamphlets on my counter for customers. He was alone with Eddy when Mason needed my help with a customer. Alice King. She was alone with Eddy when I went to the poetry section to get the book Linus had repaired. She decided she wanted to buy it."

"Wait, the book you said she refused to even touch because Linus had touched it?" Rita rejoined me on the stools and turned to face me.

"Yep, that book. She came in all weepy, talking about how it was the last thing 'her Linus' had touched." I ran the scene through my head again.

"Weird." Rita shook her head. "That woman is bonkers."

"I thought it was strange too." I hesitated, not wanting to point a finger if she wasn't guilty. But someone had poisoned my dog during that time. "Rita, what if she didn't really want the book? What if she really just wanted me to be away from Eddy long enough for her to give him the meat?" Just the thought made my stomach clench. How could I have been so careless?

Rita's brows rose as she considered. "It could be. But how do we prove it? It's not like we can go to her house and start digging through her trash or her handbags. Was there anyone else?"

"Eddy did growl at Selina's coat outside. She was being her usual sweet self." I rolled my eyes.

Rita barked out a laugh. "I'll just bet she was."

"It was bad enough Douglas came by to apologize for her behavior. But she never came in the store." I finished off my coffee and set the mug on the bar top. "Maybe she tossed Eddy something while I was looking at Douglas and asking about the library."

"Maybe." Rita looked at her watch. "I'd better get a move on if I'm going to make it to work on time today. Let me know how Eddy's doing, okay?"

I promised her I would, and she scooted out the door. Looking at the time, I realized I was going to be late, too, if I didn't get moving. I grabbed a quick shower, dressed, inhaled a bit of cereal, and headed downstairs to the store.

As I entered, Mason met me at the bottom of the stairs, duster in hand. "How's Eddy?"

"He's going to be fine, but Doctor Bledsoe is keeping hi[m] for a few days just to make sure." I gave Mason a quick hu[g]. "Thanks for helping me yesterday. I don't know what I would'[ve] done if you hadn't been here."

"It was nothing." Mason shrugged. "I love Eddy too. Can['t] let anything happen to him on my watch." He walked to th[e] counter and slid two folders out from under the counter. "[I] stuck these down here, since I didn't know when you'd be i[n] today. Did you ever get to tell Keith about the inventory sheets?"

"Oh, wow, I completely forgot to tell him before he left thi[s] morning." I inwardly cringed, knowing what was coming.

Mason's brows rose. "Before he left . . . *this morning*?" Mason grinned.

I rolled my eyes. I'd never live it down now that I'd let the cat out of the bag. Mom's voice sounded in my ear, demanding I defend my reputation by explaining we'd spent the night with me sobbing and Keith getting a crick in his neck. My stubborn streak took over. Let Mason think what he wanted. It was no one's business why Keith had spent the night. *So there.*

My fingers slid my phone out of my back pocket, and I dialed Keith's number. He answered on the first ring. "Is Eddy okay?"

"He's fine," I assured him. "I forgot to tell you about something earlier. Yesterday morning, I discovered the police officer who pulled Eddy's vet records for me also pulled another folder. Can you come get it? I want to show you something we discovered that may mean something."

"Sure, I'll be there as soon as I can."

After we hung up, I took Eddy's folder and filed it in the back room's filing cabinet and made copies of the inventory sheets fo[r] our store purposes. While I was there, I also broke down sever[al]

empty cardboard boxes the newest set of books had arrived in and walked them out to the dumpster. As I stepped back in from the alleyway behind the store, Mason poked his head into the back room.

"We have company." He gestured with his head over his shoulder. "And he seems in a grumpier than usual mood today."

Chapter Thirteen

I looked past my employee and saw not only Keith but also Frank Sutter standing by the front counter. Great. Just when the day looked to be less stressful than the one before. My gaze caught Keith's, and I raised my eyebrows. He shrugged in response and mouthed the word *Sorry*.

Striding across the store toward the frowning detective standing beside my boyfriend, I mentally prepped for the encounter by preemptively counting to ten. As I neared, I extended my hand. "Detective Sutter, how nice to see you."

Grunt. "Okay." He didn't shake my hand. Instead, he reached into the breast pocket of his gray suit and pulled out a pen and a little notebook.

Wow, rude much? I counted to ten again. "I called Keith this morning to let him know I had found something that may be pertinent to the case."

"Uh-huh." He flipped the notebook open, pen poised. "Do tell."

I had brought the folder from the back room and held it out to the inspector. "This was accidentally given to me when I went to Linus's house last Friday."

Sutter scribbled a note. "Accidentally?"

"Yes." I drew the word out slowly.

Grunt. "This is Wednesday. It took you six days to give us this folder?"

I gritted my teeth and smiled. "Detective, I'm in the middle of a monthlong grand reopening sale. I've been busy enough I hadn't even looked at the folders your officer gave me until yesterday."

Sutter sighed. "My sister's boy. His dad is pushing him to become a cop like his Uncle Frank. But I guess his mother is about to get her wish. The kid wants to be an artist, and she'd much rather see that than see him get shot at. With another write-up for carelessness in his jacket, and him only on the job two months, they'll wash him out." He shook his head. "Why didn't you give us this folder yesterday?"

"I'm sure Keith told you someone poisoned my dog, and I didn't even consider the folders again until Mason reminded me." I crossed my arms, quickly losing the last vestiges of patience with the man.

"Yeah, sorry about your dog." Sutter sounded somewhat sympathetic. "Hope he gets better."

Stymied, as this was the first kind thing Sutter had ever said to me, I stammered out a response. "Thanks. I appreciate that."

Sutter opened the folder and looked at a couple of pages. "What is this?"

"Inventory pages." I took the folder and laid them out on the counter in chronological order. "Mason and I noticed Linus had only recently begun to print an inventory every two weeks. He also highlighted that more and more antique books were missing from each new run."

Grunt. "Uh-huh." Sutter flipped his notebook closed. "It seems you think I needed to waste my time here today, looking at inventories rather than finding a killer?"

My brows shot up. "I thought you should know books were missing from the library. Rare books. Maybe it had something to do with Linus's death."

"Miss Quinn"—*grunt*—"I really don't care that the library—a place full of books—took some of those books out of inventory for whatever reasons. I doubt someone would commit murder over old books."

"My uncle was murdered over an old book," I reminded him softly.

Sutter tucked his notebook and pen into his suit's breast pocket. "Be that as it may, I have killers to catch. I don't have time to follow hairbrained ideas and search for missing library books." He turned and stormed out the door.

As the door chimes sounded at his exit, I whirled to Keith. "Ooooooh, that man drives me crazy! I know you say he gets results, but he's so bullheaded, I don't see how he keeps from getting in his own way."

Keith chuckled. "I know. He's close to retirement, and he wants a big splashy case to go out on. I don't think library books fit the bill, in his opinion anyway." He gave me a quick kiss and left, following his partner.

"What now, boss lady?" Mason asked after Keith left.

I tossed my hands in the air. "I honestly don't know. I guess it's a dead end."

"At least we can use those records to improve our own inventory runs, especially on our antique books." The door chimes sounded, and Mason turned to greet the next customer.

I walked to the back room and spread out the copies of the inventory sheets I'd made before turning the originals over to Sutter. Sitting at the desk, I studied the pattern Linus had found. Frustration bubbled up anew at not knowing what he had or had not sussed out by looking at these lines and lines of data, other than that books were missing. Were they really missing? Or was he tracking loans to other libraries? Was I making a mountain out of a molehill in my attempt to make sense of Linus's death? Maybe Mason was right, and the most we could expect to learn would be how to improve our own tracking and inventory methods.

Eddy and his grief popped into my head, and I called the vet.

On the second ring, a receptionist answered. "Hokes Folly Veterinary Clinic. How may I help you?"

"This is Jenna Quinn. I'm calling to check on Eddy. Is Doctor Bledsoe available?" I asked.

"Please hold." Silence sounded through the line. Not even tacky Muzak to listen to.

While I waited for the vet to come on the line, I restacked the inventory lists by date and slid them into a folder, leaving it open to the most recent one. An idea nudged at the back of my mind, interrupted by the vet's voice in my ear.

"Hi, Jenna. Eddy's doing fine. He's up and mobile, and his kidney and liver numbers are stable, although his appetite is a bit low right now." The sound of shuffling papers sounded through the line. "If you don't mind, to be on the safe side I'd really like to keep him through the weekend."

"Of course. Whatever you think is best." Relief poured through me.

The vet had previously stated Eddy would pull through, but hearing about his improvement renewed my optimism. I thanked him and ended the call.

My hand still rested on the inventory sheets. I slid my fingers down the line items, letting my mind run. Snatching the most recent printout, I stood. The idea rummaging around in my brain gelled into action. Walking through the store, I waved and motioned toward the front door to let Mason know I was leaving.

I drove the short distance to the Hokes Folly Community Library, folder in hand, and made my way to their rare book section. Slowly I moved down an aisle, checking books off the inventory list. At least the shelves and the inventory list were arranged by subject and alphabetized within them. The only books I had to hunt for were ones that had been mis-shelved.

An hour in and a third of the way through the list, I had discovered three misplaced books and one possibly missing book. However, I was beginning to receive odd looks from the staff. I smiled and waved, and the two librarians busied themselves with other tasks. Sitting on the floor, I made my way along a bottom shelf, continuing to check titles off my list. When I stood and rounded the corner into another aisle, I almost bumped into Douglas, who was striding toward the rare book circulation desk.

I jumped back out of the way, hoping he hadn't noticed me. I cringed when he spoke.

"Oh, hello, Jenna." He came to a halt and smiled. "Is there something I can help you find?"

Darn it, I'd been caught. I forced my shoulders to relax and returned his smile. "I'm looking at your shelving methods for your antique books, whether it's by subject, title, author, or age. I'm looking for new ideas for the store."

"Let me see your notes." Before I could respond, his hand snaked out and tugged the pages from my hands. "I may be able to make some suggestions."

Wow, that just happened. I watched as his brow furrowed.

He looked up, confusion etched in his gaze. "This is a printed copy of our inventory. Why do you have this?"

As I answered, I reached out, just as he had, and tugged the sheets from his grasp. "Yes, it is." I smiled sweetly. "When I picked up Eddy's vet records from his home, the officer there accidentally gave me a folder of inventory runs Linus kept at home. We're setting up our own inventory system at the store, and I thought it would be helpful to come here and cross-reference things, so I get a full picture of how and why you keep the records you do."

I watched his face for any signal that he thought I wasn't being completely forthright about my motivations. Since he was married to one of my suspects, I didn't want to tip my hand. They may not have had the most romantic of relationships, but who knew how much he shared of his day with her over dinner each night?

Douglas smiled again. "Ah, I see. We use the Dewey decimal classification system in this section, just as in the rest of the library. Our inventory is set to run in the same fashion, which makes it less confusing when we print an inventory run to do a visual check once a year."

That explained Linus's first two inventory runs a year apart. "I would have thought you'd do an inventory more often than that."

Douglas shook his head. "No, it's really not necessary. As patrons cannot check out these books, like they can with regular library books, we don't have the same issues with missing copies."

"Even from theft?" I snagged a book off the shelf. "I couldn't stick one in my bag and walk out?"

Douglas chuckled and crossed his arms. "Go for it." He gestured toward the archway that led to the rest of the library.

I strode across the room and stepped through the archway. An alarm sounded. As I turned to walk back to Douglas, my gaze swept across Alice, who hovered near the end of an aisle in another section of the library, a startled look in her eyes, obviously aware of the alarm's meaning because of her time working at the library. She seemed to relax when she saw it was me, and she nodded at me and smiled before turning down the aisle. I walked back through the archway into the rare book area and handed Douglas the book.

He waved a hand at the rare book circulation desk, signaling the attendant to silence the alarm. "As I said, we don't have issues with missing copies. There are tiny magnets inserted inside the spine that set off the detectors if anyone tries to leave with a book."

In for a penny . . . I pasted an innocent look on my face. "What happens if you do discover a book has gone missing?"

"More often than not, it's simply misplaced among the shelves." Douglas waved an arm to encompass the rare book section. "However, other times, it's usually a book that has been removed to resolve an issue."

"Issue?" Surely he didn't mean censorship.

"As these books are quite old, some must be handled with extreme care. They may be moved to our climate-controlled archive section and digitally scanned, eliminating the possibility of guests further damaging the book with hand oils." Douglas pointed toward a set of computers. "Patrons can view the books on those systems."

"But wouldn't those stay in inventory?" I walked toward a computer and saw instructions printed and taped to the table.

"Of course." Douglas nodded. "However, the printed inventory sheets usually contain only the books here in the main section, available for patrons to physically view. Another much shorter inventory sheet is used to check the books in the archive section. Do understand, though, there are times when we must completely remove them from our inventory. One time we discovered a book developing mildew. It was a newer book that had been donated through a patron's will. It was removed and eventually destroyed, as the methods to remove the mildew would have caused extreme damage, and we could not allow the book to contaminate the rest of our collection. Fortunately, that is an incredibly rare occurrence." He glanced at his watch.

"I'm so sorry. I've been taking up all your time." I sat at one of the computers. "If you don't mind, I'll keep looking through what you have here."

"Not at all. If you need any further assistance, one of us will be delighted to help you." He looked at his watch again. "However, I do have a meeting shortly with a donor, so if there's nothing else . . .?"

I shook my head and turned on the monitor. "Nope, I think I've got this. Thanks for the overview."

I poked around in the computer system for a few minutes, getting a feel for it before I returned to my physical inventory of the books on the shelves. I might as well be thorough before making any conclusions.

Three hours later, my stomach was rumbling, and my knees were sore from kneeling on the floor so often. My search had been fruitful, though, and I felt a sense of accomplishment. I had discovered three books missing from the shelves, and only one of the three had been moved to the archived section, according to the computer system. Two more books had been completely removed from inventory since Linus's death.

Chapter Fourteen

"Jenna!" A muffled voice came through my front door. "My hands are full. I can't even knock!"

I rushed to open the door, finding Keith on the other side holding three pizza boxes in the crook of one arm and a half case of beer under the other.

"I come bearing gifts." Keith grinned.

Before I could step back, Mason pushed past me and grabbed the pizza boxes. "Yum! Just what we need."

Mason placed the pizzas on the table next to a stack of paper plates I'd already grabbed, while Rita took the beer and slid it into my mostly empty refrigerator.

"Okay, gang, time for us to figure this thing out." I herded everyone to the table.

"Sure thing, boss lady," Mason mumbled over a mouthful of pizza.

Rita poked him in the shoulder as she took a seat next to him. "Don't talk with your mouth full."

"Yes, ma'am," he mumbled and swallowed.

I slid into the chair next to Keith. "Guys, I need your help. Someone tried to kill my dog, probably because they think he can identify them as Linus's killer. We've got to figure this thing out, and I figure four heads are better than one."

Rita sipped a beer. "You said you'd found out more today."

"I did." I nodded. "I went to the library today, under the guise of looking at how they run their inventory tracking processes. What I discovered is that two more books have gone missing since Linus's death."

Mason whistled low. "That makes"—he looked at the ceiling and counted the tips of his fingers—"between thirty and thirty-five missing books in a year and a half."

Keith pulled two pieces of pepperoni pizza onto his plate. "That's way too many at too steady of a pace to be a coincidence."

"I think your partner is missing the boat on this thing." I took a slice of everything pizza and bit into it, burning the roof of my mouth on the melted cheese. I rapidly blew in and out to cool my mouthful of pizza off before I could chew it. I shushed my mother's voice in my ear, which told me that was bad manners, by insisting it was okay because I was holding a napkin in front of my mouth so no one could see the food.

Keith shook his head. "I don't know. This could be completely unconnected. All we know for sure is some books are missing. At this point, we don't have a strong enough link to tie it to the murder. At least not in Sutter's eyes. Let's just say I can neither confirm nor deny that he is convinced the case is coming from a political angle."

"I agree with Jenna." Rita came to my rescue. "I think it's a bit too coincidental that he's tracking expensive books that have gone missing and ends up dead. What is it they're always saying on the cop shows? Follow the money. My question is, if someone's stealing books, who's benefiting?"

"And was it—" Mason caught Rita's glare at talking with his mouth full and swallowed. "Sorry. Was it a big enough benefit to kill for?"

"Hang on." I stood and walked to the bedroom and grabbed my laptop off the dresser. When I returned with it, I opened a new file and started a list. "Okay, let's write down each suspect, their motives, and how they might tie in to all that we know."

"Let's start with Mr. Prescott." Mason waved a piece of pizza while he talked, earning another glare from Rita. "He used to own Eddy. Eddy didn't like him. He knew Mr. Talbot was going to talk to that newspaper reporter."

"That could have really hurt his chances in the election next month." Rita wiped her fingers on a napkin before reaching for her beer. "As close as it is, this much sensationalism wouldn't have had time to die down. Some folks would have ignored it, or they wouldn't have cared. But he would have lost votes over the issue."

"But what about the book angle?" Keith asked. "Maybe he might need the money from stealing antique books and selling them on the black market. His campaign has to cost a fortune. But would he risk it? And how would he have gotten access to the books?"

Rita swallowed. "He's the president of the Friends of the Hokes Folly Community Library organization. A couple of years ago, they were remodeling a bit, and he had a key to let contractors in after hours. He could've kept it or made a copy once it was over."

"And from Uncle Paul's notes, he would know what was and wasn't valuable. He's been a collector for some time." I typed notes on my computer. "He was alone with Eddy too. When he came into the store, I was called away to help a customer."

"What about the lady with the fur coat? She's a bit on the cray-cray side, if you know what I mean." Mason spun a finger at his temple.

I almost snorted beer up my nose before I could swallow and let a guffaw out. "You aren't kidding!"

"Didn't you say Alice King told you about some incident where she stole Linus's car as a teenager, and he pressed charges?" Rita asked as she slid another piece of cheese pizza onto her plate.

I nodded. "Seems it kept her from going to the university she wanted, where she hoped to get a rich husband. She subsequently met Douglas, who she thought would inherit, but his father disowned him because he said she was a gold digger. She blames all of this on Linus pressing charges."

"She'd have access to keys." Keith pushed away his empty plate and leaned back with his beer in his hand. "It wouldn't be that difficult to make copies of Douglas's keys."

"Lord knows she could use the money. Expensive clothes, expensive jewelry." Rita waved her hand in the air. "And don't even get me started on how much she's spending on the ball this weekend. There's no way she can afford all of that on Douglas's salary, and she's never worked a day in her life. Her daddy gives her a small stipend each month, but not nearly enough for what she spends."

"She did make a comment recently about how surprised she was that old books could be worth so much money." I thought back to one of my recent run-ins with the rude woman as I made more notes in my Word file. "She wasn't ever alone with Eddy, but she could easily have tossed him a few balls of raw meat with crushed mothballs while my attention was on my conversation with Douglas." I shoved away the guilt that threatened to rise at my lack of attention that might have gotten my dog killed.

"As for Alice, I still think she's a strong candidate for every piece of this." Rita pointed at the computer. "Make sure you add her in."

"She did hate Linus, and at the same time she loved him." I typed as I spoke.

"That's not an uncommon motive for murder." Keith rocked his chair back on two legs until he caught my raised brows and plopped the legs back onto the floor. "Sorry. Bachelor life." He grinned.

My mind skipped, suddenly thinking of how it might be if he wasn't a bachelor anymore. *Whoa, where did that come from?* I cleared my throat. "The woman is definitely an emotional roller coaster, that's for sure. One day she can't stand him, the next she can't believe he's gone, and he's so wonderful. Then she won't touch anything he's handled, and later she demands to have the last thing he ever worked on."

Mason spun his finger at his temple again.

"He also ruined her chances at a career in antique book sales," added Rita. "And she could use the money. She's working at a gas station now. She can't be making much money to pay her bills."

"She'd have access to keys too." My fingers flew across the computer keyboard, adding notes as they came up. "It would've been easy for her to have made copies while she worked there."

"And she was alone near Eddy when she first came in the day he was poisoned." Mason reached for yet another piece of pizza.

When I finished typing, I scanned through the list, and my spirits sank. "It looks like all we've done is prove they all had a strong motive, they all needed the money, they all could have figured out what books were valuable, they all could've gotten access to keys, and they all had an opportunity to poison Eddy."

"Maybe it was like that old movie where it wasn't just one killer," Mason suggested. "Maybe they got together because they all hated him, and they all helped kill him."

Rita rolled her eyes. "This is not an Agatha Christie movie."

"There's only one way we'll know for sure who's stealing books and whether it really does tie in to the murder." I leaned forward and propped my elbows on the table. "We'll have to stake out the library at night."

"Why at night?" Rita sipped her beer. "Why can't they just walk in and take a few books out during the day?"

"Trust me, they can't." I filled them in on the alarm system the library had rigged to prevent such thefts. "Someone would have to do it after hours so they could turn off the alarm. Our stakeout will have to be overnight."

Mason whooped. "Awesome! We'll get coffee and donuts like they do on TV. Anyone own a big camera with a night vision lens?"

I chuckled. "I don't think it'll be quite as exciting as it is on TV. Remember, they get to cut out the hours where the characters just sit there. A real-life stakeout is bound to be pretty boring."

"You have no idea." Keith leaned forward and sobered. "Guys, we can't go stalk these folks or stake out the library without knowing what Sutter has planned for his investigation."

Rita snorted. "Frank Sutter's determined to ignore anything Jenna says. He'd try to prove the sky was lima bean green if Jenna pointed out that it's blue."

"Sutter's a lot shrewder than he seems." Keith ignored Rita's second snort. "He always ends up on the right track with real results. Let me talk to him tomorrow and see where he's at with everything."

I sighed deeply, knowing Keith was right. Last thing I wanted to do was screw up a police operation to catch the killer. And to tell the truth, I didn't want to put Keith in the position of hiding things from his department. That was his job, and I wouldn't let him risk that. "Fine. Talk to him tomorrow morning. If he's pursuing this angle, we'll sit back and wait. But if he's not . . ." I tilted my head and raised my hands.

Rita stood and took her beer bottle to the trash can. "If he's not, we have a killer to catch."

Chapter Fifteen

I sat at a table inside The Weeping Willow. As with previous visits, I enjoyed the play of colors across the tables and floors where light streamed through the stained-glass windows. I'd already ordered a glass of sweet tea, and I sipped it, lost in thought, while I waited on Keith. As it was only ten AM, he'd promised to meet me here for a non-lunch date after he'd talked with Sutter about the case.

My heart skipped when he swept the door open and strode through the room toward my table. Holy cow, he was hot. I sipped my tea again to hide the warmth spreading across my cheeks at the thought.

Keith plopped onto the seat across from me. "Sutter said no."

I took in the tension, the furrowed brow, and the tone. "Rough morning?"

He nodded and raised a hand to wave at our server, ordering a coffee when she arrived at our table, before returning his gaze to me. "There, now I'll have a bit of go-juice, and maybe I'll be fit for polite company." He chuckled. "Let's try this again. Hi, sweetheart. How was your morning?"

I leaned in to brush a kiss on his cheek. "It was fine. I went for a walk, called the vet to check on Eddy, and worked in the store for a bit. Nothing spectacular. Sounds like yours was a bit more stressful. Want to talk about it?"

With closed eyes, he took a long deep breath and let it go slowly. "You have no idea." His eyes opened and settled on me again. "So far today, we've talked to an elderly lady who regularly calls in to tell us there are multiple peeping Toms trying to look in her windows from outside. She lives in a third-floor apartment with no balcony. We've also gone on calls for littering outside a restaurant, two jaywalkers, and a dumpster fire."

My guffaw drew looks before I could quiet my mirth. Catching his somber expression, I cocked my head. "You're serious?"

"Dead level serious." Keith sipped his coffee, which had just been delivered.

I reached across the table and touched his hand where it wrapped around his mug. "Keith, what's going on? Why would you be going on such low-level calls? Aren't you guys a senior team?"

He flipped his hand and laced his fingertips through mine. "Honestly? I think they're trying to push Sutter toward early retirement."

My eyebrows shot up. "What about the whole Sutter's-the-best-and-even-though-he's-unorthodox-he-always-solves-the-crime thing?"

Keith raked his free hand through his hair, mussing it a bit, and I resisted the urge to reach out and fix it for him.

A deep sigh escaped his lips, and he leaned forward, propping his arm on the table. "We've been partners for five years, since I transferred here from Virginia. During our partnership, he's always been spot on."

"Until Uncle Paul's murder." I squeezed his fingers gently.

He nodded. "Yeah, until your uncle's case. He was up for promotion, and he was determined to close a high-profile case the Charlotte PD couldn't solve. It would've been quite a feather."

"You mean he was determined to prove I had embezzled and murdered in Charlotte and had then come here and murdered my uncle." I picked up my tea glass and took a large gulp, trying to give my mouth something to do other than let loose a few rude comments about what I thought of Frank Sutter. My mother's voice in my head was right. Now was not the time.

"Pretty much." Keith shrugged. "He thought if he could prove you'd murdered your uncle and then tie in your past in Charlotte and solve that, he'd be a shoo-in for the promotion."

"Well, he missed the boat on that one." I rolled my eyes and shook my head. "But he eventually got it right. You guys showed up just in the nick of time."

"Jenna, his stubborn insistence that you murdered Paul Baxter is what almost got you killed." Keith squeezed my fingers once more and let go, leaning back to wrap his hands around his coffee cup hard enough his knuckles turned white. Thank goodness for strong, cheap restaurant mugs. "The only reason you didn't die was because a junior officer we had combing through drug records found the link to the sleeping meds that killed your uncle. And even then, Sutter tried to discount it. We basically steamrolled over him to come check it out." His gaze softened, capturing me in the depths of his deep brown eyes. "And thank God we did."

"I take it the powers that be noticed his attitude?" I'd had no idea. All I'd ever heard was that Sutter was the bomb at this police detective thing. Seems he was slipping. Badly.

Keith nodded. "They did. He missed out on that promotion. Now he's desperate to have a high-profile win to regain his reputation. He's almost rabid about it."

"Why are they basically benching the two of you?" I swirled my glass, letting the little bit of tea left melt the surrounding ice cubes.

"I'm pretty sure they're giving him the proverbial rope to hang himself on this one. They're watching him closely, and they don't want him to have any excuses about a heavy case load to blame it on, like he tried to do with your case."

The "well, duh" moment hit me. "They're trying to get rid of him, aren't they? And you're caught in the crossfire for now."

"Yep on both counts." Keith swigged down the remainder of his coffee, mumbling a thanks to the server when she swept by to refill our drinks. "If he blows this one, I think they'll be offering him early retirement with a strong encouragement he take it."

"What happens to you, though?" Surely they wouldn't demote or fire Keith just because his partner was losing his grip on reality. I knew he'd moved here from a much larger town, because his mother had been ill and had since passed away. I hoped what was going on now wouldn't push him into moving again for a better position.

He shrugged again. "I'll be okay. I'm just stuck in this loop of garbage cases with him, and I can't even work on the one big case they're letting him have, since I was at the party."

"What's his angle on this? You said he said no to staking out the library. Why?" My frustration must have come out in my tone, if Keith's expression was anything to go by. I sighed. "I'm sorry. I'm not upset at you. Just the situation."

A rueful smile tipped up one corner of his mouth. "Believe me, I know what you mean. And to answer your question, Sutter is determined this is about politics. He is almost maniacal in his attempts to force the facts to fit his theory. It's worse than when your uncle died."

"Wow." I almost felt sorry for Bradford Prescott. Almost. He might have been the one to kill Linus and poison my dog. But I wasn't convinced it revolved around politics. "I take it high-end book thefts, even if it's a politician doing it, isn't glitzy enough for him?"

"Not in the least." Keith took one last gulp of his coffee and signaled the server for the check. "For him, that's about on par with peeping Toms and dumpster fires. The sad thing is, if he would solve this and close it cleanly and accurately, they'd likely back off and call your uncle's case a one-off."

I watched while he signed the check, smiling at the healthy tip he put on a tab with only a sweet tea and a coffee. Definitely a keeper. Wow, another random thought.

"What now?" I downed the last of my sweet tea.

Keith stood, placing his warm palm at the small of my back when I joined him for the walk toward the door. "I'm not sure. I'll keep trying to aim Sutter in the right direction."

"That's not what I meant." I walked through the door Keith held open and stopped on the sidewalk outside, turning to face him. "I meant about our stakeout."

"Jenna, I'm still not comfortable with you sitting in the dark waiting to catch a killer." He shoved his hands in his suit pants pockets.

"We already discussed teaming up in twos to do the stakeout. I wouldn't be alone. You or Rita or Mason would be with me." I took a step forward and placed a hand on his cheek. "I can't just sit here and do nothing. Whoever did this tried to kill Eddy. Without knowing who it was, the only way to keep him safe is to lock him in the apartment by himself all day and hope no one breaks in while I'm not there. I have to do something. Please."

Keith closed his eyes and sighed before opening them to gaze into mine. "Fine. I'm working late all week this week, so Mason and Rita would have to go with you."

Working late? On what? A rash of cats in trees or a spike in loitering? I kept my tacky giggle to myself, as joking around about his recent spate of insignificant cases wouldn't help his mood, and I didn't want to hurt his feelings. "Okay, I'll talk to them and see if they can make that work."

He stepped forward and cupped my cheek in his hand. "Promise me you'll be careful. Promise me you'll call me if you see anything suspicious." His eyes again held more than he was letting himself say out loud.

I turned my face into his hand and kissed his palm. "I promise."

Keith's shoulders dropped a little as he released tension I hadn't realized he'd been holding in. "I'll call you periodically to check on you." He brushed a kiss across my hair and turned, striding toward the parking lot at the end of the street.

Watching him walk away, I worried, not for his own safety, but for his sanity. Because of Sutter's demented determination, he'd been shoved aside to work on cases that could be resolved, in many instances, with phone calls. His disappointment and frustration must be incredible right about now. I just hoped I could keep my promises to him and wouldn't become another rock in his pocket.

Chapter Sixteen

Mason and I spent the rest of the morning assisting customers, but after lunch, the flow of customers slowed enough I asked Mason to try his hand at researching a few of the more interesting books that had arrived with my estate sale purchase. While he worked on books, I hummed softly to myself as I made a list of items we'd need for our stakeouts. Mid-October in the mountains, albeit in North Carolina, would be chilly. We wouldn't be able to leave the car running, so we'd need gloves, blankets, jackets, and tons of hot coffee or, in Rita's case, maybe tea. If we were there long enough, we'd need something to eat, so I'd likely make a few simple sandwiches. It wouldn't be fancy, but we wouldn't go hungry.

I'd called Rita, asking her to pop in for a few minutes after she got off work, so we could plan out our schedule, and around five PM, she swept through the door, jingling the door chimes as she came.

"Hey, Jenna. How's it going?" Rita planted her purse on the counter beside my notepad and leaned across to look at what I was writing. "Already planning, I see."

I flipped the pad around so she could read it. "Yep. Did I miss anything?"

"Other than several boxes of NoDoz, nope." She chuckled.

"I included coffee. That should do it for the caffeine need." I pointed to the line item on the list.

"Then you'd better put toilet paper, and baggies to put it in after it's used, on the list." She apparently caught my confused look. "Night-long stakeout, tons of liquid, need to pee frequently."

The light bulb went on in my brain. "Ohhhhhh. I hadn't thought of that. A caffeine pill would keep us up without needing to go so much. But I hadn't considered what we'll do when we *do* need to go."

"No worries." Rita slid the notepad back to me. "There's a twenty-four-hour grocery store two doors down from the library. We'll have to disable your overhead light in your car, so we don't shine like a Christmas tree when one of us needs to get in or out."

Thank goodness for a friend who thought of these things. "Now all we need to do is discuss shifts."

Rita rounded the counter and sat next to me on another stool. "I thought about that on the way here. I'm a morning person. If Mason's a night owl, we should split shifts with you. With Keith out of the picture, we can't take half a night each. Someone needs to be there the whole time. I vote it's you."

"Gee, thanks." I put my hand to my chest in a gesture of surprise. "I can't believe I won." I fluttered my eyelashes. "I'm so happy."

"Knock it off." Rita chuckled again. "It makes the most sense. You can be there to keep track of things for continuity's sake. Mason can sit with you until around two in the morning, and I can come spell him off. That way, we each get a little sleep so we can keep our day jobs. I hear his boss is a real taskmaster."

I cocked an eyebrow at her. "A taskmaster? Really?" I shook my head. "So, I don't get to sleep at all?"

"You do during the day. Mason can run the store for now." She lowered her voice and leaned in as Mason exited the back room. "It would be good for him to feel you trusted him enough to let him have full responsibility for the store."

I eyed my employee speculatively as he strode down the aisle, a laptop balanced on one arm. Rita was right. Letting him run the store would free me up to have a day off occasionally and to go to auctions on workdays.

As he approached, he looked up from the screen. "Hey, guys, look at this." He slid the laptop onto the counter and turned it to face us, leaning forward to see the screen.

An antique book filled the screen. The site's header stated it was a book auction site. I started to shrug but did a double take instead. "Isn't that my book? I mean the book I sold Alice?" I leaned in, taking in the brass bindings, gold scrollwork, green grosgrain material peeking out through a cutout on a white cover, and gold gilt edging on the pages. The Milton I'd sold Alice King was for sale on a rare book site.

My eyes quickly scanned the write-up.

"This says it's in pristine condition." Rita pointed at the screen.

"Look at what it's going for." Mason pointed to the current bid, which was twice the price Alice had paid me for it.

I reached up and swiped through the pictures of the book, which showed the book from all angles, carefully avoiding showing the glue surgery Linus had performed on it. Yep, that was definitely my book. So much for her need to have the last book "her" Linus had touched.

"It also says she picked it up at auction in Georgia from a collector, and the book had been in his family since its publication date." I pointed at the provenance section for the book.

Rita's whistle came out in a low, solemn tone. "Looks like she's up to her old tricks again."

"With Linus gone, maybe she thinks no one will catch her at it this time." Mason shrugged and propped a hip against the counter, hands in his pockets.

"The question is, however, did she kill him in order to start up again?" I closed the laptop and leaned back. "It seems like really convenient timing for her."

"While I was back there"—Mason nodded his head toward the back room—"I pulled out the printed runs from Linus's folder and checked for the books that had gone missing. I didn't find any of them up for sale. At least not on this site. I also pulled up her seller's profile, which showed her last sale happened well over a year ago."

"About the time Linus shut her down." I remembered what Phillie had said about Alice's current job situation. "She can't be making very much working at a gas station. Maybe she needed the money and grabbed the opportunity to pass the book off as pristine for a quick buck."

Rita stood and grabbed her purse. "Whatever her reason, we may need to put her at the top of our list of suspects. It could be she didn't learn her lesson back when Linus caught her, and she's been stealing the library's books to pay her bills since then. Either way, I need to get a few winks, or I'll be a zombie come two AM."

I followed Rita to the door and gave her a quick hug before she left. "I'll see you tonight."

"Don't forget the NoDoz." She flipped a grin across her shoulder as she walked through the door. "You'll be the one with no sleep to back you up for an all-nighter. You'll need it."

I chuckled as she walked away. Turning, I saw Mason heading to the back room, laptop securely under his arm. "Mason, wait." I met him halfway down the aisle. "I need to pick up a few things for tonight, so I'm heading out. You'll need to watch the counter and close up. I'll be back down for closing, and we can leave from here to head to the library."

Purse over my shoulder and notepad in hand, I hurried to the parking lot. I had checked the library's hours and knew they closed an hour before we did. By the time we got there, the sun would be down and darkness would have settled, but I figured the book thief wouldn't appear until after traffic had slowed down for the night. This gave me roughly an hour and a half to get the items I needed; get home; make coffee; dig out gloves, blankets, and a coat; dress warmly; and get back downstairs to the store before seven PM, when we closed our doors for the night.

With a short timetable, I headed to the nearest grocery I knew of, waving to Benny as I scooted through the front door. He grinned and called out a greeting as I grabbed a cart. I waved back as I rushed through the aisles. Three travel mugs, since I only owned one, and it was on its last legs. Three forty-ounce thermoses. The only one I owned had belonged to Uncle Paul and looked older than I was. I didn't trust it not to leak, and I knew it wouldn't hold enough coffee for all of us for an all-nighter. Sandwich bread, lunchmeat, cheese. Check. I already had mayo and mustard at the house. Chips. I grabbed a bag of Cool Ranch Doritos and a bag of mini pretzels. I would make coffee at the house, but I didn't want to take a bowl of sugar and a bottle of liquid creamer. I grabbed a small container of powdered creamer and a box of sugar packets for Mason, knowing he liked the real stuff, not alternative sweeteners. Lastly, I rounded the aisle into the pharmacy section, looking for a caffeine pill. One box of NoDoz plopped into the cart, and I was on my way to the checkout. Fifteen minutes. Not bad.

I turned to head toward the checkout counter, startled when I heard a woman call my name. I scanned left and right, smiling when I saw Phillie Hokes waving from across the store. Glancing at my watch, I realized I still had a few minutes to spare, so I wheeled over to the produce section, where Phillie was choosing squash.

"Benny's vegetables look really fresh today." Phillie held out a squash to me. "Might be healthy to add some to your diet." She eyed my cart of junk food and lunchmeat.

A chuckle bubbled up from my chest. "This isn't my usual diet. I promise. I have a fridge full of veggies at home."

One of Phillie's eyebrows rose. "Oh?" Her disbelieving tone matched her now-pursed lips.

"I swear. Cross my heart." My finger made an X over my heart before I lowered my voice. "We're staking out the library tonight, and carrying a squash casserole to munch on isn't as convenient as sandwiches and chips."

"Oh!" Phillie's eyes widened and lit with a twinkle. "And why are we staking out the library?"

I gave her a quick rundown of our plan, including Mason and Rita's split schedule with me. I looked at my watch again. Only a few more minutes to spare. "Phillie, can I ask you something?"

Phillie moved down the aisle and thumped a large canta-loupe before putting it in her cart. "Sure, what?"

Explaining about Alice's book auction online, I ended with, "Do you think she might have killed Linus because she was the one stealing books from the library in order to sell them online?"

Phillie turned toward me, her brow wrinkled. "I don't know. Linus kept an eye on book auction sites. He found a few for the library that way. I doubt anything stolen from the library would have been sold through the normal auction sites. He'd have spotted them right away." She reached for another canta-loupe, absently thumping it for freshness. "If she stole the books, she had to find another way to sell them."

Darn. Back to square one. "Thanks. I guess we need to keep digging."

"I did hear something that might help." She gently placed the second cantaloupe in her cart. "Bradford Prescott is think-ing of dropping out of the race because of that newspaper article this morning."

My ears perked up. "What article?" I hadn't taken time to read the paper today, but I'd snag it and take it on the stakeout.

Phillie shook her head. "Oh, it was a juicy one. Seems Bradford has been taking money from high players at big pharma companies who do some seriously nasty animal testing while touting stronger animal cruelty laws and lowered costs for seniors on medications. The companies themselves cannot contribute, because candidates can't accept contributions from business entities in North Carolina. But the folks who work there can contribute as individuals. It's quite the stink, and with the election just around the corner, there's not enough time for it to blow over."

"Wow, I hadn't heard." I checked my watch again. I really needed to go, but I also needed to hear what Phillie had to say. "I don't see how this figures into Linus's death, though."

"From what I've heard, Bradford and Becky are positioning him to make a run for the United States Congress. But to get there, he needs this congressional seat at the state level first, to lend credibility. If Bradford thought Linus had somehow discovered and was going to tell the reporter about the legal but highly unethical contributions, added to Linus's accusations of animal cruelty to Eddy, Bradford might have killed Linus to shut him up."

"But how would Linus have found out? He wasn't a politician. He was a librarian." I propped a foot on the bottom rung of the grocery cart and leaned on the handle.

"I didn't say he *did*. Simply that Bradford might have *thought* he had." She reached out and patted my hand. "Now, you've checked your watch three times already. I know you're hot to get going for your secret stakeout. Have fun with it, and be safe. Just think about what I've said, though."

I gave her a quick hug, thanked her for the information, and fast-walked toward the checkout counter, my mind spinning. As I rounded the end of the aisle, completely lost in my own jumbled thoughts, I bumped into another cart, startling me into the present.

"I'm so sorry . . ." My words froze in my mouth, and I barely kept my jaw from dropping.

"Jenna!" Alice King giggled. "Fancy meeting you here."

Behind her stood Becky and Bethany Prescott, the older of the two looking anything but pleased to have run into me at the grocery store. Becky sniffed and nodded.

"Hi, Alice." I nodded at Becky. "Mrs. Prescott." Somehow I couldn't bring myself to call the woman by her first name.

Bethany grinned widely and rushed forward to give me a quick hug. "How's Benson . . . Eddy?"

I smiled and hugged her back before she stepped away. "He's recovering nicely. Should be home in another few days."

"Recovering?" Creases lined Alice's brow. "What happened to him?"

This wasn't how I'd planned to suss out my dog's poisoner, but when opportunity presented itself . . . "Someone fed him poison and tried to kill him."

Bethany's hands flew to her mouth, squelching the anguished cry that now only squeaked out past her fingers as tears sprang to her eyes.

"Bethany Prescott, get a hold of yourself." Becky's hiss at her daughter echoed down the empty aisle. "Prescott women do not create scenes in public. Especially not over a violent mutt who should have been put down a long time ago." Venom laced her words as she spat them in her daughter's direction.

"Benson is not violent!" Bethany's shriek echoed through the store. "Daddy was the violent one, and Benson finally fought back! Now everyone knows. It's all over the papers, along with what a two-faced liar he is!"

While I had to applaud the girl for finally standing up to her mother over her beloved but abused dog, I had honestly not expected a good old-fashioned southern come-apart like this.

Becky whirled and slapped Bethany, stopping the girl's tirade and making her take a few steps back.

"This family has gone through enough recently." Becky's voice did not rise in volume, but the powerful tone commanded attention. "You will *not* disgrace this family further with your outburst. Go to the car. *Now.*"

Bethany ducked around her mother, eyes wide and her hand held to her face where her mother's had made contact, and fled out the front door.

I stood rooted to the floor, wishing I could disappear into the shelves behind me, horrified at what I'd witnessed.

Alice stepped forward. "Becky, you might want to calm down a bit. Right now, you're the person everyone is looking at."

Becky swiveled her head, taking in the faces peeking around aisle corners and craning their necks from the checkout lanes. She smoothed the front of her business suit jacket and squared her shoulders and clenched her jaw. "You're right. Thank you, Alice. We've been under a terrible strain lately with the nasty smear campaign being waged by Bradford's opponent." She clenched her fists around her grocery cart's handle. "I need to gather a few more things and get home."

Alice and I watched as she marched off, head high, seeming to ignore the stares as she passed gawking shoppers.

Alice tsked. "Poor thing. To have come so far, only to be toppled by a dog."

Before I could respond to that odd remark, Alice moved off down an aisle, mumbling about dogs under her breath.

I stared after her, unable to find words for what I'd just witnessed—Becky's hate-filled words, Bethany's outburst, Alice's odd comforting gestures. I shook my head and resumed my trip to the checkout lane.

As Benny rang up my groceries, I absently chatted with him. He'd finally forgiven me for my subterfuge after I'd moved to Hokes Folly. I'd pretended to be someone thinking of moving to the area, just to ask him about crime and a heated argument I'd heard him have with Stan Jergins, a local real estate agent. Once he'd learned I was actually Paul Baxter's niece and already lived here, he'd been chilly to me for a solid month before slowly warming to me. I'd determinedly shopped at his store at least twice a week, even though his selection wasn't as wide as the larger grocery chain stores on the outskirts of town. My persistence had paid off, and after two months, I was officially welcome in his store.

During those weeks of shopping in his store, I'd learned to find other brands for most of my grocery needs, and I rarely needed to go to another grocery store. This suited me fine, as I really liked Benny, and there were rarely long lines. Besides, small business owners needed to stick together and support each other. Okay, so Benny hadn't actually come to my store and bought books, but a few new customers had said Benny told them to stop by. Good enough for me.

After paying for my items, I grabbed the bags and hurried to my car. I deposited the groceries in the back seat and closed the door. As I opened my own door, I noticed Bethany sitting in the car next to mine, her tear-streaked face stark in the glare of the setting sun.

I tapped on her window, frowning when she jumped as if it were a gunshot. "Are you okay?" I asked through the glass.

She leaned to her left, flipped the key forward in the ignition, and rolled down her window. "I'm sorry I caused a scene. I shouldn't have—"

"Bethany, stop." I put a hand on her shoulder through the window. "You don't owe me an apology. I just wanted to make sure you were okay."

Bethany's bottom lip trembled, and she took a shuddering breath as she swiped a hand across her eyes. "I'll be fine. I turn eighteen in two months. A friend has already told me I can come stay with her until graduation."

"I'm sure your parents wouldn't want you to move out like that." I leaned back on my car's door and crossed my arms against the chill in the cooling evening air.

Bethany snorted. "Of course not. It would tarnish their precious image." She sighed and wilted. "It's always about the image. Getting Benson, showing him off. Even showing *me* off as the perfect little student, the beautiful child, and the graceful and proper daughter. Nothing else is important to them."

Wow. What did I say to that? "Your mom loves you, and—"

"No, she doesn't." Bethany shook her head. "Mama doesn't love anything except the idea of being important, of living in Washington, D.C., and being a senator's wife. She's even talked about him running for president. She wants it even more than he does. Honestly, if she thought she could get there on her own, she'd be gone so fast it would make Daddy's head spin."

Staccato footsteps sounded, and I turned to see Becky approaching.

"Bethany, roll up that window." Becky yanked open her trunk and slung several bags into it before slamming it shut. "And you"—she pointed a finger at me—"don't you think you book people—you and that mutt—have done enough damage to this family? Stay away from my daughter, and keep that damned dog away from us too." She slid into her car and slammed her door.

I got into my own car, shutting my door just in time before Becky fast-reversed out of the parking spot and squealed her tires speeding out of the parking lot.

By the time I got to my apartment and lugged everything upstairs and inside, I still hadn't fully wrapped my head around what had happened. However, I had a stakeout to prepare for. I'd have plenty of time later to process.

I dumped the items I'd bought onto the counter and started a pot of coffee. While it happily gurgled down into the pot, I pulled blankets from the closet in the spare bedroom and walked them down to my car, pouring the pot off into one thermos and part of a second when I returned. While a second pot brewed, I dug through my things, finally locating an old pair of gloves Uncle Paul had owned. They were a little oversized, but they'd be warm enough for Mason. They went into an open duffle along with a pair of my own gloves, two beanie hats Aunt Irene had crocheted—I'd kept them out of sentimentality—a couple of sweatshirts, and a roll of paper towels.

I poured the second pot of coffee into the remaining thermos and a half. With little time to spare, I quickly made eight sandwiches. I figured two each for Mason and Rita and four for me, since I'd be there all night. These went into a soft-side cooler I'd found in the pantry, along with a cold pack from the freezer.

As there was room, the chips went into the duffle, along with the NoDoz, before I made another trek to the parking lot.

I returned to the store on the street side, walking in just as Mason was ushering a customer out. "Was he our last customer?"

He flipped the "Closed" sign over and locked the door. "Yep. Just need to run through closing out the drawer, and we're good to go."

While he counted the drawer and took the bank bag to the small safe in the back room, I emptied the coffeepot and the trash, locked the back door, and turned out most of the lights.

"I need to grab my purse and the package of water bottles, and we're good to go." I headed up the staircase to my apartment.

As we reached the top, Mason turned and headed back down. "Forgot something!"

I left the doors open for him and moved through the room to the kitchen, sliding my purse over my shoulder when I got there. I reached for the package of water bottles.

"Stop!" Mason called as he entered the room, a big grin across his face. "You carry these." He held out a large box of a dozen Krispy Kreme donuts. "I called a friend to bring them over."

"Seriously?" I crossed the room and locked the doors to the stairwell before turning to take the donuts.

"We can't have a stakeout without donuts for our coffee. We need something to eat to keep us alert." He hefted the heavier package of water, still grinning. "Don't you watch cop shows on TV?"

I rolled my eyes, chuckling as we exited the apartment and headed toward the parking lot. "Only you would think of donuts for the stakeout. I packed sandwiches and chips."

"Well, now we'll have dessert."

We reached the car, loaded our last items inside, and drove to the library, only five minutes away. Seven fifteen. Not bad.

I drove the car into a corner of the now-empty lot, backed into a spot, where we'd have a good view of the front door, and turned off the engine. "And now we wait."

"Time to catch a killer." Mason grinned again and sipped coffee from his travel mug, his enthusiasm filling the car.

I only hoped it was that simple.

Chapter Seventeen

"Get down, get down!" I hunkered under my blanket, where I'd shimmied as far down in my seat as possible.

Rita had arrived a few minutes earlier, and we'd bundled a yawning Mason off to bed. Rita had taken Mason's keys earlier in the day, and she'd driven his car to the library. I would drive her home. Now we huddled, hoping the car looked empty to the driver of the Hokes Folly Outdoor Cleaners street-sweeper truck. He drove in a pattern back and forth across the library parking lot.

I peeked out, reading the slogan "We Sweep While You Sleep" written across the back of the vehicle. "They're almost to this corner. Just be still a few minutes longer."

"I'm not sure I could move now if I wanted to." Rita hunkered in the passenger floorboard, a blanket tossed across her head.

"Oh stop it. It's only been a few minutes." I peeked out again to see headlights headed straight for us. "He's on the last pass. We're almost done."

"I should've known this would happen on my watch. Mason is young. He can bend himself like a pretzel easier than I can." Rita shifted again.

Bright lights swung past us as the vehicle turned, and I peeked out again to watch as the truck slowly lumbered across the parking lot and out onto the street. "It's safe."

Rita groaned beside me. "I'll just stay here until someone can come cut me out of the car with the Jaws of Life."

"The good news is that they likely don't do this every night." I struggled to crawl out from under the steering wheel.

"At least we'll have something exciting to tell Mason tomorrow." Rita managed to turn, covering her lap with the blanket as she sat.

"He'll be disappointed he missed it." I chuckled. "He couldn't believe all we did was sit and watch the building. No streaming on his phone because of the light. Same with reading a book."

"He could always listen to an audiobook." Rita opened the door long enough to empty Mason's coffee on the ground before placing the travel mug in a large baggie and sealing it shut.

"I'll be sure to tell him that." I handed her the clean travel mug I'd brought for her and a fresh thermos of coffee. Mason and I had finished off the first one.

Steam rose from the thermos as Rita poured her mug, which she held between her knees. "You started to tell me about running into Phillie at the grocery store before we were interrupted by the street sweeper."

I mentally backtracked, picking up where I'd left off. "She thinks Bradford Prescott might have murdered Linus if he thought Linus was going to tell the reporter about his backroom contributions on top of the animal cruelty allegations."

"I don't know." Rita sipped her coffee. "Maybe. It's definitely something to consider, although I don't see how Linus would have found out."

"As Phillie put it, it didn't really matter if Linus knew or not, just that Bradford *thought* he knew."

I reached into the cooler and pulled out a sandwich, offering it to Rita, who shook her head, adding a "No thanks, not yet."

I slid the sandwich from the baggie and took a bite. Mason had polished off two sandwiches, half the bag of Doritos—I'd need to stock up again before our next stakeout—and four donuts. This was my third sandwich, and I was eating it solely to stay awake. I'd been up since six AM the previous morning, and as of half an hour ago, I'd passed the twenty-hours-awake mark. Only three and a half more hours to go before I could go home and collapse in bed. I took another bite.

"Maybe Frank's onto something." Rita's quiet voice sounded through the car.

I jerked my drifting mind back to the present. "How so?"

"If Bradford really did kill Linus, maybe it had nothing to do with the supposedly missing books." She shrugged and tucked her blanket closer in the chilly car.

"I don't know." I looked out the window, still processing the scene with the Prescotts at the grocery store. "Before today, I would have argued. But now?" I filled her in on what had happened.

Rita whistled low. "And you let me believe the street sweeper was the excitement of the day."

"I'm honestly still not sure what to make of the whole thing." I looked down at my sandwich, unable to take a bite.

"I'm worried about Bethany. But I'm also wondering if we're on a wild goose chase."

"From what you saw, they seem to have hated Linus and blame him for at least part of what's happening now." Rita shifted in her seat beside me, tugging a knee up to her chest and leaning back on the door to face me.

"Maybe so." I shook my head. "But something is still telling me those books have something to do with Linus's murder. I feel it in my gut."

"Of course you do. You're part of 'you book people.'" She grinned at me. "You want everything to have to do with books."

I rolled my eyes. "I've been called worse."

Rita sobered and leaned forward, patting my arm. "You have a deep need to help find out what happened. It's understandable. And since you can't get involved in what Frank Sutter has going on, you're focusing in on what you can do: follow the book trail. Will it lead to anything? Maybe. Maybe not. But at least it's something tangible you can do."

Tears stung my eyes, and I leaned over and tugged Rita into a quick hug. "Thanks for understanding."

Rita squeezed me back and pulled away. "As for your gut, what you feel right now is likely indigestion from all you're eating to stay awake." She gestured at the empty sandwich bags, the donut box, and the chips. "You'd better slow down, or you'll be two sizes bigger by the time this is over. And that's if we catch anyone."

I finished the last bite of sandwich and tossed the baggie into the trash bag I'd brought. "Maybe." My stomach did feel a bit unsettled, to tell the truth. "Not that there'll be anyone around to care what I look like if we can't solve this case quickly."

"What are you talking about?" Rita handed me a paper towel to wipe my hands.

"Sutter's bosses are waiting for him to screw up again so they can get rid of him. They've pulled him off every major case but this one in the meantime, and Keith is stuck in his wake." I followed with a recap of my conversation with Keith. "I'm afraid if we can't wrap this up quickly, he'll be looking to move to another city again. I can't say that I'd blame him."

"Frank Sutter needs to get his head out of his backside." Rita opened the bag of pretzels and munched one before continuing. "The thing is, he used to be a pretty straightforward guy, and from what I hear, he was one heck of a cop."

"Well, he's not now." I pulled my blanket across my shoulders. "Now, he's a bully who won't listen to anyone but himself."

I hunkered in the corner, watching the library door, lost in my own thoughts—a swirl of Keith leaving for another job, Sutter lording it over everyone that he'd been right and now he'd prove I was an embezzler and killer, and an empty library because someone stole all the books.

A hand shook my shoulder, startling me, and I realized I'd dozed off. Ugh, if that was what I dreamed on ham sandwiches, Doritos, and donuts, I needed to lay off all three. "What time is it?"

"Almost six." Rita busied herself stowing away snacks and drinks for the short drive home. "They'll be coming to work soon, and we don't want to be here when they do."

"Why'd you let me fall asleep?" I rubbed one eye and yawned.

Rita laughed. "That's why. You were beat. It doesn't take us both to watch one set of doors and an empty parking lot. Are you okay to drive?"

I nodded, yawned again, and started the car. "Yeah, it's not that far. How'd you stay awake?"

"I had seven hours of sleep last night, plus I did bring an audio book." She waved her iPhone at me.

I smiled a sleepy smile and concentrated on driving us home without dozing off again. When we arrived, we left the blankets, water, hats, and gloves in the car, only bringing perishables into the apartment. Rita dumped off her load, herded me into the bedroom and onto the bed, pulled my shoes off, and covered me up. The last sound I heard was the soft snick of the front door as she left.

I awoke hours later with what felt like a serious case of jetlag, a headache, and a rumbling stomach—whether from hunger or indigestion, I couldn't be sure. It could definitely go either way. I crawled out of the bed, not sure I'd even changed positions since I fell asleep, and walked into the bathroom. After shimmying out of my clothes, I grabbed a quick, reviving shower and walked to the kitchen to make coffee.

Cup of joe in my hands, I plopped on the couch and replayed the previous day. As much as I hated to admit it, Sutter might be onto something with the whole politics angle. Bradford Prescott's motive seemed stronger and stronger the more time went by. But I still couldn't get past the rare books missing from the library and Linus Talbot's printouts. And then there was the new information on Alice King. I shook my head. It seemed like the more we learned, the more convoluted the whole thing became. Based on the previous day's revelations, both Alice and Bradford now had even stronger motives to have murdered Linus, letting Selina drop to the bottom of our suspect list. But then, if mystery books and TV shows could be believed, wouldn't that make Selina the most likely killer? Wasn't it always the one least suspected? I sighed and shook my head. Whatever the case may be, I needed to talk to Keith and Sutter about Alice.

Reluctantly, I stood and went in search of my shoes. I wasn't sure where Rita had put them. After a ten-minute treasure hunt, I found them in the back corner of my closet. Who'd have thought?

On my way to the police station, I stopped by the vet and spent an hour with Eddy. He was up and moving better, but the vet said he wanted to keep him another couple of days, as his liver numbers weren't quite where he wanted to see them before releasing my dog. I kissed Eddy on the head and, with a lump in my throat, headed to see Keith at work.

On the way, I stopped at a bakery and picked up a bagel sandwich for Keith and a box of donuts for the department. When I arrived, a desk sergeant asked me to be seated in the waiting area. Forty-five minutes ticked by, and I returned to the front desk to ask how long it would be.

Keith walked through the back office as I approached the desk, his face lighting up when he saw me. "Jenna, what are you doing here?" He instantly sobered. "Is everything okay?"

I smiled. "It's fine. I've been waiting to see you and your partner. It's been over forty-five minutes." I hoped I didn't sound as whiny to Keith as I did in my own head.

His brow furrowed. "Why didn't someone tell me? We've been here the whole time." He turned toward the desk sergeant. "Hollister, why weren't we told we had a guest?"

Hollister held up his hands. "Whoa, Detective. I told Sutter. He said he'd get to it when he had time."

Keith's jaw clenched and his face reddened. "He'd get to it?" He turned to me. "I'm so sorry, Jenna. Follow me."

Uh-oh, more trouble in paradise. This meeting was definitely not getting off to a good start, in spite of the donuts I'd brought everyone.

As we approached Sutter, he turned, caught sight of me and of Keith's furious look, and his stance settled into belligerent defensiveness—arms crossed, lips pursed, eyes flat.

"You left her sitting in the lobby and didn't bother to tell me she was here." Keith's calm tone was laced with acid.

Grunt. "What if I did?" Sutter stepped forward. "We have better things to do than visit with your girlfriend."

"Better things . . ." Keith stopped his sentence and closed his eyes, as if mentally counting to ten. Slowly he opened them and pinned Sutter with a steely gaze. "Sutter, I've had enough. In the last three months, you've done nothing but crucify Jenna for anything and everything you can think of. Your poor treatment of her ends here, and it ends now."

Sutter stepped forward another step and dropped his arms. "Or what?"

"Really, Sutter? You think I'd damage my reputation on the job with a fistfight?" Keith snorted. "You're not worth the time. What I'd do is have you up before the board for harassment of a citizen as well as unprofessional conduct. I don't think you can afford to have more strikes against you right now."

The older man blanched, and his jaw muscles clenched. The silence stretched for what seemed like an hour, although it was likely closer to a minute, as I watched a nonverbal battle waged between the two detectives.

Finally, Sutter took a breath and turned to me with an unpleasant smile, which didn't reach his eyes, smeared across his face. "How may I help you, Miss Quinn?"

As much as I wanted to say "Never mind" and run, I couldn't do that on the heels of Keith standing up for me. I held out the box of donuts. "I brought you some donuts." I turned to Keith and held out the bag. "And an everything bagel with cream cheese, salmon, red onion, and capers on it for your lunch."

"I'm on a diet." Sutter snatched the donut box and tossed it onto a desk. "Anything else?"

I gritted my teeth and smiled again. "I have information regarding Linus Talbot's death."

"Of course you do." Sutter's fake smile stayed in place, and his soft tone slithered up my spine.

I cleared my throat. "Yesterday evening, we discovered Alice King has begun selling antique books at auction, providing false information concerning their provenance and condition."

Sutter blinked and the smile sagged. "Books."

"Yes." I nodded and rushed on. "We found a listing for a book she'd purchased from my shop, a book that had been damaged and repaired. She knew about the damage, but she lied and said it was pristine and she'd purchased it from a family in Georgia who had owned the book since its publication in 1853."

Sutter pinched the bridge of his nose and squeezed his eyes shut. "And this matters how?" The soft, low tone had gained a sharper edge.

"Linus Talbot caught her selling fake antique books. She was taking reproductions of old books, making up fake histories for them, lying about their values and their condition, and selling them to unsuspecting collectors. He ruined her in the business, and she hated him for it. A few days after his death, she's back to her old tricks. I thought you should know." I held my breath, almost jumping when I felt Keith's hand at the small of my back, his touch so soft I almost missed it.

Grunt. Sutter's eyes opened slowly. "Books." He gritted his teeth. "Books!" The word burst from his lips, the rest of his words pushing out in a shout. "No one kills people over stupid books!"

"My uncle died over a stupid book." My soft retort brought him up short.

"Miss Quinn, I would appreciate it if you would stop trying to muddy the waters with your hairbrained ideas." Sutter's tone was low, but his words came out in a growl. "Every moment I waste listening to your chatter is a moment I lose toward catching a real killer." His voice rose in pitch again. "The next time you want to talk about books, I suggest you do it over pillow talk with your boyfriend! Stop wasting my time!"

"Sutter!" A voice roared over the top of his tirade. "My office! *Now!*"

Sutter paled and his mouth dropped open. Snapping it shut, he stalked across the room toward the open doorway and the man who filled it.

Keith leaned in and whispered in my ear. "That's the captain."

"Ouch," I whispered. "I almost feel sorry for him."

A sad look flashed through Keith's eyes. "Don't. He's created his own mess, no matter how hard others have tried to help him. I wish I knew what was really going on with him. First your case, now this one. It's not like him." His shoulders slumped, and he raked a hand through his hair, an action I'd come to associate with a high level of frustration. "I hate to see him end his career like this."

I looked toward the now-closed office door, and a small bit of sympathy for Frank Sutter crossed my mind. While I hadn't known him any other way than as a bullheaded jerk, if he'd really been all Keith said, it really was sad for him to go out this way.

"As for Alice, I'll make sure it's included in Talbot's file." Keith reached out and brushed my fingers with his. "I'm glad you came."

My heart skipped at his soft touch, and I held out the bag with his bagel again. "At least you can eat a decent lunch."

Keith took the bag and opened it. "Thanks, sweetheart. I'm starving, and there's no time to run out for something else right now."

"I wish this could've been a happier visit." I gave him a quick hug and stepped back.

"Yeah, well, maybe next time." He smiled. "I'd love to walk you to your car, but I'd better be here when Sutter comes out."

With perfect timing, the captain's door opened, and Sutter stormed out, heading in our direction. However, he didn't speak to Keith or me. Instead, he grabbed the box of donuts and marched toward a door down the hallway, slamming it shut.

"Logan!" The captain's voice bellowed out again. "My office!"

I reached out and squeezed Keith's fingers once more. "Call me tonight."

He nodded once and strode across the room and into the captain's office.

Before Sutter could come out and find me unprotected, I skittered through the building and back out the front door, not slowing down until I was driving safely toward my store.

Chapter Eighteen

I set a plate of spaghetti on the table in front of Keith. "Eat up."
I smiled, happy to be ensuring he was eating at least twice
today. I'd texted him after I'd left the police station. If he could
get away between five and five thirty, I'd feed him a real meal
before he headed back to work. I'd already taken a plate down
to Mason, figuring I could at least feed him as well before we
headed out on our stakeout. He'd handled the store alone today
with no complaints.

"Thanks." Keith spooned freshly grated parmesan cheese
over the meat sauce. "This definitely beats another burger out."

"I would hope so." I laughed and sat down across the table
from him. "What happened when you went into the captain's
office?"

Keith swallowed. "This is delicious." He swirled his fork in
the noodles but didn't pick it up. "They're letting Sutter stay
until he hits his retirement with full pension in March. Then
he's being 'strongly encouraged' to retire."

"Which means he can still screw up this case?" *And how
many others over the next four months?* I stuck a bite of spaghetti

in my mouth, using it to keep me from saying something I probably shouldn't.

Keith shook his head. "No. He'll still be on the case team, but only because he's been on it from the beginning and has knowledge that's useful to the case's closure. They're bringing in someone new from Boone, LaTisha Riddick, to take over the case. She'll be here tomorrow."

"Wow. How's Sutter taking it?" I couldn't imagine him being calm about the whole thing.

"Not well. But it's either this or they'll fire him on the spot. This will be his only active case now. After this, it's administrative duties only." He ate another bite, closing his eyes. "This is really good."

I grinned. "It was my grandmother's recipe." I didn't add that it was the dish I cooked best, and I was working on the old adage of how to get to a man's heart.

I took a deep breath and dove in. "What happens to you now?"

"I'll be partnered with Riddick for the time being. I have a feeling they're trying to woo her into staying." Keith sipped the small glass of wine I'd talked him into.

"If they already had it lined up for her to come, it stands to reason this has been in the works for a while." I sprinkled a little more cheese on my spaghetti. "I wouldn't think you could call another city's police force and borrow a detective on short notice."

"You are correct." Keith reached for a garlic breadstick. "They were going to put her on the case team as a new member. But with Sutter's blowup, they're letting her head it up. If I hadn't been at your party and a witness to all that went on, I would've been the one who led the team."

"At least we have a shot at a more reasonable head taking charge, though." I grabbed a breadstick of my own. I hadn't taken one yet as I didn't want to be the only one with heavy garlic breath if he kissed me goodbye before he left. Sure, the sauce had garlic, but not like those breadsticks.

"Our latest task makes more sense too." He sipped his wine again. "The captain has had us reorganizing our case files, filling in holes, pulling out anything unsolved. It seems he's prepping us for review in order to have further grounds to get rid of Sutter."

"On the bright side, you'll be all caught up on paperwork for a while." I grinned and chomped a bite of breadstick.

Keith chuckled. "I suppose you're right."

We changed the subject, and while he finished eating, I told Keith about our close call with the street sweeper the previous night.

"Have you thought about parking next door rather than in the library parking lot?" Keith folded his napkin and laid it on the table.

"Actually no, I hadn't." I stood and took his plate to the kitchen, setting it in the sink.

"If I were the perp, I'd be awfully nervous about a stray car parked in the library lot all night long." He stood and walked to the living room area, where he'd tossed his jacket over the arm of the couch. "They might leave if they see the car, whether or not they see anyone inside it."

"Good point." I turned and walked with him to the front door. "But wouldn't I stand out just as much in the next lot over?" I racked my brain trying to remember what building was next door to the library.

"Nah." Keith shook his head as he slid his arms into his jacket sleeves. "It's Hokes Folly Feed and Farm Supply. If you park over by the trailers they have for sale, you can blend in a bit."

"Great idea." I grinned. "Oh, wait, hang on." I turned and rushed back to the kitchen counter and grabbed a paper sack, thrusting it at him when I returned to the front door. "Here."

A puzzled look crossed his face, and he slowly opened the bag, grinning at its contents. He reached inside and drew out one of the dozen Oreos I'd packed for a dessert to go.

"I didn't bake them, but it's the thought that counts, right?" I leaned up to brush a kiss across his cheek.

A deep laugh rumbled up from his chest. "They're perfect." He pulled me into his arms for an embrace. "I love . . . Oreos."

Good grief! What was I going to have to do to get the man to actually say he loved me? I knew he did. He knew he did. But somehow he had it in his head that I needed more time. I smiled sweetly at him, hoping he wouldn't miss this next hint. "I love . . . Oreos too."

Keith raised a palm to my face, his thumb sliding across my cheek, as he leaned in to oh-so-tenderly kiss me. I melted into him, my heart racing at his soft touch. When he pulled back, the chilly evening air slid between us, sending goose bumps up my arms.

His hand remained on my cheek as his intent gaze bored into me. "Just be careful. I don't want to lose you." He stepped back, turned, and was gone into the gathering darkness.

I closed the door and leaned against it for a moment before heading to the kitchen for a quick cleanup. After the dishes were in the dishwasher, leftovers were in the fridge, and counters and stove were wiped down, I made a few more sandwiches and more coffee and headed downstairs to help Mason close the store.

Rita swung by and picked up Mason's car keys again, and we told her we'd be in the Hokes Folly Feed and Farm Supply lot next door to the library. Assuring us she'd be on time, she headed out, with us locking up behind her.

When I finally pulled my car into the farm supply parking lot, I headed for the area with the trailers for sale and slid in beside them, the front of the car pointing toward the library. My angle of sight to the library's front door wasn't as great anymore, but from this spot, we could also see the back parking lot. I hadn't considered the thief might go in the back door, where we'd never see them.

Mason interrupted my thoughts. "Why are we parking here now?"

"Rita and I almost got outed by a street sweeper right after you left last night." I reached for one of the travel mugs of coffee. Might as well get a start on that caffeine.

"Oh, man." Mason huffed and crossed his arms. "I missed the excitement."

I chuckled and sipped my coffee. "I'm sure you'll survive missing out on cramming yourself into the floorboard under a blanket for half an hour."

"Yeah, well, whatever." Mason huffed again. "So, how would this whole college thing work?"

I blinked, startled at the abrupt subject change. I'd honestly almost forgotten about my offer of a loan. "Let's see, I think I'll need to see a complete work history, school transcripts, your last bank statement, and a letter of reference from your current place of employment." I struggled to keep my face straight and was proud I'd managed to say all of that, off the cuff, without laughing.

Mason's wide eyes matched his open mouth. "But . . . but . . ." His brow furrowed. "Wait a minute. *You're* my current place of employment."

The laughter I'd held in bubbled up. "Had you going for a moment, though."

He grinned and reached for his own tumbler of coffee. "Yeah."

"Honestly, there's not much to it." I grabbed a sandwich and began unwrapping it. "I'll pay for classes and keep an account of what's spent. When you're done, we'll tally up the total, and you can begin making payments once you're on your feet."

A knock at the window startled me, and I almost choked on the bite of sandwich I'd taken. I half turned the ignition key and rolled down my window, letting in a chilly breeze from the mid-October cold snap.

A Hokes Folly Feed and Farm Supply employee leaned down and swept her gaze through the car. "Everything okay out here?"

The dash clock had lit up. Eight fifty-eight PM. Closing time.

I smiled what I hoped was a friendly, nonthreatening smile rather than the demented smile of a woman who'd just had half her life scared out of her. "We're fine. We're just sitting here talking for a bit. I hope you don't mind."

The woman leaned down to look at Mason again. "Talking. Yeah. Well, they make hotel rooms for 'talking.'" She made air quotes with her fingers.

"What?" I sputtered. "No! That's not what we're doing. What is wrong with you?"

Mason leaned toward my window. "Ma'am, are we currently breaking any laws or trespassing?" He flashed her his boy-next-door smile.

Doubt flickered across the woman's face. "No. Not really."

"All we need is a quiet place to discuss a few important matters. We're doing this in the privacy of our vehicle. We're not breaking laws, as you've stated, so we'll be fine here for a bit longer." His smile stayed spread across his face.

"Um, okay." The woman took a step back. "I guess you can stay for now." She turned and stomped back toward the store, glancing back at us over her shoulder twice before walking through the door.

I stared at Mason. Who was this kid? And where had he learned to handle folks like that?

He must have caught my odd look, because he grinned widely and shrugged. "I've been reading a few books on closing sales I found on the shelves at the store. She just needed someone else to seem like they were in control of the situation."

I shook my head. "Whatever those books told you, it worked." I let my gaze sweep through the parking lot of the library again. "At least you didn't miss out on tonight's excitement."

"Hey, you're right." He shifted beside me, crossing one ankle over his other knee. "Not a wasted night after all."

We lapsed into silence, and before long, Mason softly snored, his head leaned against the window at an odd angle. Nothing was going on yet, so I let him sleep.

Thoughts whirled in my brain. Each of my suspects rolled through my head. Their motives were strong, their access plausible, and their opportunities to both murder Linus Talbot and poison my dog were present. No one really stood out over the others.

Alice King, Selina March, and Bradford Prescott blended together into one big glob rolling across a jumble of legs, gaping mouths yelling, six grasping hands reaching for Eddy and me as we ran through a thick swirling fog that slowed our progress as it sucked on our feet like quicksand. My head smacked into my side window, jarring me awake. I looked at the clock. One forty-eight AM. Damn. Mason still snored beside me. Who knew what we'd missed?

I gently prodded him awake. "Rita will be here soon. You might want to wake up enough to be able to drive home."

"Oh, wow, I can't believe I slept like this." His hand rubbed the back of his neck. "I think my neck is stuck like this."

"Don't feel bad. I dozed off for a couple of hours too." I refilled my coffee mug from one of the thermoses. "With our luck, the thief probably chose tonight to steal the books, and we'll be doing this for another couple of weeks or so before we catch them." I sighed deeply, then sipped the still-hot liquid, letting its warmth and aroma perk up my sleepy brain.

Headlights pulled into the deserted parking lot, swinging in our direction.

"And there she is now." I settled my mug in one of the console cup holders and helped Mason untangle from the blankets wrapped around his legs. He swung out of the car, and Rita took his place, and I watched in the rearview mirror as he got into his own car and drove off.

"Anything to report?" Rita tucked the blankets in around her own legs.

I shook my head. "Nothing but a nosy employee and Mason and I both falling asleep for two hours."

"Oh no." Rita patted my hand where it rested on my travel mug. "I'm sure nothing happened. We'll still catch the thief, whoever it is."

My thoughts again returned to our three suspects. "Rita, do you think we're way off base here? Would someone really commit murder over a few stolen antique books?"

"Depends on their worth." Rita screwed the lid back onto a thermos and popped the lid on her travel mug. "If they had a high enough value, even combined, it would constitute grand larceny. If it was a really high dollar amount, it could get them some prison time for a felony."

"But what if it's unrelated?" I blew warm breath on my hands against the cold snap that had taken the overnight temperatures into the low forties. "What if the book thefts have nothing to do with the murder? I mean, look at Bradford Prescott. Maybe Linus knew about the big pharma angle. Phillie said he had big plans to aim for a U.S. congressional seat in a few more years. Who knew what his plans were beyond that? Any negative press now might seriously impact his chances in a few years, even if he gets elected in November."

Rita propped her feet on the dashboard and slid down in her seat, setting her cup on her knees. "Nasty dirt always has a way of popping back out of the reaches of obscurity when an election's at stake."

"But would he have stolen rare books?" I sipped my coffee, hoping the warm liquid would wash an idea into my exhausted brain without bringing back the budding nightmare I'd had earlier.

"Maybe. If he needed the money to fund his campaign." Rita shrugged.

"I don't think he could've randomly added money to his funds. I think they'd have to keep records of where it all came from, so no candidate could cheat the system."

Rita chuckled. "I'm sure those who wish to cheat the system can. How about this? Candidate A needs donors, but each donor can only give so much. Candidate A finds new donors, slips them the cash, and lets them donate it to his campaign fund. Now you have a paper trail making it look legit."

"And the candidate's own bank accounts would likely be open for tracking to make sure that type of thing didn't happen." I turned and let my gaze sweep across the parking lot, not really expecting to see anything, but more to let my mind put pieces together. "The candidate would need an outside source of untraceable money to give to these fake donors."

"Exactly." Rita sipped her coffee. "But it doesn't mean he did it. Just that he could have a motive to steal the books and to silence Linus if he felt Linus had sussed out a piece of his possible plan. Frankly, I think Alice King and Selina March still have equal motives."

"True. Alice has a less convoluted motive. She hated that Linus broke her heart and exposed her fraudulent book sales." I leaned my head back on the head rest and closed my eyes, letting my own failed relationship play through my head. My ex-fiancé had broken my heart. Well, not broken, but at least bruised it. He'd also taken the stance that I was guilty of embezzlement and fraud and murder, even though I was acquitted of all charges. "I can see how Alice could be pushed into killing Linus, especially if he found out she was starting to dip her toes into fraudulent book sales again. Maybe she really was stealing books to sell but was using an assumed name to do it."

"Could be." Rita shrugged. "But we still have Selina March. Let's don't forget her long-standing grudge against Linus and her money-grubbing need to spend, spend, spend to prove she's the queen bee of the community. With what she has likely learned from Douglas, she could easily steal the books to sell for cash."

I opened my eyes and sagged into my seat, frustration pouring through my brain, blending the three possible killers into one again, à la my nightmare. "Maybe Mason was right and the three of them got together and killed him."

Rita laughed and nudged me with her elbow. "I know you don't believe that."

"No." I sucked in a long deep breath and held it a few seconds before letting it rush out, taking some of my anxiety with it. "I feel so in the dark about all of this."

"I know." Rita reached out and squeezed my hand. "But we'll get to the bottom of this. I promise."

Chapter Nineteen

The rest of the night had passed in idle chatter, and I'd arrived home to fall into another exhausted pile, only to dream of the Alice-Selina-Bradford blob chasing Eddy and me again. I awoke on high alert, jarred from the dream. Sunlight streamed through the gauzy curtains, and I rolled over to look at the clock. Ten thirty AM. I'd only had four hours of sleep. My head flopped back to the pillows, and my eyelids drooped, sleep pushing to drag my brain back into oblivion.

"How dare you?"

The muffled screech sounded through the closed window, and I rose up and pulled the curtains aside. Alice King and Selina March stood on the sidewalk below, and if their expressions could be relied upon, both were fighting mad.

I slid the window open a bit so I could hear their argument, not just the screeching.

"Listen, you loser hag, you run your nasty mouth anymore, and I'll have you in court for a defamation case so fast you won't know what hit you." Selina, dressed to the nines as usual, including four-inch heels, towered over Alice. "When my attorneys get done with you, your little book sales won't come close to paying the money you'll owe me. I'll destroy you and any life you ever hoped to have."

I had to hand it to Alice. As mousy as she had seemed earlier, she stood her ground with Selina. "Defamation? I doubt anyone will disagree with 'blood-sucking leech' the way you bleed poor Douglas dry. I know you hated my Linus. You blamed him because you have a crappy marriage to a good man who can't possibly live up to the glitz you want the world to see, and you have to depend on your daddy's allowance to scrape by. If you can call furs and jewelry and fancy balls scraping by. Then Linus embarrassed you in public at the bookstore thing, and you decided to shut him up permanently. You're nothing but a money-grubbing tramp who wants to impress everyone, and I hope your husband finally sees through you before you suck him completely dry like the vampire you are."

There was that "my Linus" phrase again. This woman changed her attitudes about Linus faster than the weather changed in the Carolinas.

Selina raised her hand to slap Alice but stopped before swinging. "You lying piece of trash. You'd better be careful what you say before someone shuts you up permanently." A slow nasty grin slid across Selina's face. "Just like 'your Linus.'"

Holy crap on a cookie! Did Selina just infer she'd killed Linus?

Alice opened her mouth, but a garbled squeak was all that came out. Her red face and huffing chest pushed forth another squeak before she screeched a repeated phrase. "How dare you?"

Selina leaned in, her face inches from Alice's. "I'll see you in court." She turned on her four-inch heels and stalked across the street to The Weeping Willow, leaving Alice standing on the sidewalk.

When Alice turned and headed for my store's door, I jumped from the bed, threw on clothes—I'd shower later—and forced a brush through my tangled bed-hair. Catching sight of the dark circles under my eyes from lack of sleep and the still messy look of my hair, I winced but headed toward the stairs anyway, hoping my customers wouldn't notice.

"Wow, you look horrible." Mason whistled low. "And why are you here this early? Aren't you supposed to be sleeping so we can go back out tonight?"

So much for the hope that I looked better than my mirror said I did. "I'm fine. Where's Alice?"

"Ah." Mason nodded. "I take it you saw the fight outside?" He gestured toward the poetry section. "She went that way."

"Thanks." I smiled, hoping it softened my exhausted look. "And yeah, I saw. It's what woke me."

I headed across the store in search of Alice, passing an elderly couple who stared at me with startled eyes and whispered to one another as I passed. Guess the smile didn't help.

Alice looked up as I approached, seemingly unfazed by my ghastly appearance. She smiled a slightly damp smile at me, her lip trembling for a brief moment before she drew in a deep breath and huffed it out.

"Are you okay?" I gently touched her shoulder.

She nodded. "Yes. I take it you saw the argument."

"I did." I let my hand fall from her shoulder and gestured toward the sitting area. "Want to talk about it?" I tried to put on my Perry-Mason-esque-prying-mind-disguised-as-a-friendly-ear persona.

Alice's gaze turned toward the large armchairs. "I don't want to be a bother." Her bottom lip trembled again.

Compassion warred with nosiness, and I shoved my mother's voice—chiding me for the nosiness—aside. "Nonsense. Everyone needs to vent sometimes. I'm happy I can be here for you."

I led the emotional woman to an armchair and settled her, gesturing to Mason to bring a warm cup of coffee. He arrived with a steaming Twice Upon a Time mug, two single-serve creamer cups, and several sugar and sweetener packets for Alice to choose from.

Tears sparkled in Alice's eyes as she whispered a "thank you" to Mason before he left to greet an incoming customer. Absently she stirred a creamer into her coffee. "I wish . . . I don't know what I wish."

My Mom conscience poked at me, telling me to be nice to her, compassionate about her distress, even if she was a killer. "I know you loved him."

Watery eyes looked up at me. "I did." She cleared her throat. "I thought he loved me too."

"I understand what that's like," I said gently. "I thought a man loved me, too, once, and it hurt a lot when it wasn't true."

A lone tear streaked down her face, and she pulled what appeared to be another used tissue from her purse to dab at her eyes. "Part of me wishes I could go back to daydreaming about the possibilities."

I nodded, knowing exactly what she meant, but I kept silent, giving her room to have her say.

"I said some really ugly things to him when he rejected me." She sniffed loudly. "Things I wish I could take back. I mean, it's not his fault he didn't love me. It simply is what it is."

This was a new side to Alice King, one I hadn't seen previously. This Alice was wise and reasonably calm. Maybe the two previous Alices were operating on high emotion, and this Alice had managed to come to an acceptance point. Or maybe she was just a really good actress, trying to convince others she wasn't a killer.

Alice blew her nose into the tissue, tucked it into her lap, and reached for the pink sweetener packets without sanitizing her hands. Ewww. I'd have to remember to toss the whole bowl of packets and wash the bowl.

"Did you not ever have a chance to repair the friendship?" I pushed my ick-meter aside and concentrated on comforting her.

"I was getting to the point where I could let it all go and just be friends when he found out I was . . ." Her brow wrinkled and she stirred her coffee rapidly. "He discovered something about me that he disagreed with."

"That you were selling books with false provenances?" I crossed my legs under me in the armchair opposite her and leaned back, waiting to see how she would react.

Her stirring froze for a brief moment, then resumed at a slower pace, her gaze remaining on the mug. "He discovered I was being a bit too eager to make sales, and in the process, I was over-qualifying the worth of the books inadvertently."

A nice way for her to say she was lying to her buyers. Inadvertently, indeed. "I heard he damaged your reputation in the book world."

Alice's hand trembled as she removed the spoon from the mug and laid it aside on the small table beside her chair, making a sticky ring I'd have to clean up later, but she still didn't make eye contact with me. "He did. But I'll survive."

Well, all or nothing. "And now he can't say anything any-more." I waited, but when Alice didn't respond, I added, "We saw your online book listing."

Alice's gaze flew up to mine, eyes wide and startled. She opened her mouth to say something but snapped it closed instead.

"Was that what you were arguing with Selina about?" I had home-court advantage, so I might as well press on. Even if she were the killer, she wouldn't try anything here in the store with witnesses. Would she?

Alice thumped her mug on the side table, sloshing a bit more of the sweetener-sticky liquid onto the surface. "If you must know, I saw her and couldn't contain myself. I accused her of killing Linus because she hated him. I know she did it. I just can't prove it."

"I saw you the day of the funeral, before you came into my store." I watched her closely for a reaction. "Were you following Selina?"

Alice froze, her nostrils flaring before she relaxed and shook her head. "I need to find a way to prove she's the one who hurt Linus. I thought maybe if I followed her, I'd find something. She'd slip up somehow."

My ears perked up, and I leaned forward, stopping Alice as she began to rise from her chair. "Alice, wait. Why are you convinced Selina did it?"

Spine ramrod straight, Alice perched on the edge of her seat. "Her car was still in the parking lot when I left that night. Add that to her hatred, and there you go." A head bob accompanied her matter-of-fact statement.

"You know what she drives?" I scooted to the edge of my seat as well, ready to pop up and stop her if she tried to leave before she told me what she knew.

"Everyone knows what that woman drives." Alice waved her hand in the air. "It's a Jaguar something or other. A sports car. I don't know the exact model, but it's silver and flashy and she brags about it. 'Oh, I'll be over in the Jag in a bit. Let me check to see if I need to have someone put gas in the Jag. I'll meet you there in the Jag.'" Alice did a fair imitation of Selina's hand gestures and voice tones. "It's annoying and rude, and she does it to lord it over everyone else. She bought it last year, and I'm surprised she hasn't traded it in yet for a new model." Her sneer faded into a look of pity. "Poor Douglas must have put his foot down for once."

How did I answer that? "Hmm, okay. I'll have to watch for it." Unsure what else to say, I stood when she did and followed her toward the door. "Thanks for stopping by. I look forward to seeing you when you come again." I cringed inwardly, knowing how tacky it sounded after the conversation we'd had.

"Yes. See you again." She swept out the door with all of the regality of Selina March, head high and shoulders back.

"Find out what the fight was about?" Mason stepped up beside me and leaned against the counter.

"It seems she accosted Selina in the street to publicly accuse her of killing Linus Talbot." I watched Alice walk away without a backward glance.

"Does she seriously think Selina did it?" Mason let his gaze follow mine toward the retreating figure.

I sighed and walked behind the counter, settling onto a stool. "I honestly don't know. Maybe. But maybe she did it so everyone would think, 'Hey, Alice must be innocent.'"

Mason turned to face me, propping his elbows on the counter. "Kind of a she-who-accuses-first-is-most-believable thing?"

I nodded. "I even brought up our book we caught her selling online with a false writeup. She didn't even try to defend herself. Just pointed the finger at Selina again and says she's tailing Selina to catch her in a slip-up and prove she killed Linus."

Mason shook his head. "We won't see Alice again, will we?"

"Nope." I returned my gaze to her retreating figure, tiny now as she neared the end of the street. "Not unless she's our killer."

Chapter Twenty

"I think she just took a picture of our car." Mason craned his head backward toward the farm supply's front door.

What the hell? I looked in the rearview mirror at the same lady who had tapped on our window the previous night. She'd marched out into the lot to glare at us a few minutes ago, and we'd smiled and waved at her before she'd grimaced and stormed back inside. Now, it seems she was taking photographs of my car and my license plate number. As I watched, she lowered her phone and looked down at the screen, swiping her finger across it as if to check her pictures, glared at us once more, and stomped into the store.

I shook my head and returned my attention to the library. Mason had checked out an audiobook on his phone, and he quietly sat with headphones in, listening to a Robert Ludlum novel. Left in silence, I let the whole mess swirl through my brain while keeping an eye on the parking lot. I didn't really think anything would happen yet, as even Hokes Folly Feed and Farm Supply hadn't closed for the night. It was only eight PM, and I figured the thief wouldn't make an appearance until the wee hours.

A loud knock on my window made me jump, a flashlight blinding me as it swept the car. Mason yanked out his earbuds and sat up.

I rolled down the window, prepared to give the store's employee a piece of my mind. We weren't doing anything wrong, and the woman needed to quit hassling us. "Do you mind?"

The light lowered, and Sutter's face formed in the darkness. "Why, yes, I do mind. Thanks for asking." *Grunt.*

Oh, good grief, the woman had called the cops on us! "Detective Sutter. How can I help you?"

"You can start by telling me what you're doing here." Sutter shifted, leaning down to look at Mason. "We've had a complaint about someone casing the store to rob it."

I looked at Mason and we both burst out laughing. "That's insane. We're not even looking at the store, nor have we done anything but sit in our car."

"A complaint is a complaint, Miss Quinn." Sutter stepped back. "Would you please step out of the car?

Was he serious? I opened my car door and slid to my feet as another car entered the lot and headed in our direction.

Keith stepped from his car. "Sutter, what's going on? Why are you hassling Jenna and Mason?"

"We had a complaint from this store's manager about someone casing the joint for two days." Sutter reached into his pocket for his little notebook, flipping it to a blank page once he had it in his hand. "Care to tell me why you're here?"

Keith snatched Sutter's notebook from his hand and flipped it closed, thrusting it back at Sutter. "Enough. They're here because I told them to sit here to watch the library. Is that official enough for you?"

Sutter's eyes narrowed, and his voice hissed out. "Don't ever get physical with me again, boy."

Keith's eyes went cold, and I took a step back, ready to jump into my car and slam the door shut if things got really ugly.

"Move, Jenna," Mason whispered from behind me. "I can't see."

I shifted to the side, still able to leap into my car if necessary, yet giving Mason a little bit of a view. I wouldn't deprive him of the night's excitement. He'd never forgive me.

Keith clenched his fists at his side. "Sutter, you are no longer my partner, and you have no say in what I do or do not investigate or how, when, or where I do so. You are interfering in an active investigation and need to back down."

Sutter took a step forward, puffing out his chest, his voice a growl. "No, boy, it's you who is interfering. I won't have this woman messing up my Talbot murder case." He turned, took a step, and grabbed my upper arm. "I'm taking you in."

"Drop her arm. Now." Keith's warning was low and firm, a tone which did not match the stark fury coming from his gaze.

"As you said earlier, we're not partners any longer." Sutter tugged at my arm, forcing me to stagger a few steps toward his car. "You can't tell me what to do either."

The passenger door on Keith's car swung open, and a lithe African American woman stepped from the car. "No, he can't." She stepped into the circle of light formed by Keith's headlights. "But I can. I'm the lead on your investigation. You will drop her arm now, and you will stop harassing our consulting detective immediately."

Sutter and I both dropped our mouths open at her statement.

"Consulting detective?" Sutter's grip tightened on my arm. "Since when?"

Pain shot up my shoulder, and I stumbled, gasping.

Keith grasped a handful of Sutter's jacket collar and jerked him up close. "Let. Her. Go."

If Sutter missed the threat implied in his tone, he was an idiot.

"Logan. Enough." The senior detective's voice cut through the tension.

Keith released Sutter and stepped back, and my gaze swung to the other woman, noticing her hand had slid to the grip of her gun, her feet in a solid stance.

"Detective Sutter, please release Miss Quinn now."

Apparently, Sutter's lizard brain finally took in not only Keith's rage but also the woman's action-ready stance. He dropped my arm and held his hands in front of his chest, although the superior sneer never left his face. "Fine. Whatever you say." He turned to glare at me. "But you'd better stay away from my investigation. You already lost me a promotion. I won't have you screwing up my record again."

I bit my tongue, dug my fingernails into my palms, and listened to my mother's voice screaming in my ear that I should shut up. None of it did any good. "First, my *innocence* did not screw up your record. You did that all on your own by trying to pin two murders on me so you could have a big splashy case. Second, as you have already stated you feel book thefts cannot possibly be connected to 'your investigation,' I fail to see how sitting in my car watching a library at night can in any way interfere."

Sutter reached for me again, his grasping hand barely missing my arm when I took a large step back from him.

"Sutter!" The female detective's sharp bark stopped Sutter's advance. "In the car. Now. You're done."

Sutter froze, his jaw clenching and unclenching, his eyes cold and hard. Slowly he turned to face her, his voice slithering out in a hiss. "I'll go, but I'll deal with you at the station." He stalked to his car, got in, and drove out of the parking lot.

Keith stepped forward and slid an arm around me. "Are you okay?"

I nodded, unable to speak, and sagged into his shoulder. I took a few ragged breaths, forcing myself to quell the tremble that threatened to overcome me.

Mason jumped out of the passenger door and stormed around the car. "Whoa. That was a bunch of bull." He laid a hand on Keith's shoulder. "Man, if you hadn't been here, I would've let him have it."

"I'm glad you didn't. It would've given him a legitimate reason to arrest you." Keith led me to my car door and eased me into the seat. "It's over. He can't hurt you."

I nodded again. "I know."

The other detective stepped forward. "He won't be hurting anyone again."

Keith stood and angled his body to include Mason and her in the conversation. "Mason, Jenna, this is LaTisha Riddick. She's the detective we're borrowing from the department in Boone."

"Everyone calls me Tish." She reached for my hand, shaking it when I responded. "Nice to meet the woman Keith talks about in such glowing terms."

I glanced at Keith, unsure if there was a blush staining his cheeks, before turning back to Tish. "Very nice to meet you as well, Detective. And thanks for helping with Detective Sutter."

Tish sighed deeply. "I honestly don't know what to do with him. I hate to see him fired when he's six months from retirement, but he cannot be allowed to work on active investigations."

My brows shot up. "Even this one?" Was it possible I'd been accused for the last time by the detestable detective?

"That'll be up to the captain to decide." She gestured over her shoulder toward their sedan. "But with the dash cam footage, I'm sure they'll conclude he at least needs to be relegated to filing paperwork for the next few months."

Oh, please no. They'd caught it all on video. I fought down the urge to cry. If it got out, my store would once again be entwined with the police. "Is this going to be on the news?"

Tish shook her head. "We'll keep it inside the department."

Mason pointed at the store's front door. "It might be on Facebook or YouTube."

My gaze flew to the store. The manager stood, triumphant look on her face, phone held up as if she was taping everything.

Tish strode over to the woman and they talked quietly before the woman handed Tish her phone. Tish tapped the screen a few times, handed the phone back, and shook the woman's hand before returning to our group. "I told her it was a deep undercover action, and the rest of the department had been unaware. She was quite happy to let me delete her video once I explained she could damage an active investigation, letting a criminal ring run rampant."

Keith cocked an eyebrow. "Rampant?" He snorted.

Tish grinned. I wanted to hug this woman. She was amazing, or at least a darned sight better than Sutter had ever been.

"What's this about consulting detectives?" Mason leaned on the car in a casual pose, obviously approving of the title.

"Oh, that." Tish waved her hand in the air. "I had to tell Sutter something to get him to back off, and I just finished binge-watching *Elementary*, that TV show about Sherlock Holmes." She apparently caught sight of Mason's now-dejected look. "We don't mind if you want to sit over here and watch the parking lot on the outside chance that Linus Talbot was onto something. But if you see anything, you need to call us and let us handle it."

Keith slid his fingers through mine and squeezed softly. "Promise me."

I nodded, soaking in the warmth of his hand. "I promise."

Keith dropped a quick kiss on my hair, squeezed my fingers once more, and left with his new, albeit temporary, partner.

After Mason and I slid into the car and shut the doors, I started it briefly to warm the interior. I was shivering, and I didn't think a blanket or two would counteract the deep chill I'd fallen into when Sutter had manhandled me. I leaned forward, hands at the top of the steering wheel and forehead on my hands, sucking in deep, cleansing breaths.

Mason rested a hand on my back. "Hey, I really would have defended you if Keith hadn't shown up. I wouldn't have let him hurt you."

I raised my gaze to meet his and smiled with trembling lips. "I know you would have. But I'm glad you didn't. There's no need to put you in Detective Sutter's crosshairs again."

"Are you okay?" Mason awkwardly patted my back.

"I am." I took another deep breath, letting it out slowly. "At least I will be. The whole thing just brought back some memories I'd rather not have."

Mason's hand dropped as I sat up. "Oh, yeah, the jail thing in Charlotte. I almost forgot."

I chuckled, releasing more of the tension. "I sure wish I could." I closed my eyes, squeezing out the images flashing in my brain. If there was some way I could erase that whole half a year of my life, take it out of my memory, I'd be a happy camper. I shook my head and opened my eyes. "For now, we have to catch a book thief."

Mason slid down in his seat, plugging his earbuds in again. "And maybe a killer."

Chapter
Twenty-One

The next few hours passed in a daze. Mason remained alert, although he kept his earbuds in, listening to his book. I knew without asking that he was beating himself up for not coming to my rescue. However, my own swirling thoughts of my months in jail, the rough handling, both emotionally and physically, by the police department, and the loss of my entire life sucked me down into a quagmire of regret, anger, and fear, to the point that I had nothing left with which to try to comfort him. Instead, I sat silently, drinking copious amounts of coffee and desperately trying to push back thoughts of Charlotte that threatened to overwhelm me.

Lost in the depths of memory, I jumped, a small scream bursting from my throat, when Rita yanked open Mason's door.

"Hello, hello, my little sleuthing friends." She grinned in at us, the smile slowly ebbing as she took in our somber expressions. "Uh-oh. What did I miss?"

Mason glanced at me then Rita. "I'll let her explain." He slid from the car but leaned in again before walking to his own car. "I really am sorry. I'll make it up to you, I swear."

I reached out and squeezed his hand where it rested on the seat back. "Mason, it's all okay. I'm okay. None of this was your fault. I promise. And you're the one who saved us from that awful manager who was videoing it all with her phone. Without your attention to that point, it could have gotten ugly. I'm deeply grateful." Gads, now I was babbling. I gave him what I hoped was a reassuring smile.

He nodded and pasted on a smile, which looked more like a pained grimace. "Okay." His slumped shoulders as he walked to his car said it was anything but okay.

Rita plopped down beside me and shut her door, pulling blankets from the back. "Man, it's cold tonight. I think the weather said it was going down to thirty-eight."

"Something like that." I held up a mug. "Want some hot coffee?"

Her hands wrapped around the mug as I poured, and she took a long sip before pinning me with her gaze. "What in the world did I miss?"

"In a nutshell, the manager here called the cops on us because she thought we were casing the store." I screwed the lid on the thermos and stuck it in the back seat.

"Oh, don't tell me." She leaned back and slid a foot from her shoe, tucking her toes under her other leg. "Please say it wasn't Frank Sutter who showed up."

"The very one." I nodded and filled her in on what had happened.

"And here Mason was, jealous because he missed out on the street sweeper a couple of nights ago." Rita reached for a sandwich in the cooler. "I'd have loved to see Frank's face when Keith all but punched him and Keith's temporary partner ordered him around."

I grinned. "Yeah, that part was a bit on the satisfying side."

"Seems the bully got his just dues." Rita bit into her sandwich, getting a tiny smear of mustard on her finger.

"Oh, it's not over yet." I handed her a napkin. "Once they show their captain the video—"

"They have video?" Rita whooped and fist pumped. "Take that, you jackwagon!"

"Yes, they had turned on their dash camera before they got out of their car. Everything that happened was caught." I held a hand up. "Don't get too excited, though. Sure, Sutter will get raked over the coals and will probably be put on desk duty until he retires in the spring. But if this leaks out, it's going to be ugly for my store."

Rita, caught with her mouth full, rolled her hand in a request that I keep explaining.

"Think about it. If someone leaks this video to the news, some eager reporter looking for a splashy headline will link it to Twice Upon a Time." When Rita's blank stare told me she wasn't following my train of thought, I continued. "In the last three months, the store has been linked to the following." I held up a hand and ticked my list off on my fingers.

"One, my uncle's murder. Two, my arrest situation in Charlotte, possibly a murder and embezzlement. Three, a second murder tied to my uncle's. Four, both murders being pinned on me. Five, Linus Talbot's murder. And if they can, six, Eddy's poisoning at the store, although I don't think the news media is aware of that yet." My heart twinged as Eddy's face floated through my mind. Right now, I could really use a hug from my dog. I was amazed anew at how quickly and deeply I'd bonded with the animal. Thank goodness he'd be coming home in two days. Monday morning could not come soon enough.

"I honestly hadn't thought of it in those terms." Rita wadded up her napkin and stuck it inside the sandwich baggie before tossing both into the grocery store bag I'd brought for trash.

"Yeah, well I have." I sighed deeply and leaned my head against the driver's side window, letting the cold glass help ease the tightening band of pain from a forming stress headache. "All I need is for one more police incident to be tied to the store, especially one where it looks like I'm being arrested again." I held up my hand to forestall Rita's interruption. "You know they'd edit it to get the most shock value from it, and by the time we put the full video online or somehow got the police to give some sort of statement to the contrary, the damage would already be done. It would be too little, too late."

Rita sank back into her seat, lips pursed and brows pulled tightly together. "We'll have to hope that doesn't happen." She raised her gaze to mine. "Trust Keith. It's a small department, and I'm sure folks there know he's quite attached to you. They wouldn't want to hurt you."

"Except for Detective Sutter." I sipped at the last of the coffee in my mug and reached for the thermos.

Rita laughed. "I doubt Frank would want that video to go viral. It doesn't exactly show him in the best light, and he wouldn't want his image damaged."

A grin pulled up one corner of my mouth. "True. Maybe there's hope after all."

"As my grandmother used to say, 'Don't borrow trouble from tomorrow.'" She shifted and pulled the blankets from her lap, reaching for her door handle. "After that sandwich and the coffee, I need to make a quick run to the ladies' room."

I helped her untangle from her cocoon of blankets. "I'll be here when you get back."

She stepped from the car. "See that you are. You promised Keith you'd call if you saw anything." She shut the door and jogged toward the Piggly Wiggly on the other side of the long-closed farm supply store.

I looked at the clock on my phone. Three fourteen AM. Only a few more hours to go, and I could finally get warm. I glanced in the rearview mirror, losing sight of Rita as she strode through the darkened grocery store parking lot. My gaze dropped from the mirror to the library parking lot in front of me. I swept my eyes from one side of it to the other.

In the quiet darkness, Keith's face, full of barely controlled rage, formed in my mind. The way he'd looked when Sutter had grabbed me . . . While I definitely didn't want to see Keith ever get into a physical altercation because of me, it was a strangely comforting feeling to know he would protect me if the need truly arose. The fact that he'd kept a handle on his fury was a testament to his self-control. A lesser man would've let fists fly. My ex-fiancé, Blake Emerson, shoved his way to the front of my memory, and I corrected my internal statement. A lesser man wouldn't have cared one way or another, except for how it affected his own image. Keith's determination to protect me spoke volumes about how he truly felt about me.

I startled back to the present as a brief movement at the edge of my vision caught my attention. I sat up straight, hands gripping the steering wheel, my body leaned forward, my eyes straining to see into the darkness. The tiny sliver of a moon did little to illuminate the parking lot.

There! I'd seen it again. This time I knew it was a person easing around behind the building, disappearing toward the back entrance. I grabbed my phone and dialed Keith's number. No answer. I called again. Nothing. Again. Nothing. I left a voice mail and hoped he'd hear it in time.

Frustrated, I looked back across at the Piggly Wiggly. No sign of Rita either. I grabbed a notepad from my purse and wrote a quick note telling Rita I was going to sneak around to peek at the back of the library to make sure I'd actually seen a person, and that I hadn't been able to reach Keith.

I eased my car door open and quietly snicked it closed again, hesitating for a moment as the sound seemed to echo through the darkness. Movement behind the building caught my eye again. Carefully, I crept along the line of trailers in the parking lot, somewhat masking my approach from anyone in the library lot. When I had a good line of sight to the back lot, I hunkered down and waited. Nothing moved. I strained my eyes, hunting for any sign of a person.

My eyes swept across the back of the building, catching a dark gap along one side of the door. It was cracked open, but no light spilled out. Someone had gone inside but hadn't turned on any lights.

I looked back across the farm supply store's lot toward the Piggly Wiggly. Still no sight of Rita. I dragged my phone from my pocket, shielding it inside my coat to see if I'd missed a return call or a text from Keith. Nope.

Determination pushed caution aside. We'd sat for days waiting to see if someone came to the library in the night, and I'd be damned if I was going to let whoever it was get away with more books while I sat there in the cold like an idiot.

I eased across the library's back lot, hunkered low, and ran to the side of the building, where I pressed myself against the bricks and waited. The lot remained silent and still, and I slid along the wall toward the door, trying to form a plan of action should someone emerge before I could conceal myself again.

When I reached the door, I hesitated. I'd promised Keith. But then, in a way, Keith had also promised me that he'd be available if I called. My mother's voice chided me, telling me to stop trying to find loopholes, to stop being foolish. I mentally shut her down and eased the door open enough that I could shimmy through it into the darkened room beyond.

Once inside, I gave my eyes a moment to try to adjust, finally making out the faint outline of a doorway that led, I hoped, into the main library area. I couldn't see anything but that doorway, so I shuffled my feet slowly, trying not to trip over anything. As I closed in on the doorway, my upper thigh raked across the corner of a table or desk, and I barely managed to keep a yelp from escaping. That would definitely leave a bruise. I eased sideways a step and moved toward the doorway again, finally reaching the frame. The front counter sat a few feet away, and I ducked down, scooting through the doorway and skittering underneath the solid surface.

I listened. A thud—a book dropping? I froze, breathing shallowly, trying to pinpoint the direction of the sound while mentally making a map of the library. I'd only been in the rare book section once, but I was pretty sure the sound had come from that area. I took a deep breath and slipped out from behind the counter in a crouch, tiptoeing toward the sound.

A dim light, as if a flashlight were muffled with cloth, swept out across the room, and I flattened myself against the floor near a freestanding shelf of videos. The light swept across once more and disappeared. I waited a moment, rose to my hands and knees, and crawled to the opposite end of the shelf. Easing my head out, I caught sight of the dim, bouncing light again, sweeping through the enclosed glass section where the more delicate rare books were housed.

My pocket buzzed, and the sound echoed loudly in the silent room. I ducked and fumbled for my phone, dragging it out. Keith had texted.

Sit tight. On my way.

Relief surged. I pushed the button to blank the screen again, realizing too late that, even if they hadn't heard the buzzing from the glassed enclosure, my screen light would have shone like a blazing sun in the dark room. I shoved the phone back into my pocket and leaned my head out to look for the flashlight again. Nothing. Had they seen my light or simply finished what they were doing? My stomach tightened. Logic dictated they'd use the light to get back to the door to leave, even if they were done. I'd been seen.

Flattening myself, I belly-crawled as quietly as I could, like I'd seen in war movies. I didn't need to be in here now. Keith was on his way. If I stayed put, I was a sitting duck, since they'd seen my light. I had to get out of the open aisles. After slowly crawling past two shelf sections, I rose to my hands and knees, crawling until I got behind the front counter, the door into the back room only a couple of feet away. I eased into a crouch and moved into the pitch-black room, picking my way through, carefully avoiding the furniture I'd bumped earlier.

I knew the exterior door lay just ahead, but I couldn't see its outline in the dark room. Someone had shut it. I held my hands out in front of me, stepping forward in small steps until my fingertips brushed the wall. I slid along the wall until I found the metal door, and my hands dropped to the crash bar to push it open. The bar barely moved. What the hell? Weren't these things supposed to open from the inside, even if they were locked? Some kind of safety standard? I slid my hands along the bar, my fingers catching hold of a rope looped through the bar. Blindly following the rope with my hands, I found it also looped around the leg of a piece of furniture which seemed to be bolted to the floor.

Now there was no doubt I'd been seen. Whoever I'd seen had gotten to the door first and had tied it shut. My brain worked past this and realized this meant they'd known I would come. They'd planned for this. They'd brought rope. I was trapped in the building, possibly in the pitch-black room, with a killer, my only way of escape now blocked. Fear sliced through me, shredding my self-control. I stifled the scream that wanted to erupt, pressing my hands hard across my mouth. Panic surged, and I fought against it. *Think, think, think!* The front door.

I groped my way toward the front room again, catching my thigh on the furniture once more. Tears filled my eyes, from both pain and terror, and I caught a small sob before it could make too much noise.

Freezing just inside the doorway in the darkness, I scanned the outer room and the pathway toward the front doors. Maybe

I could get out that way . . . unless someone had locked them as well. I dropped to my hands and knees and crawled, weaving my way through the aisles toward the front doors. As I reached the open entry area, I understood how an animal must feel when it runs out of woods and has to cross an open field with a predator hot on its trail. I scanned the area. All clear.

I stood and raced for the doors, not caring if I made noise at this point, skidding to a halt when I realized these weren't crash bar doors, and they were locked. Panic surged anew. As I whirled to run for a hiding place, something heavy slammed into the side of my head, hard enough to bounce it into the solid wood of the front door. My hands grasped at the door handle for balance as I fell to my knees, the room spinning. Another blow, another hard smack against the wood, and I crumpled to the floor, too dazed to move.

Unconsciousness tugged at me, and I fought to stay awake and as aware as possible. Sloshing sounds echoed in my ringing ears. A smell. What was that? It was familiar, yet I couldn't place it. I struggled through my mind's darkness, willing myself to open my eyes. A form moved through the stacks with a canister, shaking its contents out onto the bookshelves. My brain pulled a terrifying word from its recesses. Gasoline!

I soundlessly screamed at my arms, my legs, to move, to run, to hide. My ankle shifted, and my foot bumped into the back of my other leg. I raised my knee, forcing my other knee to follow it. My arms were next, sliding up near my head. I rolled over onto my hands and knees and wobbled up, vomiting as the room spun and gasoline fumes sank into my lungs.

Footsteps ran past me, and I managed to turn my head enough to see the figure unlock the front door. In a staggering crawl, I tried to follow, only to see the door slam and hear the lock click into place again as another stench hit my nose. Smoke!

My grade-school training as school fire drill officer—I'd even had the sash to wear for a month—kicked in. Fear dragged my fuzzy brain back into a weak focus. Staying as low to the ground as I could, I crawled toward the back room. Once there, I fumbled for my phone, my hands trembling as my hazy vision sought the flashlight button. Light sliced through the room and through my brain, sending waves of dizzying pain through my head. I swallowed the bile threatening to come up again, breathing as deeply as I dared in a room rapidly filling with smoke.

My hands dragged me farther into the room, and I turned and kicked the door closed, slowing the creep of smoke and fire into my hiding place. Crawling, I crossed the room toward the door. At least this time, I wouldn't hit that stupid furniture again, whatever it was.

At the back door, I slid my gaze along the rope that tied the back door closed. Rope. My brain struggled to find a way around it. Scissors. I was in an office-type setting in the back room. Desks. I pulled myself toward the closer of the three desks and yanked open drawer after drawer, screaming in frustration when no scissors appeared, falling to the floor when the scream induced a crippling pounding in my head. Who in their right mind didn't keep scissors in their desk?

Heat pushed into the room, and smoke curled in under and around the closed door. Sirens wailed in the distance as I dragged myself to another desk, desperation pushing me beyond my pain limits. *There! Scissors!* I grabbed the instrument and clutched it in one hand while I dragged myself back to the exterior door and the rope that kept me captive inside an inferno.

I opened the twin blades, my fingers and thumb in the grips, and sliced it closed. Another scream threatened, and I squelched it, knowing the pain it would cause would only slow me down. The scissors were dull. I rocked them back and forth, and tiny threads from the rope began to fray apart. Sweat popped out on my brow.

Faintly, I heard someone yell my name. Keith. He was here. I sawed on the rope frantically, fraying more tiny threads.

"In here!" My hands raised to pound on the back door.

Muffled sounds came from the other side as I sawed more threads loose, not cutting enough of the rope to make a difference.

A voice I didn't know yelled through the door. "Jenna Quinn, are you behind this doorway?"

"Yes." My voice came out in a scratchy croak, and I coughed. I sucked in a deep breath and tried again. "Yes! The door is tied shut! I'm trying to cut the rope with dull scissors!"

"Is there fire anywhere in the room?" the voice yelled.

I raised up and looked. "No, just some smoke coming in around the edges of the door I closed to the front room!"

Indistinct voices, muffled because of the door, yelled to one another, and I ramped up my efforts to saw through the rope with the dull blades.

"Jenna!" Keith's beautiful, amazing, perfect voice yelled through the door. "They've brought a saw to cut through the door around the lock. Back away and stay low to the floor. They're trying to contain the fire to keep it off the back of the building until they can get you out.

I dropped the scissors and slid backward under a desk, covering my face with a layer of my jacket to keep the smoke out.

The loud screech of the saw sent waves of intense pain through my head, and I slumped to the floor in the fetal position, my arms wrapped around my head.

A final screech, and a circular spot around the door lock fell away, and bolt cutters extended inside to snip the remaining rope. The door flew open, and within seconds, strong arms scooped me up from the floor. As we emerged into fresh air, I opened my eyes, forcing them to focus on Keith's face as he carried me toward an ambulance.

His voice pushed through my brain's haze. "You're okay. Don't leave me. You're okay."

I tried to respond, but darkness pulled me down into its clutches.

Chapter
Twenty-Two

Something jolted underneath my bed. An earthquake? There weren't earthquakes in North Carolina. Were there? Another jolt forced my eyes open. Strangers peered down at me, and straps held me to a tiny bed. I struggled to comprehend, opening my mouth to protest, but no sound came out, just a shuddering cough.

"She's awake." Keith's face swam into view. "It's okay, sweetheart. You're in an ambulance on the way to the hospital." His warm hand clutched mine tightly where it lay on the blankets.

As he spoke, I felt a sharp turn, and the ambulance slowed to a stop. The back doors flew open, and more strangers grasped at me.

Keith slid to the ground ahead of me, and I groped for his hand.

"Don't leave me." I parroted his words back to him.

He slid in between two paramedics. "I won't. I promise. I'll be with you every step they allow." He jogged in tandem as emergency room staff took my stretcher inside. "You're going to be okay."

Maybe if he said it enough, I'd begin to believe it. I wasn't sure. My head pounded, and my chest felt as if it was still trapped inside the burning library. "The books?" I gasped.

Keith's laugh eased a few of my fears. Surely if he was laughing, I wasn't dying.

"Sweetheart, leave it to you to worry about books when you're headed into the ER." He squeezed my fingers.

I did my best to squeeze back, but I wasn't sure if I'd managed it or not.

A nurse stepped in front of Keith as they approached a set of double doors. "Sir, you'll have to remain in the waiting room. We'll call you back once we have assessed the patient and are assured she's stable."

Keith flashed his badge. "Ma'am, with all due respect, we need to stay with this witness. I will not be in your way, but I will be where I can keep my eyes on her."

The nurse nodded and stepped aside, allowing Keith to follow me as they pushed my gurney through the emergency room bays to an empty slot, sliding the curtain closed around me once they'd locked the wheels and released the restraining belts.

I struggled to sit up, but gentle hands held me down until I stilled. Swiftly they moved me to the emergency-room bed, and the gurney disappeared from the bay.

A woman leaned over me, gray curls surrounding a weathered but sweet face. "Ma'am, I need you to be still for a bit longer, okay? We need to check a few things before we're ready for you to move around."

"Okay," I whispered and slumped back onto the bed.

Seconds later, another woman entered. "I'm Doctor Lincoln." She strode to my side, a clipboard in her hands. She flipped pages on its surface before setting it aside and reaching for my head, running her fingers across my scalp with a feather-light touch. "Looks like you hit your head. Did you fall?"

"No." I didn't recognize my hoarse croak. "Someone hit me with something."

Dr. Lincoln pressed her lips into a frown, and she pulled a pen light from her pocket. "I know this will be hard, but I need you to keep your eyes open for me, okay?"

I nodded, willing my eyelids to stay open as she quickly flashed her light across my pupils.

"Looks like your pupils are dilating and contracting properly. A good sign." Dr. Lincoln smiled at me and turned to Keith. "Are you her husband?"

Keith blinked, his mouth opened and closed, and he flashed his badge. "She's a . . . I'm not—"

"Yes, you are." Dr. Lincoln abruptly turned back to me. "Current hospital policy says only your spouse can be in here with you. Your husband can stay with you and move with you to a room when we have one ready. We'd like to run a few tests and keep you overnight for observation." As quickly as she'd entered, she swept aside the curtain and left.

Well, okay then. I guess I was married. For tonight anyway. I looked at Keith, and he looked as confused as I felt.

"Somehow I don't remember proposing." He grinned at me. "Or the wedding. Maybe I hit my head too?"

A chuckle burbled up, and I winced as it pounded through my head. "Don't make me laugh," I gasped.

Warm fingers slid through mine. "I'm sorry, sweetheart. I'll be more careful." Keith placed a soft kiss on my forehead.

The curtain swished aside again, and the nurse with the gray curls stepped in, pushing a computer cart. "I'm Amanda. I'll be your nurse until you move to a room. Can you answer a few questions?"

At my nod, she launched into questions about my date of birth, social security number, legal name, and insurance company, making me doubly glad I'd bought insurance the previous month.

After a barrage of questions, Amanda opened a drawer on the cart and pulled out blue gloves, pushing her hands into the protective coverings. "Just going to draw a little blood, dear."

I closed my eyes and held out my arm, glad when the last vial was drawn.

"All done now." Amanda stacked the blood vials on her cart, slid the curtain back, and wheeled the cart out, closing the door behind her.

A chair stood in the corner, and Keith slid it close to the bed and sat next to me, wrapping my hand in both of his, letting the silence of our tiny bay envelop us. The beeps and whirs and voices from the other emergency room bays faded away as I soaked in his warm strength. Periodically, he leaned in and kissed the back of my hand, stroking his thumb across the kiss each time as if to massage it in.

Amanda returned. "We're moving you to a room upstairs." She rolled a gurney into the bay. "Let's get you up and onto this thing."

With Amanda on one side and Keith on the other, I swayed to my feet and stepped to the gurney, dizzily sinking to its surface for what my brain saw as a roller-coaster ride. The brisk pace

Amanda set with the gurney still seemed to take forever before they finally helped me from the gurney onto a bed.

"Would you like help getting out of your clothes and into a gown, or will your husband help you with that?" Amanda laid a gown on the bed.

Keith's face turned a crimson color, and he coughed. "I'm sorry." He coughed again. "I need to get something to drink." Another cough sounded as he scrambled from the room.

Amanda turned to me, a grin on her face. "He's not your husband yet, is he?"

I forced my chuckle back down into my chest, so it didn't trigger a pounding in my head like before, but I let a wide smile slide across my lips. "No, he's not."

She slid my sweater over my arms and head, careful not to brush my bruised spots. "I didn't figure he was. But I won't tell."

I slipped my bra off while Amanda turned her head and held the hospital gown up as a shield, giving me at least the illusion of privacy. Sliding my arms into the sleeves, I shifted to let it drape around me.

Amanda circled the bed and snapped it behind my back. "Up we go now."

I wobbled to my feet and unsnapped and unzipped my jeans, pushing them down past my hips before settling onto the bed again.

Amanda helped me swing my feet onto the bed, took off my shoes and socks, and pulled my jeans off my legs. "There, now you'll be more comfortable." She settled the blankets around me and adjusted my bed, showing me the buttons to push if I needed to change the settings and moving the TV remote out of reach. "Can't watch TV right now. It'll make your headaches worse. Just push the call button if you need me."

Keith entered as Amanda left, his hand held over his eyes. "Is it safe to come in?"

I suppressed another laugh. "Stop making me laugh. It hurts. And yes, you can come in."

He dropped his hand and strode to my side, his eyes dark with emotion. "At least you're around to laugh." He dragged a chair next to the bed and sat, reaching out to put a hand on my arm.

I rolled to my side and looked at him. "I'm really sleepy. If you don't mind, I'd like not to talk for a while."

Keith nodded and leaned in to kiss my forehead. "Anything you want, sweetheart. You rest. I'll be here."

Chapter
Twenty-Three

"The doctor said you need to rest for at least two more days." Rita gently shoved me back against a bank of pillows leaned on my headboard. "Stop trying to be superwoman, and let your body heal."

"You shouldn't be missing work to play nursemaid to me." I crossed my arms and glared at her. The doctor had allowed me to go home after checking my vitals all day Sunday, so I'd slept in my own bed Sunday night, with Rita ensconced in my guest room in case I needed anything.

"It's Monday. Mondays are always slow. I took the day off." She calmly tucked the blankets in around my legs, speaking as if to a petulant child.

Okay, so maybe I *was* being a bit petulant, but Rita wouldn't let me get out of the bed to do anything but go to the bathroom. "It's my house, and I can do what I want." That definitely was childish, but I didn't care at this point.

"Of course you can." Rita smiled sweetly at me. "As soon as the doctor says you can."

I stuck my tongue out at her back as she left and snuggled down into the soft pillows. I wasn't allowed to read, look at my computer or phone, or watch TV for at least another twenty-four hours, because these activities might trigger headaches.

At least they'd let me shower once I was home. My clothes and my hair had reeked of smoke, and I'd refused to get into bed the previous evening until they let me scrub myself clean. Rita had positioned herself outside the bathroom just in case I fell, and she'd helped me to the bed when I exited, wrapped in a bathrobe, a towel around my hair.

Once I was dressed in a pair of fleece pants and a T-shirt, Rita had ushered me to bed, letting Keith kiss me goodbye before shooing him out the front door. This morning, I was under orders to have no electronics, no books or newspapers, not even a pencil and paper, and until he dropped by again, no Keith. That only left sleep, and to tell the truth, exhaustion still tugged at me. I closed my eyes, letting sleep have its way.

A soft tapping at my door jamb woke me.

"Jenna, are you awake?" Rita whispered as she tiptoed into the room and stood over me.

I didn't open my eyes. "I wasn't, but I am now."

"I'm so sorry. The police are here. Do you feel up to talking to them, or should I tell them you're asleep?"

I rolled over to look at her and shifted myself up to lean against the pillows. "I'll talk to them. I have all day to sleep."

Rita chuckled while she fluffed my pillows and adjusted my blankets. Maybe she had been a nurse in a past life. "Honey, you've been asleep for five hours. It's two thirty." She walked to the doorway and gestured to someone in the other room.

Tish Riddick appeared, stepping toward my bed. "Hi, how are you feeling?"

I raised my hand to my head. "Head still hurts some, but it's better."

"Thank goodness you're okay." She pulled out a little notebook, giving me flashbacks to Detective Sutter. "I don't know what we'd have done with Logan if you weren't." She grinned and sat on the chair Rita had pulled into the room.

Rita sat on the foot of my bed. "We all would have been devastated."

"I'd prefer not to talk about how everyone would feel if I had died." I shifted uncomfortably. "You had some questions for me?"

Rita jumped up to adjust my pillows again, misreading the reason for my discomfort.

"Can you tell me what happened Saturday night?" Tish crossed her legs and held the notebook poised in the air, pen at the ready.

"It's all pretty hazy. I remember bits and pieces, but not all of it." I closed my eyes and thought back. "I saw something, someone, in the back parking lot at the library. I tried to call Keith but couldn't get him. Rita was in the bathroom at the Piggly Wiggly."

"I am so sorry I wasn't there. I got caught by Mrs. Willis from church. Who knew she shopped in the middle of the night? Who does that? But she just had to tell me all about her cousin's daughter's wedding to the coroner's son. Right down to every detail, including the fact that they left for the honeymoon in a hearse. Not a good start, if you ask me." She settled onto the foot of my bed again.

Tish made a note in her booklet. "Go on, Jenna." She shot a pointed look at Rita.

"Since I couldn't reach Keith, I decided to find a spot in the parking lot where I could see the face of the person who came back out of the building."

Rita made a tsking sound and shook her head.

"Ms. Wallace, I am happy for you to remain while I talk to Jenna, but if you keep interrupting, I'll have to ask you to wait in the living room." Tish's firm tone left no room for argument.

"I'm sorry. Go ahead." Rita crossed her arms.

I wasn't fooled by Rita's acquiescence. I knew at some point she'd fume and fuss because I hadn't waited for her or Keith. Had it really been less than two days ago? I shook my head, instantly regretting it, as a dull ache settled behind my eyes. I took a few deep breaths, relaxing so the pressure would ease a bit.

Rita jumped to my side, placing the back of her hand against my forehead. "Are you okay? Is it too much? We can wait if you need to."

I opened my eyes and smiled at her. "I'm fine. Just a little headache. Really." I refocused on Tish and her questions as Rita settled at the foot of the bed again.

"If you were outside the building, how did you get locked inside?" Tish flipped to a new page.

Maybe she should get a bigger notebook, so she could write more on each page. Those little pages didn't hold enough information. Why did they always use such tiny ones? I reined in my wayward thought processes. "I couldn't find a place to hide, and the door was cracked open a bit, so I decided to peek in."

"And by peeking, you mean you decided to play hero and catch the person in the act?" Tish narrowed her eyes.

"Not on purpose." I sighed, knowing how my actions must look to the detective. "I didn't want all our hard work to be for nothing. The person had already killed Linus Talbot and poisoned my dog. I couldn't let them hurt anyone else. I had to find out who it was, so you guys could arrest them."

Tish propped her forearms on her crossed legs and leaned forward. "Jenna, that's our job. We're trained to catch bad guys. You're not."

I sighed. "I know. I know. But at least now you guys are taking the book thefts more seriously."

Tish leaned back and referred to her notebook. "Yes, I did go over the files you sent. I had already discussed it with Logan, and we'd agreed to look into it ourselves. He did convince me, however, that we could trust you to call us with anything you saw."

"Hey, ease up." Rita came to my defense. "She's already been through enough as a result of her leaping before she thought things through." She patted my feet under the blanket.

Maybe she wouldn't rake me over the coals as much as I feared. One could only hope.

Tish sighed. "You're right." She looked at her notebook, seeming to scan her notes. "Did you see who hit you and set fire to the building?"

"No." I closed my eyes again. "It's just a mishmash of images after I went in. The building was dark. I remember seeing a figure with a flashlight. There were locked doors. I remember lying on the floor and smelling gasoline and then smoke. At some point, I was looking for scissors and trying to cut through a rope. I'm sorry. I wish I could be more help."

Tish made a few more notes in her book. "It's okay. It'll likely come back to you as time passes. If you do remember something, let us know." She stood and turned to leave.

"Tish?" I called her back. "Thank you."

"For?" Tish cocked an eyebrow.

"For all of it." At her quizzical look, I elaborated. "For getting Detective Sutter to leave me alone. For helping Keith. For believing me."

Tish smiled and nodded once. "Any time." She strode from the room, and a moment later, I heard the front door open and close.

"That was interesting." Rita adjusted my blankets again.

I smiled, knowing she was fussing over me out of love, but there were only so many ways she could fix my blankets. "Rita, I'm fine."

Rita sat on the side of my bed and took my hand, clutching it tightly. "I know. Really, I do. But you almost weren't, and it would've been my fault." Tears glittered in her eyes.

I read the fear in her face, and my stomach clenched. I would've fared better if she'd given me the chewing out I deserved. But tears? "It wouldn't have been your fault. It would've been mine. I'm the idiot that charged in without backup."

"No, because your backup was busy hearing about some stranger's wedding, glad to have something to pass at least a tiny bit of the time, not thinking that anything might really happen that night." A single tear slid down her face. "I should've told Mrs. Willis I needed to go. I should've been there for you."

Although her hands enveloped mine, I squeezed back as best I could. "You're here for me now. That's what counts."

Rita sniffed loudly and reached for a tissue from the box on my nightstand, using it to dab at her eyes. "Yes, I am." She stood. "I'll bring you some lunch."

A lump caught in my throat at the realization that I meant as much to my friend as she did to me. "Thanks," I croaked out.

I slid down on the pillows when she left the room and pulled the blankets up. Before she made it back into the room, sleep claimed me once more.

My dreams became a jumble of fire, smoke, and fear. A figure loomed over me, and the smell of gasoline burned in my nose. A warm wet tongue licked the flames away. Wait . . . I struggled to open my eyes. Something thumped rhythmically against my thigh, jarring me out of my nightmare.

I raised my eyelids as Eddy licked my cheek again. I grinned and wrapped my arms around my dog, spying Keith behind him. "Hey, you brought him home."

"The vet said he was confident Eddy's going to be okay, so he said he could keep you company while you recuperated from . . . from . . ." Keith's voice caught, and he cleared his throat.

Rita strode through the door with a tray. "It's not lunchtime anymore, but here's some stew. Since it's now nine o'clock, we can call it a late supper."

I'd slept another seven hours, and I was still tired. Keith moved to my side and helped me sit up against the headboard, although he didn't fluff any pillows like Rita had done earlier. My stomach rumbled as Rita flipped the legs on the tray and set it across my lap before she shooed Eddy off the bed.

I picked up the spoon and scooped up some of the stew, raising the spoon toward my mouth. As I looked up, I froze, spoon halfway there. "Would one of you like to video me eating? That way you won't both have to stand there staring at me."

Rita chuckled. "Okay, okay." She shuffled out of the room, and I heard her clinking dishes in the kitchen, sounding like she was loading a few things into the dishwasher.

Keith sat in the chair Tish had occupied earlier, reaching down to scratch Eddy's ears while I ate.

"Tell me what you've found out." I spooned a bite into my mouth.

Keith shook his head. "Not much. As you know, it was definitely arson, you were intentionally locked in the building, and someone hit you over the head with a huge book."

"I didn't know about the book part. It's all sort of hazy." I grabbed a napkin and dabbed at a dribble that had slid down my chin. Eating soup while lounging in bed wasn't as easy as it looked.

Keith squinted his eyes and looked upward, as if visualizing something. "You were hit with *The Random House Dictionary of the English Language, Unabridged Edition*, copyright nineteen seventy-one. I think I got that right."

I laughed. "Leave it to me to get hit with an old book."

Keith smiled, but it didn't reach his eyes. "Yeah, leave it to you. Is your soup good?"

I'd almost finished the whole bowl. "I guess it was."

Rita swept in again, jacket on and purse over her shoulder. "Okay, Detective. I'm off. Take good care of our girl tonight."

"Wait, what?" I sat up straighter as Rita grabbed the tray off my lap.

"I'm sleeping in my own bed tonight, girlie." Rita nodded toward Keith. "He's taking tonight's shift to watch over you while you sleep. I'll check on you tomorrow."

Before I could stop her, she walked out of the room. I heard her set the tray on the counter and the front door open and close. Keith followed her, and I heard him turn the front door bolt. As his footsteps neared, lights disappeared from the main area in my apartment.

I stared at Keith as he entered the room, my eyes narrowed. "What's going on?"

He sat on the bed and pulled off his shoes and his jacket, arranging both on the chair in the room. Next, he pulled off his holster, laying his gun on the nightstand before turning off the lamp. "I'm getting ready for bed." He settled, fully dressed, on top of the covers next to me and opened his arms.

I slid into them and lay my head on his chest, listening to the steady thump thump of his heartbeat. "You don't have to stay here tonight. I'm fine. Really."

"Jenna, I almost lost you." His voice caught again, a slight tremble underscoring his emotions. "I think I'd prefer to keep you close for now." He dropped a kiss on my hair. "Now go to sleep."

I snuggled closer, finding a comfortable fit. A soft thud hit the bed as Eddy jumped up. He turned three times, settling against the small of my back.

My body relaxed, and I allowed sleep to tug me down into nothingness. For tonight, at least, I was the safest girl in town.

Chapter Twenty-Four

S un streamed into the bedroom, and I stretched, inhaling deeply. Coffee? The warm smell wafted in through my open bedroom door. The previous night seeped into my half-awake brain.

I slowly sat up. "Keith?"

Footsteps sounded, and Keith stepped into the doorway. "Good morning, sunshine. I have eggs ready to scramble and toast sitting in the toaster. Ready for some breakfast?"

How did I get so lucky? "Sure. Can I shower first, or am I still confined to bed?"

Keith grinned. "Nah, you're good. I'll make you take it easy, but I'm not quite the taskmaster that Rita is. Go ahead and grab a shower. Take your time. When I hear the water stop, I'll start the eggs and toast." He pulled my bedroom door shut as he left, his happy whistle echoing through the main area.

I shook my head, a silly smile on my face, and was pleasantly surprised my unthinking action didn't trigger another headache or wave of dizziness. I stood and walked to the bathroom, where I shimmied out of my fleece pants and T-shirt before stepping under a steaming spray of water.

Twenty minutes later, I emerged from the bedroom, clean, combed, teeth brushed, and dressed in old, soft jeans and another loose T-shirt. Barefoot, I padded across to the kitchen and sat on a stool, elbows propped on the bar-top counter, trying to contain a giggle.

Keith turned, my frilly pink apron wrapped around his waist, and set an empty mug on the counter in front of me before filling it with coffee. "I know you missed this yesterday."

I picked up the mug and inhaled the aroma. "Mmmm-mmm." I blew across the hot liquid and took a small sip, letting the strong flavor warm me from the inside. "I needed that."

"Wait 'til you get a load of this." Keith turned to the counter, turning back to me with two plates in his hands. "Your feast awaits." He placed a plate in front of me.

Three strips of bacon lay next to a small pile of fluffy scrambled eggs. Two slices of toast, cut diagonally, butter already swept across their surface, lay on the other half of the plate. A feast indeed.

I picked up my fork and took a bite of eggs. "These are perfect."

Keith swept the apron over his head and settled onto the stool next to me. "Mom taught me how to cook when I was in high school. She didn't want me to be one of those guys who couldn't feed himself or clean a house or wash his own laundry."

"She did a great job." I crunched on a piece of crispy bacon.

Keith laughed. "I'm glad you like it."

I glanced at the clock. "Shouldn't you be on your way to work by now?"

Keith swallowed a bite of eggs. "I'm going in a little late. Tish knows. If you're feeling better, you can hang by yourself for a while. Rita will be over this afternoon to check on you. Otherwise, I can take a day of personal leave."

"Nope, I actually feel great this morning. All the sleep yesterday helped immensely." I crunched another slice of bacon. "And today I can watch TV, so I'll have plenty to keep me company. Besides, Eddy is here." I dropped a tiny piece of bacon on the floor, and Eddy gobbled it up.

As we finished our breakfast, Keith stood and picked up our plates. I watched him as he cleaned up the kitchen, knowing he would argue with me if I said I could do it later. When done, he settled me in the living room with the remote. He knelt in front of me. "Honey, are you sure you're okay?"

I nodded. "I promise. I would tell you if I wasn't. I'm not looking for a trip back to the hospital."

Keith kissed me softly, lingering for a moment, before standing and going to the bedroom, returning wearing his shoulder holster, his jacket over his arm. "I'm heading out. If you need me for *anything*, call. I'll come." He hesitated. "I promise I won't let you down again."

I stood and followed him to the door, wrapping my arms around his shoulders and gazing into his eyes. "What happened is not your fault. It's mine. I did something stupid, and it blew up in my face. Stop beating yourself up about it."

He kissed me again, deeper this time, before stepping away. "I'll call you in a couple of hours to check on you, okay?"

"I'll be here." I smiled and stepped back, watching as he strode down the walkway to the stairs.

Alone at last, I walked through my apartment to the couch, where I sat and watched a *Murder, She Wrote* rerun. There was no way I could do this all day, though. I'd been bed-bound for two days, and today I was full of energy.

I clicked off the TV and stood, and Eddy was instantly at my feet, glancing back and forth between me and the front door. I got the message and strode to the door, where I put on a jacket from the hook, zipping it up over my old T-shirt, and snagged Eddy's leash. However, rather than go out the front door, I figured it was a better idea to go out through the store, where I could tell Mason what I was doing.

Easing down the spiral staircase, I stepped on each tread carefully, making sure the twists and angles didn't bring on another bout of dizziness. Nope, all good. As I neared the bottom, Mason caught sight of me and rushed toward me.

"Jenna, you're okay!" He threw his arms around me in a bear hug before jumping back, a worried look on his face. "I didn't hurt you, did I?"

"I'm fine." I stepped off onto the floor. "I just felt like getting out of the apartment for a while. Besides, Eddy needs a walk." I pointed at Eddy, standing patiently by the front door.

"Cool. Okay." Mason stepped aside. "Just don't be gone long. Keith would kill me if I let anything happen to you."

I smiled and patted him on the shoulder. "Mason, I won't break. I'm only going for a walk with my dog."

Mason followed me to the door and stared after me as I left. Twice I looked back, and he remained hovering in the doorway, watching my progress. I shook my head and stepped off into a grassy area at one end of the historic district, giving Eddy a place to take care of his morning business.

Eddy took his time, and I enjoyed the fresh air and sunshine, trying not to let my mind go too far into greeting-card territory. Every day is a gift. Life shares sweet promise with those who open their eyes. The sun is shining, the birds are singing, and it's a beautiful day to be alive. At this rate, I'd be ready to work for Hallmark.

Done with sniffing, exploring, and marking his territory, as he did every morning, Eddy tugged toward the store. The wind had picked up, and while I wore a warm jacket, Eddy did not.

We entered the store, and I walked behind the counter to sit, draping my jacket over the other stool.

Door chimes rang, and Rita rushed in, take-out bags over her arm. "Hey, girlie. I figured you'd be upstairs."

Mason approached, rubbing his hands together. "What did you bring?" He sniffed the air.

Rita plopped a bag onto the counter. "Yours is in there. It's chicken fried rice and steamed dumplings from the Chinese place near the inn."

Mason sat on my jacket, jumping back up when I tugged at it. "Sorry." He reached for the bag. "I'm starving. I didn't have time for breakfast."

Rita shook her head. "You're always starving. It's the natural state for a young man of your age." She waggled her fingers at me. "Let's take ours upstairs."

I followed her up the staircase, Eddy at my heels.

Rita spread out a series of square boxes on the counter. "Dumplings for us, lo mien, fried rice, and moo shu." She reached one last time into the bag and brought out a tall plastic container. "And let's not forget the egg drop soup."

Mouth watering, I grabbed bowls and plates, along with silverware and napkins, and slid them across toward the food. "I am perfectly able to prepare lunch for myself, but I can't say I'm disappointed you brought over Chinese."

Rita scooped a helping of lo mien onto her plate and sat. "I figured you might want the company, stuck in the apartment all day. Little did I know you'd make a break for it the moment our backs were turned."

"I went to walk the dog." I slid onto the stool next to her and reached for the moo shu pancakes. "Eddy's bladder waits for no man."

"Fair enough." Rita nodded. "How has the rest of your morning been?"

I slathered brown sauce on the pancake and filled it with the moo shu mix before rolling it. "Boring. I'm not used to just sitting around by myself anymore."

"I know." Rita twirled noodles onto her fork. "But it won't be forever. Just until we're sure your head is okay."

"Either way, I don't want to harp on what happened. Tell me what's going on at the inn. Distract me." I took a large bite of the rolled moo shu.

"Not much, now that we're done cleaning up the mess from Selina's event." Rita ladled soup into a bowl. "It took the staff two days to fix everything."

"Fix?" I wiped my fingers on a paper towel. "She broke stuff?"

"Oh, honey, you have no idea." Rita stood and walked into the kitchen, opening a cabinet door and retrieving two glasses. "She got drunk and pitched herself a hissy."

"Do tell." This was a lot more fun than thinking about the meaning of life, à la greeting-card style.

"It seems Douglas went behind her back and told the staff and the caterers to use less expensive items where possible." Rita

250

returned to her seat with glasses of sweet tea, sliding one toward me.

"Thanks." I took a sip and set the glass down. "I take it she discovered it?"

"She did." Rita twirled more noodles. "And she was not happy. As I said, she'd had too much to drink at the open bar, and she dropped a glass. Rather than shatter, it merely cracked and a few pieces broke off. She'd been too preoccupied to realize it wasn't the crystal she'd asked for but rather a cheap, heavy glass that wouldn't shatter into a million pieces if dropped."

"Oh, man, I wish I'd seen that." I took another bite of my moo shu.

Rita grinned and reached for her back pocket. "But you can." She pulled out her phone. "One of the servers started videoing after Selina had picked up two more glasses and threw them to the ground, trying to make them shatter like crystal. It's on YouTube now." She tapped her screen a few times and passed me her phone.

I propped the phone up on her PopSocket and hit "Play." Selina March filled the screen, screeching at the top of her lungs.

"Where the hell is my crystal? I asked for crystal, and this crap isn't it!" Selina staggered, falling into the bar but failing to catch herself before she ungracefully plopped to the floor.

Two male bartenders ran to her aid, each taking one of Selina's arms to help lift her to her feet.

"Get your lying hands off me!" Selina smacked at the two men. "Don't touch me!" She rolled to her knees and inched up onto her feet, her hands still splayed on the ground and her backside pointed directly at the rest of the room and the camera. Her bejeweled hands groped for the bar top, and she tugged herself upright, catching one of her stiletto heels in the hem of her dress, which seemed to be made of some delicate, bright red, frothy material. A loud rip sounded as the sharp heel tore a gaping hole down half of the skirt in the back.

Douglas crossed the room at a jog, shoving his way through the ring of onlookers.

Selina turned and caught sight of him, pointed, and let a bloodcurdling scream fly. "You! You did this! You ruined everything!" She picked up another guest's half-empty drink and threw it at him.

Douglas sidestepped the flying glassware, and it splattered against another partygoer's tuxedo, red wine soaking into his white shirt like a blood stain.

"Selina, stop it." Douglas continued his path toward his wife.

Selina did not stop. She stepped to another table, the crowd parting, and grabbed handfuls of food, turning to throw this at her approaching husband. "You made me get cheap food"—several slightly mashed petit fours sailed in his direction, falling short—"so we could keep costs down"—two handfuls of what seemed to be stuffed mushrooms came next, their stuffing scattering as they hit the ground in front of Douglas—"but it looks like a tacky potluck"—iced crab legs sailed next, two of them hitting Douglas in the chest—"instead of an elegant ball!"

Douglas reached her and caught her wrists before she could throw the handfuls of what looked like oysters on the half shell. "Enough, Selina!" The rage fled from his face as she crumpled in a frothy, red pile, sobbing. He slid to the floor with her in his arms, rocking her back and forth.

"I hate you." Selina weakly pounded on his chest and hiccupped. "You made me be poor. I hate being poor. I should have been rich. Richer than the whole town. And Linus Talbot screwed it up. And now he's dead. It serves him right. But I got stuck with you instead, and you screwed it up too."

Douglas continued to rock her. "I know. I'm sorry. I love you." He stroked her back and kissed her hair.

"I hate you," Selina repeated, sobbing to punctuate it. "But I'll show you. I have ways to get money. I don't need you."

She struggled to stand, and Douglas helped her to her feet. The crowd was silent, although a few people were whispering to friends behind their hands.

"I think the party is over." Douglas scooped his wife up in his arms like a hero of old.

Selina promptly puked all over his shirt and her lap, but Douglas never broke stride as he carried the woman he loved—although I couldn't figure out why—from the room.

Stunned, I looked up at Rita. "Wow. Just wow."

Rita reached for her phone and stuck it into her back pocket. "I know. It almost makes you feel sorry for her."

I wasn't so sure about that, but I didn't argue. "I don't get it. She thinks she's poor?"

Rita shrugged and took her plate to the sink, having finished her lunch while I watched Selina's meltdown. "Rich, poor. For some folks those terms don't mean the same things as they do for everyone else."

I took a bite, chewed, and swallowed. "I tell you what, though. I've never been to a potluck with a chocolate fountain, free-flowing drinks, Champagne, snow crab legs, and oysters on the half shell."

Rita chuckled as she closed the food containers. "I guess you haven't lived, then."

"Oh, and you have?" I cocked my head at her.

"Nope, and I doubt I will." She put the food in the fridge. "I prefer potlucks with casseroles and dips and messy ribs."

"I doubt the caterer is thrilled having their food compared to a tacky potluck and thrown on the floor in a tirade for the world to see." I popped the last bite into my mouth and stood.

"Who knows?" Rita grabbed her purse. "She wouldn't let anyone know who they were. Probably not fancy enough for her."

I followed her to the door. "I'd bet they're glad now."

"Probably." Rita gave me a quick hug. "Take it easy this afternoon, okay? I'll check back in tonight."

I promised her I would and shooed her out the door, Selina's tirade still in my mind. More specifically, her last words before she was carried out. How had she phrased it? Something about not needing Douglas and having ways to get money without him. I thought of the book thief. Could the person I'd seen destroying the library be Selina March? Had she been the one who tried to kill me?

Chapter
Twenty-Five

The rest of the afternoon passed in semi-boredom. I'd napped, binged on more *Murder, She Wrote*—there was a marathon on TV—and had walked Eddy a couple more times. Both Keith and Rita had stopped by, but I'd refused to let either of them disrupt their schedules to spend the night with me again.

When Wednesday morning's sun sent fingers of light through my window, I awoke feeling refreshed and ready for a real day, not a day of being treated like I was breakable. Enough was enough. After walking Eddy and grabbing a bite of breakfast, the two of us went down to the store.

"Are you sure you're supposed to be back at work yet?" Mason poured a mug of coffee and handed it to me.

"It's been three and a half days." I accepted the mug and inhaled the aroma. "The doctor even said I could drive by today, so I figure I'm good to go."

Mason's expression said he didn't believe me. "I guess it's okay as long as you don't strain yourself."

The door chimes tinkled, and Mason moved off to greet a customer. Eddy and I went to the back room, where I poured

255

over the last few days' receipts. Mason had done well in my absence. He definitely deserved that raise I'd given him.

At lunchtime, Eddy and I went upstairs, and I rummaged in the fridge for leftover Chinese food.

Eddy whined softly at my side.

"Sorry, buddy. I don't think you can eat this stuff." I reached for a package of cheddar cheese slices. "But maybe you can have a bite or two of this."

Or could he? I wasn't sure if he was supposed to be on a limited diet after his recent poisoning, so I grabbed my phone and called the vet's office, waiting patiently until he came on the line.

"He can have a few treats, but you know table food isn't the healthiest food for him anyway." The vet's firm tone sounded through the phone.

"I know, but it's just a tiny bit here and there." I reached down to scratch Eddy behind the ears. "I'd definitely never feed him raw ground beef. He probably wouldn't eat it anyway after getting so sick when he ate it last week."

"Jenna, I never said he had ground beef. I said *a* hamburger." I heard pages rustling. "As in a cooked hamburger, with onions, spices, cheese, a little bit of mushroom."

"Someone slipped him a whole hamburger with mothball flakes inside?" How had I missed that? I think I'd have noticed Eddy gobbling down a Big Mac.

"How he ingested it, I cannot say. I can only say what he threw up." More papers rustling. "I'd like to see him in another week to run one more blood panel for liver numbers, if you don't mind. But the likelihood is that he's just fine."

I thanked him and hung up, my mind stuck on the fact that I'd missed my dog eating a hamburger. Something niggled at the back of my mind, but I couldn't put my finger on it. Maybe my memory wasn't quite as up to snuff as I'd hoped after the whack on the head.

Refusing to spend the afternoon racking my brain, I returned to the store for the last few work hours of the day. Eddy greeted customers, play-bowed and ran down the aisle with two young children, and napped in the sunshine pouring in through the glass front door. All in all, a good day.

After we closed, I returned to my apartment, looking forward to another episode or two of *Murder, She Wrote*. I was getting hooked on that show. A firm knock propelled me off the couch and to my front door.

Keith stepped inside, to-go bags in his hands. "I brought dinner so you wouldn't have to cook." He leaned in to kiss me.

I pulled one of the bags from his hand and opened it on the way to the kitchen, peeking in at the contents. "What did you bring?"

"Hmm, let's see . . . slug soup, dirt balls, and last week's boiled cabbage." His expression remained deadpan.

I moaned and rubbed my stomach. "Sounds delicious. I can't wait."

"I stopped across the street and picked up a few things." He opened a couple of Styrofoam clamshell containers.

Heavenly smells of hot wings, beer-battered onion rings, cheese sticks, and stuffed mushrooms filled the air. I placed the items on the counter, inhaling deeply as I lifted each dish from the bag.

Keith grabbed plates from the kitchen, handing one to me across the counter. "I thought finger foods would be fun tonight."

"It's perfect." I popped a stuffed mushroom into my mouth, savoring the mix of flavors. I froze. Hamburger. Onions. Spices. Cheese. Mushroom. Wasn't that what had been used to mask the flavors of the mothball flakes? I grabbed a mushroom and squished it on my plate, peeling through it with my fingers.

"Honey, what are you doing?" Keith handed me a napkin. "Is there something wrong with the mushrooms?"

"This . . . this is what poisoned Eddy." I gestured at the demolished mushroom on my plate. "Where did you get these?"

"The Weeping Willow." He stepped to my side, prodding at the mess with a finger. "Are you sure?"

I nodded, reaching for my phone. "I need to talk to them." I searched for The Weeping Willow and pressed the phone icon on their web page to call them.

"Thanks for calling The Weeping Willow. This is Lily."

"Hi, I live across the street, and I'm thinking about hosting a get-together. Do you guys cater? And if so, do you offer stuffed mushrooms on the catering menu? I love those things." I waved a dismissive hand at Keith's odd look.

Lily's perky voice sounded through the line again. "I know we do catering, but the owner handles that side of things. I'd be happy to pass your information along to her when she's in tomorrow."

Frustrated, I plopped onto a stool. "What time will she be in?"

"Sometime after ten. Would you like to leave a message?" Paper rustled in the background.

"No, thank you. I'll try to call back in the morning." I touched the end icon on my screen after we said our polite good-byes and dropped the phone to the bar top.

"What was that about?" Keith slid an empty plate in front of me.

I reached for the closest to-go box and opened it. Mushrooms. I pushed them away. "I talked to the vet today. He said Eddy was poisoned with a mix of cooked hamburger, spices, onion, mushroom, and cheese mixed together with the mothballs."

Keith nodded. "I gathered that much from the mushroom destruction earlier."

"I also talked to Rita today. She had a video of Selina having a complete meltdown at her event on Friday night. During her tirade, she threw stuffed mushrooms, among other things, at her husband." I picked up my phone and showed Keith the YouTube video.

"You weren't kidding about a meltdown." Keith handed my phone back after he'd finished. "You're thinking because Selina is a suspect and she had mushrooms at her event, maybe she poisoned him?"

I nodded. "Am I stretching it a bit too far?"

Keith's brow furrowed. "I don't know. Maybe. Eddy was poisoned two days before her event, so it's not like she scooped up some of the leftovers to take home for her mad-scientist plan."

"I know." I sighed. "But I feel like there's some connection there. Maybe I'm wrong. Maybe I'm just desperate to find out who did this, so it'll all be over." I stared down into my empty plate. "How do you do it?"

"What?" He crunched an onion ring.

"Come so close to getting the information you need, only to have to wait longer or not get the information at all." I reached for the container of hot wings and slid three onto my plate.

Keith shrugged. "Welcome to the life of a detective, sweetheart."

"Doesn't it bother you?" I snagged a cheese stick and dipped it into the sauce Keith had opened while I was on the phone.

"Every day. But it's part of the job." Keith bit into a hot wing, sauce staining his fingers.

I shook my head. "I don't know if I could do it. I'm not that patient."

Keith's gaze met mine, and a slow smile spread across his face. "Sometimes being patient brings the most amazing results." He winked at me.

My stomach flip-flopped, and I almost choked on the bite of cheese stick I was swallowing. Lord, this man would be the death of me. I could see the headlines now. *The Bookstore of Death Claims Another Life: Owner Chokes on Cheese Stick.*

Eddy whistled softly at my feet, and I glanced down to see his gaze glued to the cheese stick I still held in my hand. Tension broken, I laughed and broke off a piece for my furry roommate, dropping it to the floor for him to gobble.

Okay, so I shouldn't encourage him to beg at the table. But after all he'd been through, I figured that training could wait a few more days. I shoved aside thoughts of murder and poisons, refusing to allow them to mar an evening with my two favorite guys.

Chapter Twenty-Six

I sat at a bar-height table at The Weeping Willow, waiting for the owner to appear. I'd arrived early, but it seemed she was late, due to a traffic accident delay on her way to work. By ten fifteen, I had ordered a sweet tea, so the staff would quit eyeing me oddly. At ten thirty, it was still too early for lunch, and I'd eaten a healthy breakfast consisting of a pop tart and a glass of chocolate milk—okay, I'd channeled my inner six-year-old that morning—so I sat nursing my sweet tea, hoping it didn't add too much to my ongoing sugar high.

At 10:43, the door swung open, and by the reactions of the staff, who all became very industrious, I guessed the woman entering must be the owner. One of the servers caught her and whispered to her, pointing in my direction. The woman glanced at me, nodded and waved, and walked into the back room.

A few minutes later, she greeted me at my table, sans coat and purse. "Hi, I'm Willow Gaddon. Lily says you're looking for a caterer?" She laid a thin, bound book of some sort on the table and slid onto an open stool, an expectant look on her face.

I winced, hating that I'd misled the woman before I'd even met her. But I was worried that if I told her I was trying to find out if someone had come in and had used her food to poison my dog, she might clam up and refuse to talk to me. I shoved Mom's voice aside and kept up the pretense.

"Yes, I'm considering a party, but I'm really not sure yet. I may not have it." There, I'd at least left it open that this might not turn into a job for her. "I live nearby, and I thought I'd find out if you catered."

"Aren't you the lady with the bookstore across the street?" Willow gestured in my store's direction.

Crap. She knew who I was. But then, what had I expected? "Yes, I am."

She turned and eyed my store suspiciously. "Oh, okay."

Was she kidding me? Did she think if she catered, someone would get murdered during her event? I took a deep breath. *Let it go, Jenna.* I smiled.

With less enthusiasm than she'd had when she got to the table, Willow slid the book across the table to me. "Here's my catering menu. Let's see if there's anything that piques your interest."

I opened the book to find a catering menu printed, a picture of each item as it would be displayed on the serving dish next to each description. After looking through the pictures, I noted there were lists of suggested items that went well together, or I could select items à la carte.

"There are a lot of selections." I flipped back to the beginning and slid my fingers through the pages of offered dishes, locating each of the things Selina had thrown at her husband.

"I try to ensure each client has the catered event she wants, rather than limiting the menu to what I like." Willow smiled, although it didn't reach her eyes.

I widened my eyes and raised my eyebrows, hoping I wasn't laying it on too thickly. "I see several things Selina March had at her event. The food was amazing. Were you the caterer? She wouldn't tell us who did it. She said it was her little secret."

Willow nodded, and this time her smile was genuine. "Yes, I catered for her."

"Wow." I slid my gaze over her menu again. "She has the best taste. She must eat here often." I glanced up.

"No, not really." Willow shook her head. "They called three days before the event. Seems there was a problem with her caterer."

Problem with their caterer? More likely that Douglas demanded she spend less money. "And you put it together that fast?" I widened my eyes again in mock amazement.

Willow leaned back and crossed her legs. "Normally, I expect more time, but when Selina March calls . . . let's just say she can make or break a business with her reviews of service. So I made it happen. They dropped by the next afternoon to taste samples, and I delivered on time."

I had no doubt Selina's acid tongue could destroy a business with the local women. If Selina really was the queen of local high society, others would follow her lead, even if they disagreed with her. It was like grown-up mean girls.

"You sure couldn't tell it was a rush job." I slid the book back across the table. "Everything was delicious. I'll definitely consider you if I host that party."

The wary look returned to Willow's face as she stood. "I appreciate that. Thank you for inquiring."

My stomach sank when she cast another sidelong glance at my store before hurrying to the back room. I had to get this murder solved, and fast, before I ended up as the town's little shop of horrors.

I grabbed my purse and stepped outside. When I walked across the street and into the bookstore, Eddy greeted me at the door.

"Hey, sweet boy." I scratched his back and grinned at his bicycling leg. "Have you been good?"

"He licked Mr. Hickle's granddaughter's lollypop. Then he stuck his nose in Mrs. Hickle's purse and snagged one of his own." Mason stepped from behind the counter, drawing my attention. "Not his best day as a salesman. We had to chase him through the store so he didn't eat the thing, paper, stick, and all."

I looked back at Eddy. "Really?" I cocked my head at him.

At my scolding tone, he sat and wagged his tail, head bowed a little.

Unable to even pretend to be mad at him, I pulled his leash from under the counter and snapped it onto his collar. "Maybe a walk will settle you down a bit."

Eddy bounced to the door, and we set out. Twenty minutes later, Eddy was calmer, and my stomach was telling me it was now late enough to be lunchtime. I left Eddy with Mason and headed to the parking lot, dialing my phone as I went.

Selina March's voice trilled a happy answer. "Hello?"

"Hi, Selina. It's Jenna Quinn from Twice Upon a Time. How are you today?" I put her on speaker as I got into the car and laid the phone in my lap.

"Oh, it's you." The disdain dripped from the phone line. "What do you want?"

I buckled my seat belt and started the car. "I'm on my way to the inn to have lunch, and I thought you might want to join me. My treat."

"Lunch." Selina paused briefly. "With you. Why?"

Okay, so this might be a bit harder than I had considered. "I thought maybe we could start over. I know you're very important to the women of the town . . ." Where was I going with this? *Think, think, think.* "And I'd love it if you'd help me start a women's tea and book group at the store. I think the other women would love to know what you enjoy reading." I rolled my eyes, knowing I'd likely come up with the lamest possible idea to get Selina's attention.

"And by tea, you mean . . ." Selina's voice trailed off suggestively.

"Um, wine?" I hated the pleading tone in my voice.

"Hmm. I'll consider it."

"And lunch today to discuss it?" I eased into the Hokes Bluff Inn's parking lot and slid into a space.

"If you're buying, that would be fine." The haughty tone had returned to her voice. "I'll be there in half an hour."

Relief surged through me as I ended the call. I left my car and took the two-mile carriage ride to the hotel. On the way, I called Rita to let her know I was there for a visit, and she met me in the lobby.

"Why on earth are you having lunch with Selina March?" Rita pulled me into a hug.

"I think Douglas poisoned Eddy." I stepped back, not wanting to wrinkle her soft coral day dress which made my jeans and light sweater seem boring in comparison.

"Wait, you're having lunch . . . *food* . . . with a woman whose husband you think poisoned your dog . . . with food." Rita looked at me like I'd lost my mind.

I nodded and moved to one of the settees in the lobby. "I talked to the vet. He said Eddy was poisoned with a mix of cooked hamburger, onions, spices, cheese, and mushroom."

"Oookay." Rita dragged the word out slowly as she sank to the settee beside me. "And?"

"They had The Weeping Willow cater her party." At Rita's blank look, I continued. "The stuffed mushrooms. The ones she threw at Douglas."

"I'm still not seeing how Selina throwing mushrooms at Douglas two days after Eddy was poisoned equals Douglas poisoning your dog or killing Linus, since we're pretty sure the two are linked." Rita crossed her ankles and placed her hands in her lap, the picture of an early twentieth-century woman.

"They went to The Weeping Willow to taste the mushrooms the day Eddy was poisoned." I leaned forward. "I think Douglas had mothballs with him, because he knew Eddy could identify him, and he grabbed a few mushrooms during their tasting."

"I don't know." Rita cocked her head. "You think he could've done it under Selina's hawk-like gaze? She watches his every move."

"Maybe she went to the bathroom and he stuck them in his pocket." I stood and paced in front of the settee. "He did come into the store later and would have had time to give them to Eddy. It all adds up."

"Could be." Rita caught my arm. "Sit down. Guests are staring."

I plopped onto the settee. "He had access to the books, and with the way Selina goes through money, he'd definitely need it. I'll bet Linus talked to him about the missing books too."

Rita shifted her skirt out from under where I'd unceremoniously dropped myself next to her. "If you're so convinced it's her husband, are you sure you want to confront her with it? Why not go to Keith?"

"Not until I have something more to go on than a hunch." I stood, pulling Rita up with me, and walked toward the front porch, where it wouldn't seem so odd if I paced. "Keith is already under scrutiny for how things were handled with Detective Sutter. I can't drag him into this on random hunches."

"Do you want me to eat with you so you have a buffer of some sort?" Rita sat in a rocker, watching me pace.

"No." I turned and walked back past Rita. "I'll handle it. I don't want her to think it's a setup."

"Okay." Rita stood. "Then I'd better scoot before she arrives. Let me know when you're done."

After promising her, I continued to pace, mentally going over my approach, hoping Selina didn't see through my amateurish attempts to interrogate her. Intent on my thoughts, I jumped when Selina spoke behind me. I whirled. "Selina, how nice to see you."

"I'm here. Let's get this over with." She brushed past me into the lobby.

Well, we were off to a great start. "Let's go get a table."

We entered the dining hall, a massive room with two huge fireplaces, one at each end. Originally housing an incredibly long dining table, the room now held a series of small tables, with more on the porch outside several sets of double doors, which stood open to the balmy autumn temperatures.

The server led us to a table outside.

"Absolutely not." Selina turned and walked back inside. "I have no desire to fight bugs off my food."

Next, the server tried a table beside a tall bank of windows, sunlight streaming in to brighten the setting.

"And have the sun wrinkle my skin? Are you kidding?"

The table in the corner across the room from the windows drew more censure.

"Now you're putting us near the kitchen entrance. What kind of place is this?"

Elliot strode across the room, hands outstretched toward Selina's. "Mrs. March. How delightful to see you."

She took his offered hands, and they leaned in to air-kiss each other.

"What brings you here today?" He smiled at me and turned back to Selina. "Planning another party, are we?"

Selina tilted her head and offered Elliot a pout. "We are trying to find an appropriate table to eat lunch, but your staff cannot manage to find us a decent spot to eat."

Hot pickles on a crouton, was this woman in high school? From mean-girl persona to pouty flirty girl in the blink of an eye. I couldn't keep up with her.

Elliot tucked her hand into the crook of his arm. "I have just the spot. It's my personal table, the best one in the room."

A guffaw rose up from my chest, drawing a raised eyebrow from Elliot. I ducked my head and coughed several times, hoping it covered the laugh, and meekly followed Elliot and Selina to a table in a semiprivate nook, a shaded window overlooking a garden area. It was beautiful, and I knew this was not Elliot's private table. However, there was no need for Selina to know this.

She purred and preened as he settled her into a chair.

"I'm sure you'll be quite happy here. Not too much sun, and the view is quite soothing." He gestured to the server, who had hovered nearby. "Nadia will be happy to ensure your service is on the same level I would receive."

Selina missed the wink he offered to Nadia as he turned to leave the dining hall. Man, he was good.

We ordered drinks, which Nadia brought immediately.

Selina sipped her cocktail. "So, what's this book club thing? And do we have to actually read books?"

"Well, yes, that's sort of what a book club is for." What did she think a book club would do?

"I don't read." She waved a dismissive hand in the air. "I find it tedious. I'd rather wait for it to be made into a movie instead."

I nodded with what I hoped was a considering look. "That could be interesting." No way in the world would I host a movie club in the store.

"And tea?" Selina took another long draught of her cocktail. "No. Just no. Maybe martinis." She giggled at her own joke. "See what I did there? Mar-TEA-ni?" She emphasized the middle syllable.

Was this woman serious? I watched as she downed the last of her cocktail and motioned at Nadia with her glass. Had she even tasted it?

Nadia appeared at the table with a smile and another cocktail. "Are you ready to order yet?"

I grabbed a menu and quickly scanned it, choosing a salad with grilled chicken, feta cheese, apple pieces, and walnuts, and encouraged Selina to choose the same. If I didn't rush her through this meal, I'd be broke from the amount of alcohol she was downing. On the other hand, it might make her easier to question.

"Selina, I hear you had The Weeping Willow cater your event here last week." I sipped my sweet tea to offset the nervous dry mouth I'd developed.

She nodded and chugged more of her drink. "I did. Although I wanted to have Delilah's cater instead. They're in Raleigh. Their food is divine and all the rage."

Was she kidding? "Isn't a four-hour drive one way a bit long for a caterer to come?"

"Now you sound like Douglas." She put on a mocking expression. "It's too expensive. We can't afford it. You'll have to make do."

I wasn't going to get a better opening than that. I leaned in, patting her forearm. "I'm so sorry you have to live like that. It's not fair."

Selina swigged her drink again. "No, it's not. It's never fair. But he doesn't even care that I had to buy a car that was last year's model. I don't care that it was new. They'd swapped to the new model, and I should've gotten one."

I shook my head and tsked. "I can only imagine. I'll bet he even makes you store your furs with mothballs."

Tears filled Selina's eyes. "How did you know? I took it to the cleaner, and they said they'd gotten the smell out."

Bingo! "You poor thing. I'm so sorry. It must be awful."

"It is!" Her wail drew stares, and she downed the last of her second drink before dabbing at her eyes with a napkin.

"You're so strong to persevere, though." I patted her arm again. "I'm sure you're an inspiration to others." Gads, could I lay it on any thicker?

Selina dropped her crumpled napkin at the edge of the table for Nadia to take away when she brought our food. "I'm sure I am."

It was all I could do not to roll my eyes at the long-suffering look, and I was grateful when the salads arrived. "Look how beautiful the salads are. I'm sure they made them extra special since we're at Elliot's table."

Selina sniffed and looked at Nadia. "I'll take mine to go, and I'll take another one of these." She held up her empty glass.

By the time Nadia returned with Selina's third drink in less than half an hour, I was halfway through my salad, gobbling as fast as I could. No way was I giving her time for a fourth. I hoped I didn't have indigestion later.

I took my last bite as Selina chugged the last of her drink. "Look, we finished together. I'll get the check." I waved frantically to Nadia, shaking my head when she made a tilting glass motion with her hand.

Nadia brought the check, and I left enough cash to cover the tab, plus a healthy tip.

I stood and moved to Selina's side of the table, leaning down to thread my elbow through hers in a best girlfriends gesture. "This was fun. We'll have to plan this again soon." I smiled as I helped her to her feet.

Selina swayed a bit, straightened, picked up her purse, and walked with me to the door, surprisingly steady on her feet. "I'll think about it."

There was the snooty Selina I'd come to know and love. I held the dining hall door open for her. "I'd be happy to drive you home." I figured I'd be safe enough since Douglas would likely be at work. Plus, it would give me a chance to poke around and find the mothballs, so the vet could compare them to what Eddy had thrown up.

Selina shook her head and stumbled, recovering quickly. "No, thank you. Douglas is coming to pick me up. He should be here"— she flipped her wrist and looked at her watch—"right about now."

Crap. I didn't want to see Douglas. "That's great. Let's get you a carriage. I need to run to the ladies' room before I go, but we don't want to keep him waiting. No telling what he'll keep you from buying if he's upset."

"Good point." She nodded once and strode toward the front door, her gait steady.

I guessed she had experience at drunk walking, but I did thread my arm through hers again as we descended the stairs from the porch. No need to tempt fate.

Selina swayed a bit as the carriage driver and I helped her inside, and I quietly tipped him, mouthing a silent apology before he pulled away.

I sucked in a breath and released it. This had better pay off. I waited a couple of minutes, giving Selina time to get to the parking lot and leave with Douglas. Satisfied enough time had passed, I got into the next available carriage, calling Rita on the way down the lane.

"Yes, she's gone." I answered her immediate question.

"Did she say anything incriminating or just drink herself under the table?" Her voice came out punctuated with a half chuckle.

"You heard?" I propped my arm on the side of the carriage and rested my forehead in my palm.

"Oh, honey, everyone heard. It's all anyone is talking about. After what happened here last weekend, it's no wonder."

"At least I did get some information. Douglas makes her store her furs at home with mothballs." The carriage rolled to a stop and I stepped out.

"I've heard that can be really hard to get out of a fur. Not that I've ever had one." Rita snorted.

I walked toward my car, scanning the lot for Douglas and Selina, catching sight of her fancy car pulling out onto the street. "Neither have I. But whether it's good for a fur or not, the point is that Douglas had access to mothballs."

"True. What's your next step? Tell me you're not going to break into their house or something."

I could hear the concern in Rita's voice, and I rushed to allay her fears. "Nope. But I will tell Keith about it tonight, now that it's not just a hunch anymore."

"Okay, girlie. Just be careful. I need to get back to work."

We said our goodbyes, and I stuck my phone in my back pocket before digging in my purse for my keys. They always seemed to fall to the bottom of my purse.

A soft scratching sound from behind me caught my attention. As I turned to locate the source, a hard object pounded into my head, and the world faded to black.

Chapter Twenty-Seven

I sat on the beach, watching the surf rhythmically roll in and out, in and out. The waves grew taller, and the sound increased, until it was a deafening roar. I tried to raise my hands to cover my ears, but I couldn't move them. The ocean faded to nothingness, but the roaring continued, and my head began to pound with the same rhythm. Something cold lay across my face. The cold felt good. It helped the pain in my head. What was cold and hard like that? Wait, it wasn't against my face. My face was against it. The floor.

I cracked my eyes open, and images swam into view. A tile floor. Cabinets. A stove. A kitchen? I was in someone's kitchen? My arms ached, and I tried to move them. I shifted my feet. I wasn't paralyzed. I wiggled my fingers and tried to bend my wrists. Something held them together. I was tied up. Why was I here?

Rita. I'd been on the phone. Something had hit me. Hard. That wouldn't be good for my concussion. Rita would fuss at me.

The fog began to recede, and voices rose above the roar in my head. I struggled to make out what was said.

"Are you kidding me? You brought her here?" Douglas March strode into the room.

I knew it! Everything had pointed to him. I'd tell Keith tonight at dinner. Maybe I could look around for mothballs before I went home. Mothballs. What a fun word. A giggle escaped my lips.

"She's waking up." Douglas leaned in and looked at me. "Now what do you want to do with her?"

"Douglas, she has to die." A woman's voice came from around the corner. Selina was in on it too? And I'd just bought her lunch! How ungrateful could you get? I would never offer to take her to lunch again.

"What are you talking about?" Douglas whirled.

"Selina too." The woman spoke again.

Wait, what? I took deep breaths, trying to quell the roaring in my head and the rising nausea that threatened to give Douglas a close-up view of what I'd had for lunch with his wife. Unable to hold it back, my salad forced its way up, spewing across his floor.

"Don't let her choke to death," the woman said. "She needs to die in the fire."

Small hands dragged me back from my vomit and rolled me more toward my stomach. If I could just turn my head to look at her. I tried to shift and cried out at the pounding in my head.

"If you'd just left well enough alone." The woman moved her hands off my back. "I don't want to do this, but you've given me no choice."

"I'm not letting you murder two people." Douglas's firm voice sounded from across the room.

"I've already killed Linus for us, love. Two more won't make it any worse." The woman laughed.

"You killed Linus? Why?" Douglas shifted and stepped closer to the counter behind him. "And what do you mean 'for us?'"

"So we can be together, silly man." The woman laughed. "It'll be perfect."

The roaring receded further, and my head cleared a bit. I knew that voice. But from where?

"Be together?" Douglas's voice held incredulity. "What the hell do you mean by that?"

"Darling, I know you love me." The woman giggled again. "I love you too."

"Love you? I don't love you. I barely know you." Douglas eased a few more steps toward the counter.

"You don't have to hide it just because Jenna's here." The woman's foot shoved me in the shoulder. "She won't be able to tell anyone."

I couldn't tell if the woman was watching me again. I chanced it and shifted a little, rolling a couple of inches toward my back and waited for the pounding caused by the movement to stop.

"I love my wife." Douglas straightened his spine and stopped his slow creep toward the counter, now at his back.

"Pfffffff." The woman snorted. "Puh-lease. That woman has treated you like dirt for years. There is no way you actually love her. She sucks you dry financially. But I have money for us. Almost a million dollars I've been saving from the book sales."

"Book sales?" Douglas placed a hand on the counter. "What book sales?"

"That's the best part, darling. I stole them from your dumb library. Linus almost ruined everything. He was about to figure it all out. I couldn't let that happen. Not when we're so close to having a life together. And since I burned down the library, now no one will ever know I stole the books, and you'll have a perfect reason to move away." She clapped her hands behind me.

Douglas's brow furrowed and he hesitated. "You burned the library? The books?" His voice trembled as if in mourning for the lost history.

"Darling, keep up. Of course I burned it. Miss Nosy Pants"—another shove to my shoulder from behind—"figured it all out. I saw her at the library with you when you were telling her all about how books were safe there." The woman giggled again. "I also overheard her at the store, talking to someone about watching the library to catch me. But I got away again. I did think to take a few more of the really rare books to sell. We'll have all the money we need to start our lives together once we're married."

Douglas clenched his fists. "I. Love. My. Wife. I won't let you kill her. Or Jenna either."

The woman stepped over me, striding to Douglas, placing a hand on his chest, her back to me. "Darling, stop saying that. I know you don't mean it, but it still stings."

Douglas gripped her wrists and pushed her away. "I do mean it. Now get out of my house. I'm calling the police." He turned and grabbed his phone from the counter.

If she would just turn. She was familiar, but my addled brain wouldn't pull up a name or a face. The woman stepped to the counter and picked up a frying pan from the dishrack.

I tried to yell a warning to Douglas, who had raised his phone to his ear, his back to the crazed woman with a skillet. Nothing came out but a squeak as I watched her raise it and slam it down on Douglas's head. He crumpled to the floor, and the woman reached for the phone, pressing the screen, probably to disconnect the nine-one-one call.

She stood and stepped across Douglas's inert form, turning to kneel by his side and place a hand to his chest. Alice King. Sweet, sad Alice King. And now psycho Alice King. "You'll be okay, darling. I'll nurse you back to health."

Alice stood and looked at me. "Now see what I've had to do?" She shook her head. "The things we do for the men we love."

I tried to speak and coughed instead, wheezing past the burn in my throat from throwing up. I swallowed a few times and tried again. "You can't do this."

"Oh, honey, I can, and I will. I've hated Selina for how she's treated poor Douglas. The man has been a saint, putting up with her. I finally get to kill her, but I had to wait so it would all be perfect. I've been following Selina around since Linus died, making sure it all points to her." She stepped across me and returned with an umbrella, which she fed through my bent elbows behind my back. "I saw this in a movie once. This'll keep you in place while I set up Selina's suicide. She's going to be so filled with remorse for killing Linus, she's taking a bunch of pills and will accidentally"—she waved her fingers in the air as air quotes—"knock a candle over and set her own house on fire. I had to improvise a bit to include you, though. You're going to die trying to rescue her. Then you'll both be out of Douglas's and my way, and he won't even have this stupid house holding him back." She patted me on the head. "I really am sorry you got involved in all of this."

When her footsteps faded toward another part of the house, I grappled with the umbrella. I couldn't roll. I couldn't hook it through anything to shove it out of my elbows. I was unbalanced enough from the knock on the head, there was no way I was going to stand up without help. My hands brushed my back pockets, my fingers connecting with something hard. My phone! Alice hadn't seen it stuck under my sweater.

I inched it out with my fingertips, hoping it was on. "Siri, call Keith." Please let my voice be strong enough for it to understand.

"I'm sorry, I don't understand."

I swore and cleared my throat. "Siri, call Keith."

I'd never heard a sweeter sound than my phone saying, "Calling Keith Logan, mobile."

I couldn't see the screen, so I couldn't risk hitting the end icon trying to fumble for the speakerphone icon. I could hear the faint ringing. *Please, please pick up.* A strangled cry rose up when I heard his voice.

"Hi, sweetheart. What's up?"

I shifted my hands to the side as much as I could, trying to stick my phone toward my hip, giving a better chance of being heard. Keeping my voice to a loud whisper, so Alice wouldn't hear, I said, "Keith, help me. Alice has me—"

"Hello? Jenna? You there?"

He couldn't hear me. Footsteps sounded again, and they were getting closer. No help for it. I opened my mouth and shouted at the phone. "Keith! Help! It's Alice! She has us all at Douglas and Selina's—"

Alice yanked the phone out of my hand and pressed the screen, fury in her eyes. "How did you get this?" She threw the phone across the room. "You're going to spoil everything."

"They know where I am, Alice. They're coming." I struggled against the umbrella, desperate to move away from the woman.

"It won't matter. They'll be too late." Alice grasped my heels and began to drag me, my head grinding against the floor.

Pain blinded me again, but my sense of self-preservation pushed through, and I kicked at my captor, breaking one foot free. I needed time for Keith to get there.

"Stop it!" Alice grabbed at my loose foot.

I continued to swing it wildly until she dropped the other foot. I was free. I tried to shift but caught her kick in my stomach, the pain doubling me into a fetal position.

"Now see what happens?" Alice calmly picked up my feet again and began to drag.

At the doorway to the hall, I shifted and jammed the umbrella across the opening.

Alice sighed deeply. "You know you're just delaying the inevitable." She dropped my feet and moved to step around me. "I guess I can understand, though."

As she stepped across me to get through the doorway, I flipped to my side, tripping her on the umbrella. Alice screeched as she hit the floor, and I gave myself an internal fist pump.

I tilted my head back to see where she was and watched as she dragged herself to the cabinets and pulled herself up using the counter. Another cry escaped as she stood, and she instantly rubbed her knee.

Alice reached for something on the counter and her hand came away holding the skillet she'd used on Douglas. "I'll solve this right here." She limped toward me.

Desperately, I wriggled, trying to put more distance between me and the crazy woman waving the large piece of metal with a handle. The umbrella hung on a corner of the rug and I was stuck, my stomach sinking at the look of glee that crossed Alice's face. I couldn't even raise my arms to deflect part of the blow.

Alice limped at a half jog, awkwardly trotting toward me, swinging the skillet high over her head.

"Drop it!"

I tilted my head back to see Keith and Tish rushing into the room.

Alice screeched, all of the hurt, rage, anger, and betrayal she'd ever felt seeming to pour out in that horrible sound. She raised the skillet higher and began a downward swing.

A blur flew across me as Keith tackled her, taking her backward. When he connected, the skillet flew from her hand, and I watched in slow motion as it fell toward my face, connecting with my forehead, blacking out the world.

Chapter Twenty-Eight

A strange beeping sounded in my ears, and I slowly cracked my eyes open.

A whisper hissed to my left. "She's awake. Go get Keith."

I shifted, moving my arms across a soft sheet, startled at the tube extending from my elbow. I opened my eyes wider.

Another voice. "Miss Quinn? Jenna? Can you hear me?"

"Yes." My voice came out a soft rasp.

"That's good. I'm Doctor Callum. Can you open your eyes a little wider?" A man in a white coat leaned over me, his dark hair a contrast to his pale skin, even in my blurry vision.

I struggled to open my eyes.

"That's great. Now I need to check your pupils, okay?" Without warning, he swung a light across my eyes, blinding me and sending shafts of pain into my brain.

I clenched my eyes shut and tried to turn my head. Something pulled at my forehead. I raised a hand and felt bandages.

A soft hand grasped mine. "It's okay, Jenna. We're here. Let the doctor do his job. He's just making sure you're okay."

I heard the tremble in Rita's voice. What was wrong with me? I opened my eyes again, my vision clearer, and tried to sit up, but the doctor pushed me back down.

"Let's be still a bit longer, okay?" He motioned to Rita.

Rita squeezed my hand. "I'll be right back. I'm going to talk to the doctor a moment."

A nurse in white scrubs with pink kittens on them bustled into the room and busied herself checking my IV tube and the monitor readouts. Behind her, I could see the doctor in the hallway, speaking to Keith and Rita.

After a few moments, Rita returned to the room without Keith. I looked around her, searching for him. Why wasn't he here? I needed him. I wanted him here.

Rita pulled a chair close and sat, picking up my hand again. "You're going to be okay." She squeezed my fingers. "The doctor says your eyes are fine, and you're responsive."

I raised a hand to my forehead again, touching the bandages. "And this?" I rasped out.

"You had a nasty gash on your head, and they had to stitch it up." She pulled my free hand away from my face. "Don't mess with it yet."

"She hit me with something." I searched my fuzzy memory. "Twice." I hesitated. "Once. The skillet was dropped. Why does she keep hitting me in the head?"

The nurse shifted behind Rita. "She needs to rest now."

Rita squeezed my fingers again. "I have to go, but I'll be just outside. I promise."

As she left the room, the questions pushing through my head faded, and darkness took me again.

* * *

I opened my eyes again, this time to a darkened room, the same soft beeping emanating from the machines beside my bed. A solid snore rattled from my left, and I looked for its source in the dim light.

A nurse bustled in, checking the monitors. "Oh, good, you're awake. Are you feeling better?"

Mason shifted in the chair in the corner and sat up. "Hey, you're awake."

Why was this so surprising? "How long?" My dry throat wouldn't form any more words.

The nurse picked up a cup from the bedside table and spooned a few ice chips into my dry mouth. "Three days since you last opened those peepers. It's Monday morning." She changed my IV bag. "I'll let the doctor know you're awake."

"I'll go get Rita." Mason rushed from the room, almost colliding with the nurse in his haste.

Moments later, Rita, her clothes rumpled and hair a frizzy mess, strode to my bedside and picked up my hand. "Good morning, Rip Van Winkle."

I chuckled and instantly regretted it, as the action caused my head to pound. "Where's Keith?"

Mason shook his head. "Fine. Rita and I are here, sleeping at your bedside, but all you want is the hot cop."

Rita elbowed him. "Stop it. Don't make her laugh." She turned her gaze to meet mine. "He had to leave about fifteen minutes ago. It's almost seven AM. The District Attorney is questioning him in preparation for Alice's trial."

After only four days? "Isn't that awfully soon?" I tried to reach for the ice chip cup and missed.

Rita slid another spoonful of ice chips into my mouth. "It's an election year. The DA wants things to happen fast, so it looks good for him in three weeks. I think the actual trial starts next week. Her attorney isn't happy, but he got overruled. It's a pretty open-and-shut case, since Keith and Tish caught her in the act of trying to kill you."

"And Douglas?" Guilt washed through me at having assumed he was capable of murder or of poisoning my dog.

"He's fine and home." Rita sat in the chair next to the bed. "Selina's okay too. She was only passed out from drinking. Alice had left the pills in her car and was on her way to get them when you called me. Selina's mothering instincts have finally come out, especially after she found out Douglas was injured trying to save her."

"Where did the money come from for Selina's habits if Douglas wasn't stealing the books?" How had I been so wrong?

"When his father died, he left half of his estate to the library and half of it to Douglas." Mason sat on the foot of my bed, jumping up when I winced at the movement. "Sorry. Anyway, he told Selina it had all gone to the library because he knew she'd blow their share if she knew. He's been coving her major buys and trying to rein her in as much as he can so they don't end up broke by retirement."

The nurse bustled in with a tray and set it on the foot of the bed. She rolled a bed table from the side of the bed, positioned it across me, and placed the tray on top. "You can't have a full meal, but the doctor says you can have some Jell-O." She lifted the cover from the plate and revealed two Jell-O cups, both lime, before leaving the room. My stomach rolled in protest.

"Hey, Jell-O." Mason leaned over and looked. "I love lime. Can I have one?"

"Sure. Knock yourself out." I grinned when he shot me an odd look.

I slid my gaze to Rita. "Where's Eddy?"

"Phillie Hokes is puppy sitting." Rita pulled out her phone and opened her photo app, flipping through pictures of Eddy and Phillie in her yard, standing proudly by a sapling. "Seems Eddy is helping her garden. He keeps digging holes in odd places, and for fun, she's sticking plants in them. So far, I think she has two new trees and an odd, zig-zag row of rose bushes from where he tried to catch a mole."

I repressed the laugh that wanted to come up, raising my fingers to touch the picture of Eddy and Phillie. "Tell her thank you for me."

"I'm sure she'll be by now that you're awake." Rita dropped her phone back into her purse.

My eyelids drooped, and I fought to keep them open. "How's the store doing?"

Mason grinned. "We're selling like gangbusters. Everyone wants to come by and hear the latest news on how you're doing. I'm managing to sell a lot of books to them once they're there."

I smiled, struggling against the sleep that tugged at me. "Sounds like you have things in hand."

Rita stood and motioned to Mason. "We both need to go home and shower. I need to check in at work, and Mason needs to get the store open for the day. Those books won't sell themselves."

I nodded a tiny bit. "I understand. I'll be here when you get back." My eyes were closed before they got out of the room.

* * *

When I opened my eyes again, late afternoon sun streamed in the window. Keith sat in the chair across the room, eyes on his phone, tapping away at the screen as if sending a text.

I watched him for a moment, drinking him in and remembering the way he'd dived across me to rescue me. "Hey." I smiled a sleepy smile at him.

Keith's head snapped up. "Hey, yourself." His voice was tight, the set of his jaw tense.

My smile slipped. "Everything okay?"

His brow furrowed, and he tipped his head to one side briefly. "Sure. Everything's fine. Why wouldn't it be?"

Wow, okay. Change of subject. "How's the case against Alice?"

Keith sighed. "Her trial starts next Monday."

"Will she go to jail?" I shifted and reached for the bed buttons, tilting my bed up a tiny bit so I could see him more easily.

Keith shook his head. "Not likely. Her attorney is already prepping an insanity defense. In light of her crazy ramblings, the DA's office isn't going to disagree. I figure it'll end up with a plea deal before it even gets to court, and she'll end up in an institution."

"At least she'll get help." I lifted the bed a bit more. "Why did she think Douglas loved her?"

"Seems he'd been nice to her when Linus broke her heart. He'd told her she was a nice lady, and any man would be proud to be with her. She took that to mean that he wanted to be with her himself." Keith let out another sigh. "I honestly feel sorry for her. She stole all the books to get money so she and Douglas could run away together."

"You guys must have had some inkling it was her, right?" I still couldn't believe how much she had fooled me.

"We suspected." Keith nodded. "Once Tish looked at the library's inventory printouts, she set up a couple of the new recruits on computers, digging for any crumb of information about the missing books. It took time, but a few collectors posting about their new acquisitions led us to a bookseller in Raleigh. His reputation was impeccable, so no one questioned when he came up with very rare manuscripts for sale to his high-end buyers."

"Weren't the books marked by the library, though?" I winced when I furrowed my brow, and I concentrated on relaxing.

"He had made a stamp like the one the library uses when they remove a book from circulation, and he was marking them, so buyers wouldn't suspect. And he was careful not to sell more than one to any single buyer too." Keith leaned forward and propped his elbows on his knees. "Fortunately, he kept very careful sales records, so we should be able to recover most of the stolen books. Since neither of them spent much of the money, we can refund the clients a lot of what they paid."

"That's great." I was running out of things to ask about the case. "So she sold the book she bought from me under her own name . . ." I hoped he'd fill in the blanks for me.

"So she wouldn't have to give the bookseller a cut of the profit. Her end goal was to build up her own name in the book sales world again." Keith raked a hand through his hair. "That and live in her own fairy-tale land of love and lust with Douglas March."

As we talked, Keith still hadn't gotten up, come across to hold my hand, or stopped scowling. The tension radiated off him like a heat wave.

"I'm going to be okay." I lifted the bed a few more inches, now in a semi-reclined position, but up far enough I could make eye contact without straining.

Keith clenched and unclenched his jaw a few times, fire blazing in his eyes. "I know."

My heart sank. "What's going on, Keith? Are you angry at me?"

His jaw worked back and forth a few times before he shot out of the chair and paced the floor. "Yes, I guess I am."

"Why?" I held my breath. Something told me this was a make-or-break moment.

"Why?" Keith whirled to face me. "Why? I'll tell you why. Because you almost died, that's why." He resumed his pacing.

"And how is that my fault?" A dull pounding popped up behind my eyes, and I struggled to ignore it. "I didn't intentionally go anywhere near Alice. She somehow found me and took me to Douglas and Selina's house."

"She said she was following Douglas, which it seems she'd been doing for about two years, pretending she was his wife, and she overheard Selina telling him about your lunchtime conversation. She put two and two together and figured she'd better step up her game and get you out of the way. She waited for you to come out and whacked you over the head with a first aid kit she kept in the car." He stopped at the foot of the bed and stared at me, a flood of emotion flashing in his eyes.

"A book, a first aid kit, and then a skillet." I reached up to touch my bandaged forehead, glad the bandage was smaller than when I'd first awakened Friday morning. "She sure did like to whack people on the head."

"It's not a joke!" The words exploded from his chest.

"No, it's not!" I yelled back, done with his attitude. "But if I can find a way to laugh about it, through the pain that is now shooting through my head, then you damned well had better try to laugh with me! What is wrong with you?" I sat up, glaring at him.

Keith stepped closer, his fists clenching the footboard on my bed. "What's wrong is that I love you and I almost lost you!"

I sagged back against the bed, eyes closed, willing the pounding to stop, tears sliding down my cheeks. This. This was how he finally told me.

The mattress shifted as he sat on its edge. A gentle finger wiped a tear away, and I heard the whish of a tissue being pulled from the bedside box. "I'm sorry. I know I failed you again." Keith dabbed at my eyes, soaking up my tears.

I opened my eyes. "Then it's not really me you're angry with. You're angry with yourself."

Keith's hand withdrew, wadding the tissue before dropping it onto the bedside table. "Maybe."

"Uh-huh." I tried to go for the Vulcan eyebrow cock but failed when it pulled on the stitches on my forehead. I let the eyebrow drop.

Keith sucked in a deep breath and let it out in a forlorn sigh. "I don't want to hurt you or let you down."

I reached a hand up to his face and touched his cheek. "Then stop being an idiot."

His brow knit and he drew back. "What?"

I dropped my hand to the bedsheets. "I love you too. Don't you get that?"

"But I blew it. You almost died. Twice." A tremble laced his voice.

My eyelids sagged as sleep clutched at me again. "You saved my life, Keith. That's why it's only an almost."

Keith stood. "You're sleepy. You need to rest."

I grasped his hand. "Don't go."

He stood stock-still for a moment before lacing his fingers through mine. "I'll be here when you wake up. I promise."

I held on when he tried to move away. "Don't go." I tugged on his hand, pulling him closer.

The bed sagged again, and I slid over to make room on the tiny mattress. Keith's warmth spread through me as he lay down next to me, wrapping his arms around me. "I won't. I'll be right here. You rest now."

I let sleep take me, relaxed, knowing I was the safest—and luckiest—girl on the planet.

Acknowledgments

Thank you to my wonderful husband, George, whose love and support continue to push me on through my writing journey. I love you. Thank you to my eager, skilled, and very thorough beta reader, Pat Rohner, who remains ready to beta read my manuscripts on incredibly short notice and with tight deadlines. Thank you to Chief Mitch McElveen, Manning Fire Department, who answered all my odd questions on how a library might burn, fortunately understanding I was not planning a real crime. Thank you to Chief John Schomp, Wharton Fire Department, Ret., who patiently offered advice and answers on the behavior of fire and later took the time to read and critique my fire scene. Thank you to my amazing agent, Dawn Dowdle, whose unflagging belief in my writing abilities has far more of an impact than she realizes. Thank you to Crooked Lane Books for making my publishing journey an incredible one and for continuing to let me share my stories with the world.